Wings of Eventyr

Book Three

by Ellias Quinn

ISBN 978-1-944755-06-5

Published by Second March, LLC | THE WOODLANDS
www.elliasquinn.com

For humble leaders.

Table of Contents

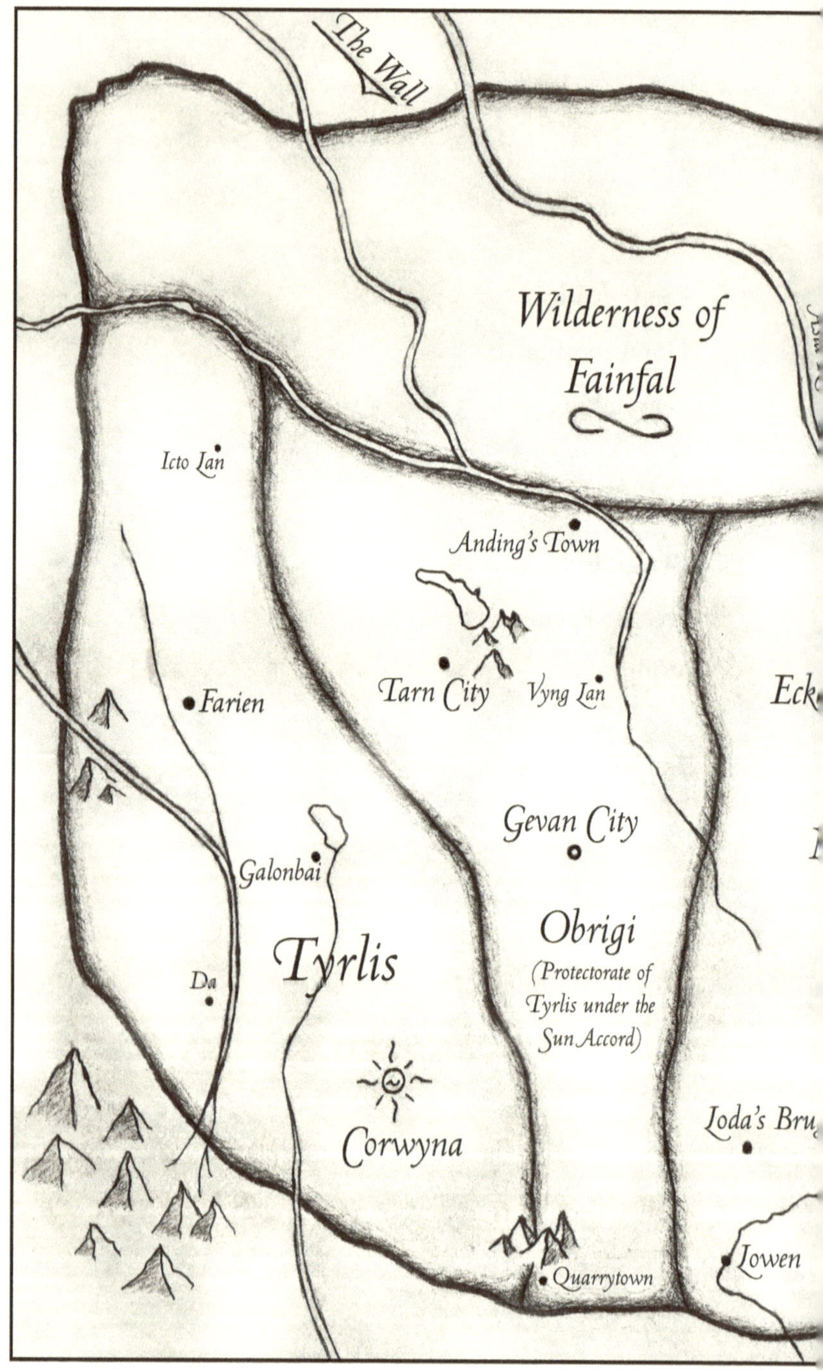

The Wall
Wilderness of
Fainfal
Icto Lan
Anding's Town
Tarn City
Vyng Lan
Eck
Farien
Gevan City
Galonbai
Obrigi
(Protectorate of
Tyrlis under the
Sun Accord)
Tyrlis
Da
Loda's Bru
Corwyna
Lowen
Quarrytown

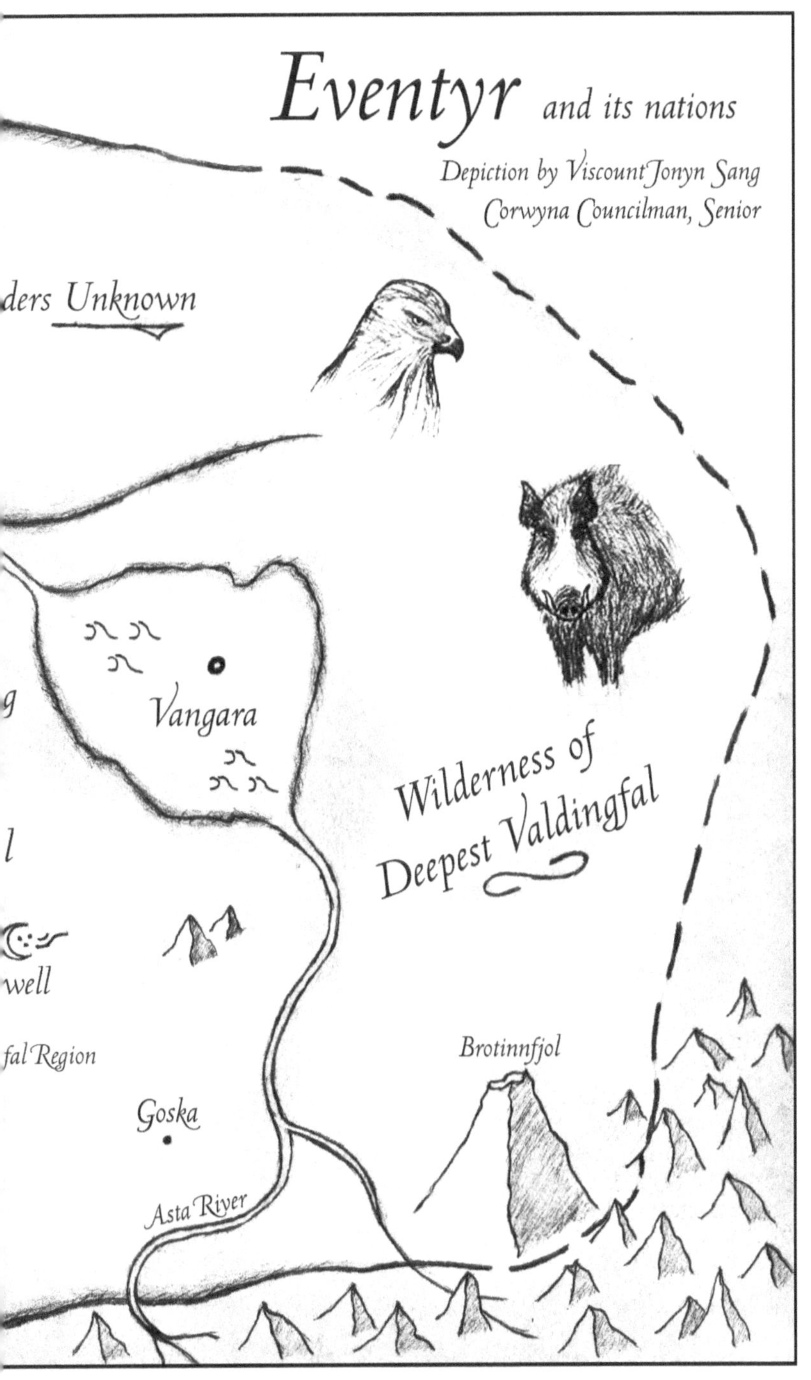

Eventyr and its nations
Depiction by Viscount Jonyn Sang
Corwyna Councilman, Senior
ders Unknown
Vangara
Wilderness of
Deepest Valdingfal
g
l
well
fal Region
Brotinnfjol
Goska
Asta River

Velana dri alva,
drimesk ermoli.
Dri dyri ajarten,
driskur erusi.

Velana dri alva,
kothym ervanoss.
Den hjardan erglir,
den valdri erveross.

Velana dri alva,
olakot, kodu.
Eletsol
Ranycht
Nervoda
Brandur
Sangriga
Obrigi
Kyndelin
Skorgon

Velana.

Awaken the fairies,
the forest is young.
The animals await,
the sun is new.

Awaken the fairies,
their home is alive.
Its heart is clear,
its guardians are true.

Awaken the fairies,
all of them, rise.
Life
Night
Water
Fire
Light
Earth
Animal
Crawler

Awaken.

Prologue

A sharp *plink-plink-plink* woke Yaric from his dozing. He blinked, breathing in deeply, and sat up. Dark shadows were cast by a tall candle on a dish, while his wings illuminated the dirt wall behind him. Indents marked the candle down its length to represent time, and three nails lay at its base, having fallen out when the candle burned to where Yaric had pushed them in.

He blew out the candle and focused on his wings. It was second nature for him to imagine the sun going down and to turn that image into action. His wings, rays of light shining from his back, diminished until they were hardly noticeable. He wrapped the candle, dish, and nails in a cloth and shoved them into his satchel while pulling on his cloak's hood. Then he moved to the cobwebbed entrance of the small dirt burrow. Fresh night air blew across his face and sharpened his mind. The moon sat at the peak of the sky, framed by blades of grass as wide as Yaric's waist and leafy branches farther above.

He stood well hidden in the grass stretching high over his head. He was in the land of Obrigi, and not too far away was the Obrigi-Nychtfal Fortification – an elaborate name for a simple wall, constructed to keep squabbling alva apart and prevent illegal trade. But the leaders who'd had the thing built rather liked illegal trade, when it was for goods they desired. Yaric's employer, Councilwoman

Lyria, was one such leader and had quite the taste for information. Which was why Yaric now searched in the moonlight for a stand of narrow trees. He floated upward, turned…and spotted it. Fly low, hurry over, keep his wings dim.

He passed by a couple of the ghostly white tree trunks and then heard a high whistle. Could be a bird call. He hovered in place and whistled back, imitating the call. Two low-pitched whistles near the ground came in reply. He repeated them and added the higher whistle at the end.

A figure revealed itself from out of the grass at the base of a tree a length away. Yaric quickly floated to the ground to meet it.

The figure was a dark-skinned Ranycht girl, thin and ragged. Her bird-like wings were folded tightly on her back. She opened a bag slung over her shoulder, pulled out a stack of papers tied with cord, and looked up at Yaric with huge, luminous eyes of yellow.

He reached out, drawn to her steady stare. Ranycht. Strange. Night creatures. So different from a Sangriga such as himself. Then again, he made his living lurking about at night.

At the same time as he reached, he offered a pouch of payment in his other hand. They made the trade smoothly. The girl was young, but practiced. Yaric understood having someone small and unassuming run the borders, yet he couldn't help wondering why anyone let children get caught up in smuggling. He thought of his own son and daughters. The Ranycht girl with her serious expression no longer seemed strange.

She felt the weight of the pouch and inspected a few of the coins inside. Yaric peered down at the papers, letting his wings glow very little as he checked them over. The scribblings and phrases he saw were in the handwriting of his usual contacts across the border. The girl's wings spread out with a quiet *whoosh*.

"Thank you," Yaric said in a low voice.

Her broad, pointed ears twitched. "Thank you," she whispered. And in a whirl of soft wind and feathers, she flew off.

Be careful, he wanted to call out after her. Instead, he went the other way, retracing his path to the cobwebbed burrow. Once inside, he let his wings glow freely and untied the papers.

Yaric began to skim through it. There were maps marked with the movements of important alva and armies through the forest. He found a note saying that many Eletsol of different clans were travelling as one. Odd. His employer had a particular interest in the alva Nychta Olsta, so when he caught her name, he slowed.

Olsta was moving about eastern Eventyr and occasionally disappearing into the wilds. The thickets and caves she ventured into were haunted, cursed, the homes of sleeping spirits, or so the locals said. And the locals were afraid, for what could she be doing, except…waking these malevolent spirits? Yaric paused. More like she was overseeing secret storehouses and operations.

He read on. Skorgon surrounded her, of course, but she had attracted followers of another kind – Ranycht who concealed their identities and wore the symbols of the Myrkharen cult. A dangerous lot. He'd heard tales of atrocities committed by the Myrkharen across Eventyr.

Nychta Olsta still held the Book of Myrkhar, which terrified the alva she ruled over in her newly established Ranycht Dominion. Some alva had begun to escape, it was rumoured, dispersing westward to get away from the Dominion's control and the dreaded Book.

Yaric wasn't sure if he could go so far as to believe the Book was a mystical piece of work created by an Elder. It disturbed Councilwoman Lyria, however, and that was good enough for him. She'd be interested to hear what these papers held. And disappointed that in all the pages there was no mention of the outlaw four who travelled the forest: the Sangriga scholar, the Obrigi farmer, the Ranycht criminal, and the girl without wings…

1

Makeshift Magician

Dewdrop and Olnar, the riding beetles, stood with saddles and supply packs strapped to their iridescent shells. Matil and Simmad lifted a leaf-covered slab of meat from the ground onto Dewdrop. The beetle took the extra weight with hardly a twitch of her antennae.

As Matil caught her breath, she went up to pat Dewdrop's head. "I'd like to be as strong as you, Dew," she said.

Khelya, towering over her friends, lifted one end of a mass of ivy while Dask flew to lift the other end over a pile of leaves that concealed a huge rabbit they had just… restocked their food supplies from.

"Wish I could take some of the pelt," Dask said, landing and folding his black-feathered wings. "It'd bag us a good amount of sgeldings."

"I don't think we'll need as much meat as we took." Khelya picked up her large spear. "You can sell the extra."

"Eh, on second thought, we shouldn't even try to sell anything in town," he said. "Soon as we're in Nychtfal we'll be outlaws again." He pouted. "And I'm so hungry I could eat half of what we packed up."

"That's a big claim for a little twig," Khelya said.

"Okay," he said, "*you* could eat half of what we packed up. Tree-legs."

"*Excuse me?*"

"Er, Dask," Simmad said weakly. His wings of light shimmered as he walked toward them. "Your- your arm is bleeding."

Dask held up his right arm to inspect it and widened his green eyes. There was a slash on the side of his forearm, a thin line of blood seeping from the wound. "Hm. Y'know, I wondered why my arm was stinging."

Matil winced.

He let the arm fall and ran his left hand through his shaggy black hair. "There's always gotta be something. We spook a weasel who's just killed a rabbit – the weasel runs off thanks to Kyndelin animal magic. But then a crow smells fresh rabbit, comes down, and we have to *fight* it until it has enough of Simmad's flashy light magic and flies off. I'm starting to think crows don't care about Kyndelin magic. Remember those crows we met in the quarry a while back who – I'm pretty sure – were gonna beak-shank us?" He grimaced.

"Crows are terrible for crops," Khelya said. She tightened the brown cloth headband she wore over her blonde hair. "They're plain evil, in my opinion."

Simmad wiped his forehead. "They're simply scavenging for food to survive."

"I mean, I guess *evil* ain't the right word…" she said.

"No, they're evil," Dask said. "Stone cold." He clapped his hands. "Okay, alva. I hear water pretty close. Let's go get cleaned off and have meat for dinner. We still have a ways to go before we get to Ecker's Brug, and Dyndal's sister won't wake herself."

As the sun began to set, Matil, Dask, Khelya, and Simmad went down to a plant-shaded, trickling stream not far from the rabbit, where they waded into the shallow water to rinse off. When Matil was clean, she went to Dewdrop and Olnar waiting at the edge of the water. Digging through a pack on Olnar, she retrieved strips of cloth and a jar of salve for Dask's wound.

Dask lifted his slashed forearm out of the stream. "That Sangriga light ball didn't get bright enough to chase off the crow right away. It did the job eventually, but, Simms, make it brighter next time we're in a fight, okay?"

"It was as bright as I could make it." Simmad shrugged his lanky shoulders. "If I were a magician, perhaps…"

Dask snapped his fingers and then paused. "Ow." He stuck his other hand in the jar of salve that Matil had opened for him. "That gives me an idea," he said, slathering the salve on his forearm. "We need to find a magician. Doesn't matter what kind of alva, since apparently we take all kinds. We'd beat anyone or anything in a fight if we had a magician."

"Ansi's a magician, and he didn't keep us from gettin' caught," Khelya said.

Dask tapped his chin. "True. But he did get us out of a riot with some very impressive magician stuff."

"You mean magic," Simmad said.

"No, I mean sandwiches," he said.

"You…what?"

Dask covered his eyes. "*Yes*, I mean magic."

"What about Dyndal?" Matil said. She laid a strip of cloth over Dask's wound and tied it in place with another strip.

"Ah, yes!" Simmad said, standing up straight. "We do happen to have with us a being of immense power." He patted the large pendant hanging from his neck, a red wooden toad.

"A being of immense power who could barely fight off his snaky girlfriend," Dask said. He smiled as Matil finished binding the wound. "Thanks, Matil."

Matil gave a small smile back. She busied herself putting the salve away and tried to ignore how her heart had jumped when he said her name.

"Besides," Dask went on, "we haven't seen his face in two days. When's he coming back out of that dumb necklace?"

Simmad looked down at the pendant. "Soon, I- I'm sure."

"Y'know," Khelya said, "Ansi made himself stronger at the riot by sharing magic with other magicians. And remember when I turned invisible from sharing magic with you? Can we give Simmad…*our* strength or somethin'?"

Dask frowned. "I can't imagine a Ranycht making light come out of a Sangriga."

Simmad stroked his dark blonde goatee. "Though cross-kind magic is not my area of expertise, I once had a lengthy conversation with a professor who was both obsessed with the subject and violently opposed to it. She frightened me, if I'm being quite honest. The path to wisdom is fraught with danger and odd teachers. But where was I…right! According to her knowledge of historical record, sharing magical strength is likely possible."

"Then shouldn't we try it?" Matil said, petting Dewdrop's blue shell plate. "Just in case?"

"I wouldn't if I were you," came an unfamiliar voice from the other side of the stream.

Matil and Dask had their knives out right away. The four alva looked up at the gravelly bank opposite them.

A quick count revealed eleven Ranycht men standing amid the grass at the top of the bank, a couple lengths away. Their dark clothes and brown skin, like Matil's and Dask's, allowed them to blend in with the shadows of late day, but their large, brightly-colored eyes stood out as they watched the strange group. Some kept their feathered wings open, ready to fly. Most had spears in hand – battered and rusty weapons, but weapons nonetheless.

Matil tightened her grip on her knife. She could see the barely-controlled hostility in their faces.

"This is Dominion territory," the voice called.

It came from a stocky Ranycht in the middle who held a short sword. He began sauntering down the bank toward the water, the other ten Ranycht following behind. The man had brick-red eyes and an uneven mane of black hair.

His black and brown wings were folded on his back. "I'm Captain Hagen of Northfalinn, and *though* this situation as I find it is very suspect…I extend a hand of friendship to my Ranycht brother and sister over there."

Matil glanced at Dask. Hagen was talking about the two of them.

"I'd highly recommend you take that hand," he went on, "because the boys and I are about to protect this land from invaders. Including any Ranycht who turns their back on kin by standing with said invaders."

Dask's eyes darted around, and then he looked at Captain Hagen. "You know we're in Fainfal, right? Eletsol territory?"

"Old borders," Hagen said. "We haven't seen any Eletsol since we got here, so we're simply making use of unclaimed land."

Dask lowered his voice. "Yeah, wait till the Eletsol come back from their seven-day feast…" He spoke up again, "What's the Dominion, anyway?"

Hagen rested his free hand on his hip. "Been out of Nychtfal for a while? No wonder you keep such poor company. You need some time in the homeland."

All of the Ranycht on the bank were slouching and glaring at the group.

"You're right," Dask said with a tense smile. "I'd really like to get back home. I just need to know who you are first."

"Sure," Hagen said, impatience entering his voice. "I'll tell you exactly what you need to know. The Ranycht Dominion is Nychtfal reborn. We're the voice of every Ranycht who's been stepped on by the magistrates or who lost family to the Massacres. All those who've put up with decades of disrespect from the Obrigi. All those who were executed by the Sangriga just for being a birdwing. We're finally standing up and looking out for our own."

Dask nodded thoughtfully. "Sounds pretty good. If the two of us Ranycht join you, you'd let the Obrigi and Sangriga go free, right? As long as they didn't enter, uh… Dominion territory?"

"Dask," Matil whispered in dismay.

Khelya and Simmad looked at Dask, confused, but neither one spoke.

"We'd have to take them in," Hagen said. "Just for questioning. There are spies all over, and who knows what kind of mission those two could be on?"

Dask adjusted his fingers on his knife. "What if I said they were on a mission from Thosten?"

Hagen chuckled. "Can't be. Thosten's on *our* side."

"And what makes you figure that?" Khelya said, planting her spear in the shallows.

A few of the Ranycht pointed their weapons down at her.

"You shut up," Hagen said. "Let your friend speak for you."

"Oh, nah, I just had one more thing," Dask said. "You didn't mention Matil's wings."

Hagen's red eyes flicked over to Matil. "What?"

"The fact that she doesn't have any."

Matil froze.

"You know who she is." Dask's bat-like ears went back. "You know who *we* are. And let me guess…there's a pretty nice reward on our heads."

Hagen opened his mouth and paused. "I really don't want to hurt a fellow Ranycht. You'll be safe if you come with us peacefully."

"*I'll* be safe," Dask said, "but no one else? Yeah…unfortunately for you, I don't want my fellow alva to get hurt."

Matil started to smile, and she saw Khelya doing the same.

"So no," he added. "I'm not joining your stupid club." He shot straight into the air.

Matil's braid whipped in the downdraft from Dask's wings, but when she looked up, he had disappeared above the ferns and reeds.

"Okay." Hagen waved his sword. "*On 'em, boys!*"

The Ranycht on the opposite bank flew up and dove toward Matil, Khelya, and Simmad. Hagen stayed where he was, watching for Dask.

"Khel, watch it!" Dask yelled from wherever he was.

Khelya lifted her giant spear and swept it between her and the ten charging Ranycht. They fell back, flapping their wings haphazardly, and then scattered. Matil shoved Dewdrop and Olnar towards some concealing grass.

One Ranycht swooped around with his spear aiming for Simmad. Matil launched herself at the attacker, tackling him into the water. She sank her knife into his arm. He howled, struggled as his wings splashed around, and pushed her off.

Matil landed on her back a few steps away with the wind knocked out of her. She rolled to her feet and into a crouch. Her opponent lifted himself up and, with a powerful flap of his wings, flew high out of her reach to attack Khelya. Matil stared after him in frustration.

Khelya lunged and swiped her spear at the rowdy attackers. Simmad stayed behind Khelya, holding a globe of light in his hands. His face burned red with the strain of getting it to grow. It was the size of his head and Matil couldn't look directly at it with her light-sensitive Ranycht eyes.

One of the fighters got too close to the light and shied away from it. "Thiffen!" he burst out. "Rat-snout lightning bug!"

"Sunspawn," another one yelled at Simmad. The light was keeping them away from Khelya's back.

One young fighter rushed toward Khelya with his spear on course for the side of her neck.

"Look out on your left!" Simmad called.

Khelya twisted, grabbed the shaft out of the young man's grip with her free hand, and knocked him in the head with the end of his own spear. His wings and body went limp as he fell. Still holding the Ranycht-sized spear, Khelya whipped it around and jammed it through another fighter's shoulder, where it stuck. He screamed and splashed into the stream. The remaining group of Ranycht bunched closer together in their attacks.

A few of them swooped past Matil on their way to attack Khelya from the side. One flew low to the ground. Matil jumped and grappled one of his legs.

"Git off!" he yelled.

She sliced as close to his ankle tendon as she could before slipping off and thudding onto the bank of the stream. The fighter slammed into one of his buddies and they both veered off course. The wounded one aimed for the other side of the stream, away from Matil, where he flopped to the bank. He groaned and crawled into the tall grass.

After that, the others kept their distance from the ground. Matil could only watch as they focused their attacks on Khelya. The giant alva had a line of blood along her upper arm and a red spot on the shoulder of her tunic. Matil hoped the wounds weren't deep. Her ears twitched at the sound of a wordless yell. Dask's voice. She looked up.

Now she saw Dask, though it was hard to follow his movements. He blazed through the air above the stream, hitting one of the fighters, soaring back up, and diving to hit another one. His harrying kept them confused and vulnerable to attacks from Khelya. Matil had never seen him fight so hard. He was bound to get tired soon. She *wanted* to help him. She desperately wanted to help. But without wings, what could she do?

Captain Hagen hurtled toward Dask from the side, his sword raised.

Matil stepped forward. "Dask!"

Dask abruptly shut his wings. As he dropped, Hagen passed above, missing his attack. Dask opened his wings, spotted Hagen, and swooped around to tackle the red-eyed Ranycht in midair. They were a whirl of feathers and limbs.

In the scuffling, Hagen dropped his sword. He fumbled for a small axe strapped to his belt.

A flash of light pierced Matil's vision. Simmad had made his light orb much brighter, just for a moment. A couple of the Ranycht fighters veered away from him, stunned by the flash. A few more of those flashes, and maybe they would retreat!

The two fighters landed and closed their eyes, but they recovered quickly. As they leaped back into the fight, Matil exhaled, disappointed. Even if Simmad could make more flashes, it wouldn't be enough. The light had to be stronger.

Where *was* Dyndal? The Elders were supposed to help alva, especially in moments like this. They hadn't even gotten the chance to try sharing their strength—

No…no, maybe now was their chance. Matil estimated the distance between her friends. Simmad and Khelya stood back to back. She edged towards Khelya, just outside the Obrigi's reach. The three of them on the ground were close enough together. Dask would need to get away from Hagen.

"Let's try it!" Matil called out. "Sharing magic! Simmad's light!"

"Okay!" said Khelya. A Ranycht flew toward her, thrusting his spear at her right side. She blocked it and grabbed his leg with her left hand. The Ranycht squawked as Khelya flung him aside. He went spinning into the water in a flurry of feathers.

"How does it work?" Simmad said.

Khelya swung her spear in a savage arc, warding off two fighters. "Take it when you feel it an'…I guess just do your magic!"

"All right…" Simmad's voice wavered.

"Dask," Matil shouted. "Get to us if you can!"

"I heard," he grunted back, twisting Hagen's axe-holding hand. "Gotta make sure I don't *die* first!"

Hagen dropped the axe, but grabbed Dask's forearm with his other hand. "I don't…understand…traitor dungbasks like you," he said, panting.

Dask grinned. "Me neither." He broke out of Hagen's grip and looped downward, but Hagen went in for a heavy punch to Dask's jaw.

Matil gritted her teeth as it connected.

Dask reeled. His wings stopped flapping for one beat as Hagen swung his fist back for the next punch, but Dask shook his head and kicked his opponent in the gut. Hagen fell back, doubled over, while Dask pulled his wings in for an unsteady dive. Before he reached the ground, he pushed them outward to slow his descent. He staggered to a landing, chest heaving as he sucked in air, and held out his right hand to Khelya.

Khelya knelt and thrust the butt of the spear into the stream bed before wrapping her right hand around Dask's wrist. With her left hand, she grabbed Simmad's shoulder and pulled him to her side. Matil splashed over behind them. Dask put his hand on Matil's shoulder while she put her hand on Simmad's back, completing their circle. The Sangriga's tall frame trembled.

"When- when should I—" Simmad made an exploding motion with his fingers.

"I'll tell you when," Dask said.

Hagen flapped downward, still hunched over from the blow. Khelya briefly let go of Simmad to bash the head of an oncoming attacker with her fist. Other Ranycht were recovering from injuries or retrieving fallen weapons. One of them grabbed his spear, spat to the side, and opened his wings. He nodded at two others, who rose into the air with him. Another fighter started running at the four alva.

Matil let her eyelids fall halfway, screening out the approaching Ranycht. Her mind reached for the power, the 'muscle' she used for her own magic that allowed her to fade into the shadows. Instead of using it to conceal herself, she imagined pushing that energy toward Simmad.

"Now!" Dask said. He pulled Matil closer and threw his wings around her in a tent of darkness, pressing his eyes shut. She realized what he was doing. She shut her own eyes tight.

Her strength suddenly left her, draining her like she'd been fading for half a day. Her body sagged, but she stayed standing. Then came the yells and bellows of pain. Even Khelya groaned.

"Can't see!" shouted one of the men.

"They can see *us!*" another one said. "Go! Fly!"

There was a sharp cry very close by.

Dask opened his wings, revealing the twilit stream to Matil. She dropped into a crouch. The Ranycht fighters were stunned – a couple of them covered their eyes with their hands and some landed in the waist-deep water. One struggled to fade, his arms and legs disappearing with the rest of his body still visible.

Simmad was lying with his head on the bank and legs in the water, unconscious after his magic surge. A fighter scrambled to get out of the stream on the other side while Khelya pointed her bloodied spear towards him.

"Still can't see," one of the men said, panicking.

"Mat chesa," Hagen spat out. He lifted his voice. "Retreat! Fall back!" He squinted his eyes and careened back the way they had come. The grass at the top of the bank waved as he crashed through it. "Fall back," he yelled again.

The Ranycht fighters followed in the direction of his voice. Behind them, two Ranycht lay still, one on the far bank and one face-down in the water.

Khelya started forward and then hesitated. "Do we go after 'em?"

"Nah," Dask said, chest heaving. "They'll get their sight back eventually. Probably."

Simmad sat up. His wings glowed softly in the falling night. "So…" he whispered. "It worked?"

"It *really* worked," said Khelya.

"And now let's make ourselves scarce," Dask said. "Careful and quiet, guys."

2

The End of the World and Other Light Topics

Matil, Dask, Khelya, and Simmad looked over their shoulders constantly as they set up camp for the night in a moss-padded grotto. Matil's ears twitched with every *too-whit* and *crrraaa* and rustle of the underbrush. Khelya stuck her spear in the ground and tied the beetles' reins to it. The grotto was covered on all sides by mint plants. The plants' refreshing smell was so strong that the group felt safe enough to prepare dinner – in haste.

They lit a fire and took a small amount of the leaf-wrapped rabbit's meat they had fastened to Dewdrop's shell. Once the food was cooked, they covered the flames in dirt. Watching the fire go out was satisfying, but the orange and white tongues of fire had imprinted on Matil's vision, prickling her nerves.

Each one of them held a twig with juicy chunks of rabbit meat speared along the length. Dask gnawed into his portion. After some indelicate chewing, he sighed happily.

Simmad, cheeks full of food like a chipmunk, inspected the toad pendant that hung from his neck. "Amazing," he said through the food, bringing the red wood closer to his squinting blue eyes. He swallowed his mouthful. "Dyndal of the Green, Dyndal the Young Spirit, Dyndal who changed the course of the Asta River and fought Igsun's blood-drinking fawn…*is in this toad.*"

"Amazing!" Dask said. "Fan-*tabulous!*"

"I *know!* Oh…you're mocking me, aren't you?"

He smirked. "Simms is catching on. And turn down those wings before we get jumped, will ya?"

Simmad dimmed his wings and went back to marveling over the relic.

"Be nice," Matil said to Dask.

Khelya was scrutinizing the pendant, too. "I wonder when he'll come back."

Dask took a swig from his waterskin and then wiped his mouth. "Something bothers me about this 'waking the Elders' deal. You all saw that fight between Din-din and Snake-face, right? Well, except for you, Simmy."

Simmad cleared his throat. "I- I saw the important bits."

"Okay, sure. You saw the flying snake ghost lady—"

"Kanay," he corrected.

"Yeah," Dask said, "Snake-face. Before you fainted, you saw her kill an alva and almost get the kid, too. And our Elder buddy couldn't do anything to protect them."

Matil looked down and pulled her feet closer to herself, away from the smoldering fire pit. She had thought that waking Dyndal would be the end of it. That they'd be able leave the situation in the Elders' hands and watch as everything worked out. Instead, the struggle had been so close between the two ancient beings – nothing more than ghosts, yet Kanay had hurt flesh and blood.

Khelya pursed her lips. "You're forgettin' the part where Dyndal fought 'er off so she couldn't get the rest of us. So she couldn't get Matil."

"Matil's only in danger *because* of the Elders," Dask said. "Whatever the Elders really are, they've caused a lot of trouble. From the stories you guys keep telling, that's what they used to do when they were awake, too. Fight each other and make life impossible for us alva." He looked up at Simmad. "Hey, before I kidnapped you, didn't you say something about the world ending when the Elders wake up?"

"What? Oh!" Simmad's eyebrows rose. "You heard that?"

"We were watching you for weeks before I made my move," Dask said.

"*Dask*," Matil and Khelya said at the same time.

The Sangriga looked around at them, his cheeks and ears turning pink. "Did- did you hear me recite any poetry?"

"I'm *kidding*, that was the first time we ever saw you." Dask chuckled. "Poetry, huh? We oughta make you do a recital sometime."

"You'll have to kill me first," Simmad said.

"O…kay," Dask said. "I can respect that. Anyway, where was I?"

"World ending," Khelya said.

He pointed at her. "Yeah. I was just gonna say, the world ending is a big issue that we should maybe consider before we go waking up any more Elders. Or half-waking-up, or whatever this loo-loo business is."

Matil frowned as she took in his words. Which was worse? The world ending or Nychta taking over Eventyr?

"But," Simmad said, looking dreamily upward, "can't you imagine the great honor of being present as the final events unfold?"

Dask rolled his eyes. "If by great honor you mean agonizing death, then sure, I can imagine it."

"There are things that're s'posed to happen before the world ends, right?" Khelya said. "They can't all happen right away. I mean, I never thought they could."

Simmad nibbled at a chunk of meat. "Yes, the prophecies in the Chivishi – if one believes them – are clear about what must happen. In that, erm, vague, prophetic sort of way. I have found additional manuscripts that indicate how some of these things *may* happen, quite plausibly, and I've done calculations based on them. They came out to fifteen weeks or so, starting from the time I did the maths. I reckon it's been two or three weeks since then." He looked thoughtful. "Considering how everything's gone so far, it *could* take…erm…I may need to review my calculations now that we ourselves have awakened an Elder's spirit."

"So this is all," Dask twirled his hand, "in theory."

"Well…yes," Simmad said.

"Then I won't worry about the world theoretically ending." Dask stood and leaned out of the grotto to spit out gristle. "But I still think the Elders are a bad idea."

Matil looked at him, pleading. "I think they're the only way."

He sighed. "If they're really the only way, fine, I'll stop complaining. I just want us to fly into this thing with eyes open." He leaned out again to tear part of a mint leaf from a plant.

"If you fly into something, eyes open or closed, you will crash," came a familiar voice. "It took me a while to learn that, myself."

Dask nearly fell out of the grotto. Khelya squeaked and Simmad choked on his food. A softly illuminated specter sat across from Matil, between Khelya and Simmad.

"Hah!" the specter said. "I got you!"

The specter was like a cloud imprinted with the image of a muscular, golden-skinned man. Matil could sort of see the grotto wall through his foggy form. He was taller than Simmad, shorter than Khelya. His smiling face was bright and confident, with ears sticking out that curved back like Eletsol ears. His dark orange hair spiked up all over like a clover flower, and his eyes had no whites or pupils – they were filled with rippling shades of green. He wore only baggy green pants with a gold sash around his waist. Springing from his back in the shape of wings were thick layers of leaves.

With the surprise past, Matil's racing heart slowed in relief. "You're back."

"L-L-Lord Dyndal," Simmad said, ducking his head.

Khelya also lowered her head.

"Ah, fie!" The Elder Dyndal brought his fist down on his transparent knee. "You are all corpses, I say. No sense of humor."

Dask plopped himself back down between Matil and Simmad. "Wanna hear a funny joke about two Ranycht, an Obrigi, and a Sangriga fighting for their lives against ten angry guys earlier today?"

"Eleven," Khelya said.

Dyndal looked around at the four of them. "It sounds like that is not a joke."

"You're stinkin' right it isn't. We coulda used some help. Where were you?" Dask ripped off a piece of the mint leaf with his teeth and started chewing.

Dyndal bowed at the waist. "I deeply apologize for my absence and am grateful and pleased that you survived." He sat back, rubbing his chin. "The duel with…Kanay… and the healing I aided – oh, they would be nothing in my true body, but in this form they drained me. So I have been in a senseless state within the pendant, only capable of recovering my strength. I appeared here just as I had gathered enough to leave."

Khelya leaned in closer, awestruck.

"Whatever," Dask muttered.

She shot him a scowl.

"Are we—" Simmad cleared his throat. "Are we truly going to wake Lady Shora?"

"Yes, we will wake my sister," Dyndal said, "as long as we are bound for Ecker's Brug. What is our position now?"

Dewdrop the beetle tapped Dask with her antennae, so he turned and rubbed her shell. "Heading south," he said. "Still in Fainfal, but almost to the border with Nychtfal."

Matil placed her hand on the other side of Dewdrop's blue shell. She looked up at Dyndal. "I think Nychta wanted to stop us from getting to you. The—my—the alva with the Book of Myrkhar. Nychta. She captured the hermit, Hasyl, and then she sent her Skorgon to attack the Eletsol."

"She found Hasyl?" Dyndal said.

Dask stretched out his legs beside the remains of the fire pit. "His house was trashed and guarded by Skorgon when we got there."

The Elder's eyes darkened. "The Book must have told her where to go. My poor friend. May he yet live. As for the Book-bearer, she would have tried to find our sleeping bodies and…perhaps wake us, or leave us under watch so that we could not be awakened."

"Wouldn't she try to kill you while you're sleeping?" Dask said.

Simmad put his pointer finger up. "Elders have only ever been killed by other Elders."

"Indeed," Dyndal said. "You, however, reached me first. Now, the Book no doubt has her looking for the resting places of the despicable Saikyr, whom we chained with our power before the Hibernation began. If they remove the chains with spells from the Book, the Saikyr will be free as soon as the waking is complete."

Dask recoiled. "Thiffen. Then why not leave you guys asleep so they don't get free?"

"You may do so," Dyndal said. "If you want to fight Nychta and the Book on your own."

"Oh, nice," Dask said. "We have such a *wealth* of *good* options. Matil?"

Matil nodded apologetically. "Let's keep going."

"Okay," he said. "We'll keep going, then. Tonight I've learned that I will forever be known as Dask, Bringer of the Apocalypse."

Dyndal gave a hearty laugh. "I am beginning to enjoy your level of disrespect."

Dask pinched the bridge of his nose. "Thanks. Now we need a plan for getting through Nychtfal. We're almost at the border, and apparently there's this new thing called the 'Ranycht Dominion' that's on the lookout for us. Any ideas?"

The group was quiet. Talking about the Dominion made Matil think about alva she had met in Nychtfal; Dask's old friend, Kerl, and Brenna the spy, whose son Amacht died at the hands of Nychta. Matil appreciated what Captain Hagen had said about standing up and looking out for each other, and she hoped that the Dominion – whatever it was – would protect Kerl and Brenna even though it wasn't safe for Matil or her companions.

"We could be more sneaky," Khelya offered.

"No matter how sneaky we are," Dask said, "we are still a big, tall, blonde Obrigi—"

"I'm short," Khelya said glumly.

"Okay, we're a big, tall, *short* Obrigi and a ridiculously pale Sangriga. Someone will see us. I'm trying to think of routes that might make us harder to find, but I don't know what the situation is like in Nychtfal since the last time we were there."

"Should…" Khelya looked at the ground. "Should Simmad and I stay behind?"

Matil's mouth opened and then shut. She didn't know what to say.

"That's a last resort," Dask said. "We'll go through all our ideas before we consider splitting up." His brow wrinkled in further thought and his sharp green eyes drilled into the dirt-covered fire pit.

Matil watched him, warmth growing in her heart. An inescapable smile lifted the corners of her mouth.

"What about disguising ourselves?" Simmad said.

Dask looked up and Matil looked down. "I thought about disguises already," he said. "It's not realistic. Even if we could disguise *you*, there's no disguising Khelya unless we put a squirrel tail on her and call her a Kyndelin." His expression brightened. "Hey, would that work? And we could find some dead birds and slap their wings on Simmad and Matil!"

Khelya and Simmad both stared at him in horror.

"What?" Dask looked at Matil. "Is it a bad idea?"

Matil shrugged. It was kind of disgusting, but if she had to, she'd do it.

"I was thinking more of…what we Sangriga do," Simmad said. "Using light magic to assist in creating an illusion. Many battles have been won and many palaces robbed with such techniques."

"Oh." Dask looked put out. "You can do that?"

Simmad squinted. "I—well, erm, *I* can't really. Not a magician," he mumbled.

"You can't do that," Dask repeated. He shook his head. "Look, guys…dead birds. It's not a bad idea."

"Friends," Dyndal said. "As amusing as that sounds, there is another way. I can help you create illusions."

Dask crossed his arms. "I thought you said you didn't have a whole lotta strength at the moment."

"*Dask*," Khelya said.

"*Khel.*"

"Dead bird man reasons well," Dyndal said. "I need more time to recover for their creation. But the illusions that I form will use your strength instead of mine."

"I guess we'll see how good these illusions are," Dask said. "I'm ready to sleep. Pretty sure it's our firefly's turn to take first watch."

Dyndal looked offended. "Do you have no wish for a bedtale *from* a bedtale? Very well. Go to sleep."

"Oh, no, we *do!*" Simmad said. "Please tell a story, it would be incredible. Beyond imagining, I dare say."

Dask made some reluctant noises in his throat and then shrugged. "All right, if it's not too long."

Matil and Khelya exchanged radiant grins.

Immediately Dyndal spread out his hands, his eyes fresh and lively like waving grass, and said, "Listen well to my tale, alva of Eventyr. I now recount Olen and Stal and the Time They Both Almost Died."

Dask clapped. "My heart's already pounding with suspense."

Simmad glared at Dask and tapped two fingers over his own mouth.

"The twins Olen and Stal," Dyndal began, "Elders of the Second Generation, were great hunters and beloved by the forest. But the two knew well and took it as simple fact that alva loved Olen, while Stal was the greater hunter. It was only in jest, then, that Olen proposed to his brother a contest to see which of them was the superior Elder. Stal accepted the challenge with a laugh. They were to race to track down the legendary great-quail."

Dyndal stood up to better accommodate his extravagant arm motions. "Each went in a different direction. Stal made headway by picking up on the tiniest of tracks and signs left behind. Olen followed the rumors and sightings that alva reported. In the end they came to the same place. Both could tell that the great-quail was near, and they had hunted for so many days that the contest's goal now burned in their hearts. Without even having caught their quarry, they argued over which brother was superior. It turned into a fierce fight, which Stal won, leaving an injured Olen to heal. Stal soon found the great-quail rumbling through the bushes, and he lifted his mighty javelin.

"Olen's voice called out through magic, asking Stal for help. Stal believed it must be a trick and ignored it. However, just before he threw the javelin, he stopped. He couldn't bear hearing Olen's voice growing more and more desperate. Stal ran back to his brother, who was overshadowed by a Ranycht with white wings and three horns on her gray head – the witch Huldra. Just as she prepared to curse Olen, a sphere of shadow forming in her hands, Stal pierced her with his javelin. She was not killed so easily. The witch cursed Stal instead, sending him into painful darkness and then…a void." Dyndal closed his eyes as he let it sink in.

Matil looked at Dask. He was only watching the ground, though his ears leaned toward Dyndal.

The Elder opened his eyes. "Stal returned to his senses. He lay in bed. At the foot of the bed was Olen. It had been a week since the encounter, and, as far as Olen could tell, both the great-quail and the witch had fled too far into Deep Valdingfal to track.

"'You let go of the great-quail to save me,' Olen said in disbelief.

"Stal replied, 'What did you think I would do? We are brothers. We should act as brothers.' And he would have no more talk on the matter, saying it was hard enough to lose one's prey without dwelling on it. The contest stayed unwon, and the two did not care. But they had many new things to jest about for years to come." Dyndal surveyed his audience.

"Is it true?" Simmad said.

"Olen himself told me the tale."

In her excitement, Khelya's hands were pressed together so tightly that it looked painful. "Sounds like it must've happened before Stal went bad!"

"Stal went bad?" Matil said, aghast.

Dyndal nudged a pebble with his foot. "This story took place long before."

So much for the happy ending. Matil absentmindedly rubbed at a rough, warped patch of skin on the back of her right arm. In the story, Stal had been heroic. He almost died saving his brother. She shuddered. How did they change? How did alva – and Elders – go bad?

Pale eyes. The dagger. Crell's face. Amacht's blood. Flames. She paused, her fingertips resting on the damaged skin. Suddenly she knew that this was a scar from before. From Nychta's life.

Simmad's voice interrupted her reverie. "Is it really my turn to be the lookout?" he said.

"You got it, Sparky," Dask said, piling his blankets in a far corner of the grotto.

Dyndal spread his hands. "You all may sleep, friends. My body rests with the Eletsol while my spirit follows the pendant, so I can watch over you in the night. You continue to do Eventyr a great service. Sleep."

3

While You Were Sleeping

Khelya stretched up to the leaves and bent from side to side, getting all the sleep-tangles out of her muscles. It was such a good morning. Light streamed through the wild green forest. Bugs crawled and buzzed all over, working hard. And this good morning, she had woken up to hear an Elder – an *Elder* – hoping she rested well. *An Elder*. She sighed in contentment.

When Khelya was a girl, she had lived for her telvogir's stories about the Elders. A bittersweet pang hit her. Her ma's grandpa had been old, very old. It was his time. But she still missed him. He'd have liked Matil a lot, and even Dask and…she smiled. Simmad.

"Time to go!" Matil said, walking up behind Khelya. Despite her cheerful tone, there was a worried tautness on her face that she'd had ever since learning she was connected to Nychta.

Khelya gave her tiny shoulder a nudge. "Is Lord Dyndal ready to disguise us yet?"

"He told us he'll need a little more time," said Matil.

They walked down from the cluster of mint plants. Dask and Simmad were saddling the beetles alongside ghostly Dyndal, who grinned up at the tree canopy.

They set off with Khelya walking, Matil riding Dewdrop, and Dask in command of Olnar while Simmad sat back-to-back with him. Dyndal walked beside Khelya.

Khelya couldn't stop sneaking glances at the Elder. She was, hands-down, the luckiest Obrigi in Eventyr, getting to travel with none other than Dyndal. A common Obrigi farmer such as herself didn't deserve the honor. But, even though it shouldn't be possible, it felt downright comfortable.

"What happened whilst I slept?" Dyndal said, breaking the silence. "Do not leave out any detail!"

Dask smirked. "That's a lotta sky to fly."

"I- I- I could—but he's right," Simmad said, not meeting Dyndal's eyes, "there's- there's, well, centuries, and, er… *every detail…*"

"I know some history," Khelya said hesitantly.

Simmad's head bobbed in emphatic agreement. "You go ahead, then."

She thought back to the books in school. The Time of Loss…where did it start? Chapter five! Yes. Okay. She could see it now. "After the Elders entered the Great Hibernation, every kind of alva lost whatever blessings had been bestowed on 'em. Without the Elders keepin' the forest in balance, too, the nations fell into turmoil. Succession wars and territorial disputes were vicious and om-nee-present durin' this period, which came to be known as the Time of Loss."

Dyndal gaped, his glowy eyes swirling.

"But, um," Khelya slowed down in her recollection, "a hundred years later the paper mill was invented. Books got cheaper to make. That was good."

"Inventions!" Dyndal said in relief. "Tell me more about those."

Khelya and Simmad took turns describing ones that came to mind. At mention of the geared crane, Dyndal sighed.

"Hasyl spoke much of invention and new ways of doing things," the Elder said. "I wonder what it was like for him to watch Eventyr change."

Khelya felt a weight on her heart. She'd never met the hermit, but she'd been in his home. In Obrigi, buildings were the same wherever you went. Sure, they had different functions. Still just walls, roof, and a floor. For all Khelya had loved her poor, burned-down house, she knew if she could see it again, something would be missing. Eventyr had spoiled her. Outside Obrigi, buildings became alva. There were fat houses and thin ones, uneven walls, lopsided roofs, styles of all kinds, decorative beams and knobs and bits and bobs that made no sense but were—goodness, the buildings seemed to smile or frown at Khelya depending on their moods. It took her breath away.

The hermit's home, with its mechanical devices, skylight, and herbs, had given her a feeling that she couldn't name, like she'd met the man and sat down with him for a meal. Somehow she knew they would've had a lot to talk about.

Dyndal walked ahead of the group. "If only Hasyl had been born an Elder in my place. He had a good enough sense of humor for it, and more sense in general."

In time he again strolled jauntily beside the others, asking them rapid-fire questions about themselves. Some answers were short and others were long, like a story that Dask got into telling about a gang operation gone sideways.

"…swear, the knife was this close to my neck," Dask was saying, "but I twisted backward – and looked really good doing it – until I completely fell over. Then I sorta scooted out on my wings till I could jump up and fly outta there. Escaped with a tiny scratch. *That's* where this scar came from." He pointed at a white line under his jaw.

Each of them wowed and oohed and aahed. Matil's purple eyes were bright. She always looked at and listened to things with deep interest, like she didn't want to forget a thing. Having a friend like her was very different from Khelya's past.

Having friends at all was different. She remembered a boy who had once taken her lunch basket and held it out of reach. "They don't let shorties go to class," he jeered.

Then she remembered the first conversation she'd had at her new school. "You just said 'ain't'," someone told her. "Doesn't that mean you're slow?"

Another time, "You haven't picked a job yet?" That alva had laughed and walked away.

"Your family moved here," a voice whispered in her ear. "You can't be one of us."

"Don't read ahead in the book," some teachers told her.

"Five marks for raising your voice," many more teachers said.

One girl spoke to another as Khelya walked behind them. "Don't do the project with Khelya. She's mean."

"Good thing she was born smack in the middle," said her second-oldest brother to the family. "When she can't make no money, we'll just pretend she doesn't exist."

"Lady Obrigi," Dyndal said. "Khelya, yes?"

Khelya was jarred back to the present. "Yes, sir?"

"What is your surname?"

"I…I'm not really sure." Khelya looked at the ground. "I had one, an' now I kind of…have a different one. Epalen. But I don't even know if it's the right one."

"You have not chosen a trade yet?" He scratched his head. "Do Obrigi still hold that tradition?"

Her shoulders fell. "Yeah, we do."

"She's working on it," Dask said. "It's hard to choose between interesting occupations like construction, farming, walking, and fighting evil."

Khelya pointed down at his head. "Exactly."

Dyndal chuckled. "Very good. There were great Obrigi who did not settle on a name until late in life after many accomplishments."

"*Really?*" she said. Could she do that, too?

"Indeed," said Dyndal. "Your time may have forgotten them, as they lived long ago. Yet a well-considered name may prove more helpful than one chosen quickly that seals a bitter fate. And what of Master Long-Ears? Any family?"

Simmad touched his chest. "Me?"

"Of course, you!" The Elder held up his hands to the sides of his own head. "You have the longest ears."

"Oh." Simmad patted his ears. "So I do. Ahem, er, family. I've got parents and loads of sisters. I go down to visit during festivals. My aunt and her husband live near them. She's the one who introduced me to the academic world! Not that I've…done much with it."

"That is not good," Dyndal said. "Cherish your gifts. From now on we will help you. Your aunt will be made proud."

"E-excuse me?" Simmad said.

"Do you have a wife?" said Dyndal.

He had to take a moment to catch up. "N-no, not—I don't even have prospects, so a wife is out of the question. No one would take me."

"That's not true," Khelya said, indignant. Everyone looked up at her. Her neck and face heated up. She took off her headband to re-tie it. "Someone would take 'im. Why not?"

Matil nodded. "Sure. You shouldn't give up."

Dask gave Simmad a doubtful look. "You two think so?"

"No prospects," the Sangriga repeated sadly. "No future. The world may end soon anyway."

"Come now," Dyndal said, "you do not know when the world will end."

Simmad looked up brightly. "Do *you*, sir?"

"No. I will not be here when it does happen, but that is all I know." He flexed his arms. "I hope that I stay for a long time."

"Almost to the border, folks," Dask said as he checked the map.

"Let us stop here," said Dyndal. "There is something we must do before crossing, and I think I have enough strength for it now."

Those words seemed to echo around Khelya's empty stomach. "I saw taters back there a little ways." She pulled a large knife out of her pack. "If we're gonna stop, want me to get some for lunch?"

Everyone liked the idea of taters – who wouldn't? – so she went into the bracken to search.

"Found 'em!" she yelled to the others through the undergrowth. She set the knife to the side and got to work digging with her hands around a potato plant whose clump of leaves came up to her head. When she'd revealed one of the domed brown roots of the plant, she looked around for her knife. Something colorful caught her eye against the forest's greenery.

It was an alva several steps from her on a low ridge. He was a little taller than Khelya, but she knew immediately that he wasn't an Obrigi. Out of his unruly, clay-red hair stood two sharp ears lined with fur. This man was a

Kyndelin wearing ragged clothes. A beard ran savage over his angular face and stuck out at the sides. His eyes were fixed on something far away. Khelya was experienced enough to recognize what the dark circles under his eyes and staring into space probably meant: He needed sleep.

Matil had told her about the last time they came across a Kyndelin. While everyone else was sleeping, a mousy guy took their supplies. He'd either been a bandit, or he'd gone wild. Khelya didn't know much about the mysterious Kyndelin except that they used their magic to protect other alva from animal predators, and sometimes they lost themselves in the animals they could turn into. This red-haired man definitely looked lost.

Khelya grabbed the knife from the ground and stood cautiously. She wondered briefly how to address him, and decided that simple was best. "Hey, there! Shoo! Git along!"

He twitched and his ears went straight up at the sound of her voice. He looked at her in astonishment, revealing the brilliant copper color of his eyes. Khelya studied them in fascination before realizing she was in a stare-off with an intense and possibly wild opponent.

"What is it, Khel?" Dask shouted.

"There's- there's a Kyndelin," she replied, glancing back through the bracken and then again at the strange man. "I think he's wild!"

"Do you need help?" came Simmad's voice.

"I dunno," Khelya said.

"If she doesn't know, she's fine," she heard Dask say. She rolled her eyes.

The man still observed her without a sound. Khelya held the knife out threateningly. She was about to speak again when his face changed slightly. She tried to figure out what was different.

He had smiled. What tipped her off was that his eyes narrowed, crinkling at the corners. Now she saw the reserved smile buried in his unkempt beard.

Khelya watched him uncertainly. Her voice lowered. "You're…not wild?"

He shook his head.

"Oh, thank Thosten." She relaxed her knife arm. "Do you need food or somethin'? We could, uh, share the tater." She gestured at her partially-excavated potato.

A different look washed over the Kyndelin's face, pale and mortified. Khelya only had a moment to realize it before he turned and dashed off. His legs became black paws, and the last she saw of him was a thick, white-tipped red tail swishing through the underbrush and out of sight.

She whipped around, thinking that there must be something scary behind her. Nope. Just leaves. Maybe he was afraid of *her*. But that couldn't be right. He'd just smiled at her. Huh. Probably missing some tools in the box.

After Khelya gathered enough, she climbed back with potato slices under her arms. The other three alva were discussing something with Dyndal. Their beetles roamed nearby plants for food.

Dask looked up at her. "The Kyndelin didn't hassle you, did he? Is he still there?"

"Long gone," said Khelya.

"Good," he said. "We're gonna do something crazy."

"Oh?" She set down the potato slices. "I'm scared now."

Dyndal – she still couldn't believe it was him – turned with a smile. "You will all be Ranycht."

Khelya tilted her head, wondering if she'd heard right. "Sir? Even with magic, how would that work?"

"What little power I have, combined with light," Dyndal put a hand on Simmad's shoulder, "and shadows." He set the other hand on Dask's shoulder, but Dask shuffled away, ruffling his wings. Dyndal gave him a side-eyed glare. "Shadows," he repeated, reaching across to put the rejected hand on Matil's shoulder. "Matil is easy enough to disguise. We need to change her eyes and give her a pair of wings. Simmad will be made to look like a Ranycht and should keep his wings snuffed out at all times. I can remain unseen when among others. You, Khelya, prove the most challenging, since we will essentially create a puppet."

"A puppet?" Khelya said. She knelt down to start building a fire for the taters and beckoned Dask over to help.

"A full illusion," said Dyndal, "to mimic your motions. The rest of your body will be invisible."

"Not again," she whined.

Dask snickered as he emptied a waterskin into their pot.

"Is there a different way?" Matil said, her ears going down.

"Hey, if it means I can go with you, I'll do it." Khelya broke apart the slices and plopped them into the pot over the growing fire.

Dyndal clapped. "Let us begin! Dask, Matil, and Simmad, join me. Be warned, when your magic leaves you, it may cause dizziness. Put your hands in the middle, yes, like so…"

Khelya looked up from stirring the tater bits. Closing his eyes, Dyndal took their hands in his. Each of them began to glow strangely, like shadows and sunlight running across their skin at random. The glow concentrated at their hands and then permeated Dyndal, finally subsiding.

Simmad fell to the ground in a heap. Matil gasped.

"Mr. Simmad?" Khelya cried. She scrambled around the fire to his body.

Dask wobbled woozily, bent down next to the fallen Sangriga, and burst into laughter. "He's *snoring*."

Dyndal crossed his arms defensively. "I did tell him it might…daze him. Is he well?"

"Oh, he'll be fine," Dask said.

"Then we must hurry. I shall make Simmad's disguise first."

Khelya turned back to make sure the pot didn't boil over. She added thyme from one of the packs. Dyndal began to wave his hands over Simmad, using magic to transform the unconscious man. Meanwhile, Dask entertained himself by sticking his hand through Simmad's new double-sized nose illusion.

"Come on, just try it," he said, "it feels really weird."

"If it feels as weird as it looks, there's no way that's happening," Khelya said.

Simmad's nose shrank to normal size.

"What's going on…?" He sat up, caught sight of his right hand, and yelped. His hand was less than half its usual size.

"I beg your quiet," Dyndal said. "I am concentrating." He looked at Simmad and choked back a laugh.

Afterward, he managed to change Simmad's skin, hair, ears, and wings. The pale Sangriga was now a tall Ranycht with dark skin and hair, as well as elegant brown wings. His eyes were the same familiar blue, but larger and rounder in shape. His long slender ears had become broader. Dyndal examined his handiwork proudly.

Matil was next, and she couldn't stop smiling. Khelya figured that even if her friend couldn't use them, it would be great for Matil to get wings.

"I will give you dark brown wings, to match your hair," said Dyndal.

"Wait," Matil said, suddenly panicking. "Can you make my hair and wings darker?"

Dyndal stretched his transparent fingers. "Good idea. You will look even more different."

He made her eyes pastel blue, and then gave her black hair and wings almost as dark and shiny as Dask's. Matil twirled to admire them.

"Look at those, they're great." Dask pointed up and down her wings. "I guess our Elder did something right, huh? Look at those."

"Thank you," Matil said quietly to Dyndal.

The Elder's eyes were a cheerful light green. "You are most welcome."

Dask walked up to him. "I wanna look nothing like me. Mustache preferred."

Dyndal laughed. "Very well." He cracked his knuckles and then moved his fingers through the air.

A few moments later, Dask's wings changed from crow-black to brown with black stripes. He turned around. Khelya and Matil looked at him in stunned silence.

"What?" Dask said. "He didn't turn me into a weevil or anything, did he?" It was a strange thing to hear Dask's voice come out of a stranger with shaved head, broad features, and a very thick brown mustache. He unsheathed his knife and studied the reflection in the blade. "*Oh*. Wow-ee. I'm not sure what to think."

Matil giggled. "It's perfect. Definitely not you."

Dask held out his hand. "What the lady said. You've done it again, ancient one."

Dyndal gave a dramatic bow. Turning to Khelya, he said, "Now it is your turn. Any requests?"

"No, sir," she answered.

He fixated on Khelya before waving both of his hands in front of her. The tips of her fingers began to prickle. The prickling spread up her arms and through her shoulders. She lifted her shoulders with a shiver. That prickle was the feeling of someone else's magic. There was something different than what she was used to, though, a strength running through it like a wild rabbit's muscles tensing to spring. It felt so much bigger than her that she was afraid she wouldn't be able to control it.

My magic, she told herself. It was such a funny thing to think. Obrigi didn't have magic…but Dyndal had pointed out it was in the Chivishi that they did. So they must. The prickling vanished and Khelya saw that she, too, had disappeared. She'd never get used to not seeing herself.

Dask flew around her, marveling at how complete her camouflage was. With more hand gestures, Dyndal created a phantom standing about Matil's height, covering Khelya's right leg. It grew solid and became a girl very much like Khelya, from what she could tell looking down at her, just with brown hair and even darker brown skin. Then the big ears and feathered wings came along. Khelya forgot the strangeness of the whole event when she saw those tawny, glossy wings. The sight of 'herself' with wings made her giddy.

"You're so pretty," Matil said excitedly. "Not as pretty as normal Khelya, but close."

Khelya laughed. "Aw, you just shush up."

She moved around awkwardly, testing the Ranycht that she had become. The illusion waved her arm, wiggled her head, and jumped when Khelya did. Dask pretended to shake her hand. She got carried away and accidentally knocked him over with her invisible arm. "Sorry." She picked him back up.

"Whoa," Dask said as her invisible hands set him down standing. "Yeah, this is gonna take practice."

"Right you are," Dyndal said. "When next we come upon a village near nightfall, let us see how you do round true Ranycht."

"It would be a fascinating experience," Simmad said, "but isn't it dangerous?"

"Oh, come off it!" Dyndal grinned. "Anything without risk is boring."

Simmad looked downcast. "I wouldn't say that, Lord Dyndal. Reading is fun."

"Paper cuts, eye strain, the discovery of unwanted knowledge." The Elder waved his hand. "Reading has risks, which is why you find it entertaining."

"I've never thought about it *that* way. B-but I don't think that's why I like to read…"

"What if we do get caught?" Matil said.

"Our shiny green ghost has a point," Dask said. "We should test the disguises somewhere we can escape easily. If things go wrong, the Brug ain't a place an Obrigi or a Sangriga would wanna get trapped."

"Then I get to go to a Ranycht town for the first time?" said Khelya.

Matil's reluctance seemed to melt away at her enthusiasm. "Yep!"

"And to make things a bit safer…" Dyndal closed one eye and pushed his palm toward each of them.

Khelya felt an added burden like she was wearing a heavy pack, only it was all through her body.

"A veil now falls between you and other alva," he said. "As long as the disguises are in place, alva will be urged away from each of you by something they know not, for if they laid hands on you they might notice that the wings have no substance, or that there is a concealed mass hovering over little Khelya's head. With this veil, they will not want to go near you."

"Excellent!" Simmad said.

Dask tapped his chin. "In disguise, you'll be Geck," he said to Simmad, "and Khelya can be…Livi. I'm thinking Volf for myself. Matil, you should have a Ranycht name, too. We could call you Yuna."

"Yuna's good," black-haired Matil said.

"Geck," Simmad tried out. "I'm Geck. Right, better get the accent sorted. 'Wherrre arrre yoo.'"

Dask shook his head. "Too much arrr. Just don't talk much."

Khelya sighed while looking down at little Livi, who sighed with her. She didn't like the idea of pretending to be someone she wasn't, but at least she'd fit in for once.

4

At Your Own Risk

The Nervoda representatives were a pool of blue and green on the Ambermeet's warm floor with Princess Karimis, their ambassador, at the centre. Man and woman alike let their slick black hair flow back alongside their downward-sloping ears, and the fabric of their gathered robes shimmered like liquid.

Many of them were heaped with jewelry, but Karimis's sole accessory was a headdress made from iridescent shell fragments. She gazed about at the Council members with appreciative and careful eyes of a deep sapphire colour. Her features were typical among the Nervoda – heavy eyebrows, long nose, and round jaw, a beautiful and proud face of the kind a sculptor would carve onto a statue. All of the Nervoda present had pale skin like that of the Sangriga, only with a sallow tint. Lyria imagined that living underwater denied one the healthy glow that sunlight provided.

"Hail, Council of Tyrlis and Lord Owynth," Karimis said in her purring accent. Vangarans like her spoke their own language between themselves and sounded very different from Nervoda elsewhere. "We bring plentiful greetings from King Delos and all of Vangara."

The entire Council bowed graciously, and then the princess began to speak about trade. The Nervoda king was apparently nettled that their routes to Tyrlis now required extra work to get through or round the Fortification. Owynth could only offer apologies, but the overall tone was pleasant because their traders continued to profit. It came time for the Council members to ask their questions.

Lyria and one other rose from their seats.

"Sorigan," Owynth said with a nod.

Sorigan, an old countess bent under a pile of jewels in her hair, waved both hands at Lyria. "Stay up, I shan't take long." She turned to Karimis. "Dear princess, you would do me great honor by attending a ball I happen to be throwing this evening. Even our own king – long may he live – is due to attend!"

Oh, she "happened" to be throwing a ball? Knowing Sorigan, it would be Nervoda-themed, with Nervoda cuisine and water-woven cloth draped everywhere. Lyria had heard much about the countess's parties, though she'd never been invited.

Owynth smiled tightly. "Please leave invitations for after the Council is dismissed."

"Oh, good Calo, I am altogether too eager, aren't I?" Sorigan gave the Council members near her a charming smile.

"Let us speak afterward, Lady Sorigan," Karimis said politely.

Several other Council members rose now to speak, but Owynth said, "Lyria." They floated back into their chairs.

Lyria looked down at the princess and bowed slightly at the waist. "Hail, princess. Have your alva made any moves regarding the Ranycht Dominion?"

"Scouting, yes," said Karimis. "It is our determination that the Dominion poses no threat to Vangara. They have not yet made contact of any kind."

"If, for example, they made war with us," Lyria said, "would you be able to offer aid?"

Karimis looked sympathetic. "The king has promised his alva that he will not put them in danger unless Vangara itself is threatened. I am certain, besides, that your military might is a great salmon to the Dominion's tadpole." A chuckle went round the Ambermeet, and the princess smiled.

Lyria had expected as much. The Nervoda were fair-weather friends and everyone knew it. No doubt some Council members would wonder where Lyria's wits had gone. She'd kept herself steady and clear-spoken, but behind the mask boiled desperation. The Dominion, the Book, the Skorgon…Other alva weren't concerned with those things. They hadn't been through what she had. Nevertheless, she wouldn't wish that experience on anyone.

"I urge you, princess," Lyria said, "keep your eyes on Nychtfal. Keep watch, or the tadpole may grow and become a monster." She bowed once more and sat down. Her immediate neighbors shot puzzled glances at her.

* * *

The Council recessed much later, leisurely filing out of both doors onto the suspended walkways on opposite sides of the Ambermeet. The sunset's rays caused the giant amber teardrop to glow red around its edges, and its walkways glowed yellow with the wings of many Council members. Everyone gabbled and gossiped about the Nervoda delegation, whilst Lyria wanted to scream at all of them. She thought she just might have, if a hand hadn't closed over her shoulder.

"Councilwoman," came Nider's voice, much too close in her ear.

She tightened her fingers around her staff and turned. "What is it, Councilman?"

He looked genial, his yellow eyes smiling and reddish-blond hair flowing loosely. The Council members filing out behind them groused, "How rude to stop in the exit," or, with significant glares, "Some alva lack propriety."

"Thought I'd pull you aside," Nider said. "I only want a quick word in private."

Nider wanted a word with her? Even through a hostile lens, her curiosity was piqued. "Nowhere too private."

"Oh," he said, as if he thought she were adorable, "you stress too much, Lyria. It's how you got those emaciated cheeks. Now come along."

Once his back was turned, she made a gargoyle face at him and followed at a safe distance. He led her across the walkway into one of the tree buildings between which the Ambermeet hung suspended. There were only a few alva walking and floating through the halls as the day came to a close, but they were enough to satisfy Lyria's caution. She greeted them conspicuously as they flew by. Nider chose a door high up on the wall, and she checked the room before going in. It was dim, but simply furnished, with no closets or desks large enough to hide someone. Nider must be trying to settle her concerns somewhat.

When Lyria came in, she didn't close the door all the way. He allowed it.

"I was impressed when you spoke with the princess," he said, pacing calmly about his half of the room.

Lyria raised her eyebrows at him. "I can't imagine that anything I've done would impress you."

He chuckled. "You'd be surprised. I've noticed more and more your confidence. Your daring. It only today occurred to me how entirely unsuitable your behavior is."

She was strangely relieved that he'd said the last part. Being complimented by Nider felt all wrong. "Is it? Funny how alva have such different viewpoints. I believe I comported myself with courtesy today. But if you can't give me that, then at the least we can agree I'm not a total boor."

Nider stopped pacing. "Those who ignore their place get hurt," he said. He looked serious, his expression void of menace or mockery. "That was the reason I held you back."

"What? Held me back?" She tried to remember a time when he might have stopped her. He couldn't mean asking to talk with her just a moment ago.

"The riot," he said. "Surely you remember."

Fury flushed Lyria's cheeks. The riot. "So finally you admit that it *was* your doing."

"It would have happened at some point, Lyria. And the farther you and the other commoners had gone, the worse you'd have been hurt in the end. I saved you from that fate."

"*Saved?*" She laughed harshly. "I'm dreaming, aren't I?"

The corners of Nider's mouth lifted. "You're lucky my words don't make sense to you. Oh, but I doubt luck will let you avoid the consequences of your actions for much longer. If only Owynth had taken you off the Council back then, after the riot. You'll regret not having stayed in Galonbai where you belonged, with your oafish father."

Lyria dug her nails into the wood of her staff. It took all her restraint to keep from swinging the staff's triangular metal headpiece at him. "My father never spoke an unkind word about anyone," she said in a low voice, "much less the dead. What does that say about you, a nobleman?"

"It says that I'm not an idiot. Most alva deserve unkind words. The dead ones especially." He tut-tutted. "Where has our country gone, that a cloth-monger's daughter would attempt to shame a count?" He stepped closer and locked his eyes onto hers, his yellow irises murky in the shadow. "What are you doing here, Lyria?" he said softly. "This is not your place."

She closed her other hand around her staff, but otherwise didn't move. "It is my place." *Snake*, she wanted to add. "I belong on the Council. As much as your birth earned you a seat, my work has earned me the same."

"That you had to work for it is a sign you'll never belong here. No matter what fine official's robes you wear, your blood is as common as dirt."

She glowered up at him. "Have you gone out of your way just to blow sour breath at me, or was there some point you wished to make?"

Nider smiled, and suddenly Lyria's stomach turned with how close they were. Stepping back would show her to be intimidated, so she met his haughty stare. The amusement on his face grew, however, and she knew he could sense her discomfort.

He began to speak in a warm murmur that sent chills all through her. "Bid the Council farewell, Lyria. Leave."

She nearly jumped out of her skin when Nider put his hand near hers on the staff.

"There," he said. "I've told you now. It will be your own fault when you die."

* * *

"Ha-*ah!*" Lyria yelled.

Her training staff cracked against the bucket head of a dummy. It flew off and banged against the stone wall of her cellar. She whirled around to chest-jab a second dummy, who bent back from its weighted base. Another bucket soared across the cellar, followed swiftly by a broom that had served as one dummy's arms. Her flurry of smashing left no dummy undemolished.

Gasping heavily, Lyria slowed to a stop. She gave the slaughtered dummies a wobbly, sportsmanlike bow, set her staff against the wall, and grabbed a rag to wipe the sweat and hair from her face. She took another look about at the dummies. With a hopeless groan she sank to the floor, her brown practice robes bunching up.

He had never before confronted her directly. Everything remained veiled in etiquette to the point where she often doubted that he was the one who'd destroyed her first great cause. Yet there he was, confirming it.

She scowled. "Collied rat-spawn."

Insulting her father.

"I doubt yours even loved you."

Threatening her.

Lyria rubbed her face. "Blazes."

When it came to the Council, anyone could be bought. Those with sprawling households of gossipy servants and party guests endangered themselves far more than those with tight circles of allies. And those who kept their circles so small as to be squares or triangles were better off still. While imprudent Council members fell from grace amid scandals or found that a careless word implicated them in treason, Lyria had got on pretty securely without close associates. Alva disregarded her outside of the Ambermeet because she shunned connections, but she'd scraped up enough respect with those who mattered that she could make a difference inside of the Ambermeet. Her self-defense skills had also thwarted the kind of cheapjack assassination attempts that bitter Council members would commission once before giving up. On the whole, Lyria was safe.

No, she *had been* safe. The old rules weren't enough anymore. Isolation was her shield of choice, but if Nider's powerful allies on the other side took notice, they could use that heavy shield to crush her.

She leaned her head against the cold wall and closed her eyes. "Can I stop?" she whispered. Her mouth felt full of thistledown. "Can't I just…stop?" Tears traced her cheeks. "Let me be that pitiful thing – that thing he wants me to be."

At last she sniffled, wiped her eyes and nose on her sleeve, and stood. With a wry look upward, she said, "Or *you* could help me. I've heard you're good at helping."

5

In Memory

Crossing into Nychtfal at midday, Matil and her friends saw an unmanned watchtower built into a tree trunk. There would be more alva around soon, so Dask told Dyndal they should have their disguises ready on short notice. Dyndal enthusiastically practiced disguising the alva while he floated above them. He wiggled his fingers and their appearances changed, first to their Ranycht disguises, then to their true forms, and back. Each time, the alva grew more comfortable with the disguises using their strength.

Turning her head, Matil could see her illusory wings out of the corner of her eye before they vanished. She'd been glad they weren't like Nychta's. Now an idea occurred to her. If Dyndal's spirit could give her wings like these, could the awakened Elders give her real wings? She imagined racing Dask, or flying just to feel the wind on her feathers, or breaking the tree canopy to see the stars in full glory.

Matil brought Dewdrop alongside Olnar. She looked over at Dask, who was sitting backwards on the beetle while Simmad sat up front. "What does flying feel like?" she asked. She saw his hesitation and guessed what it meant. "Don't worry about me. Be honest."

"Well, it's…useful," Dask said. "Very convenient."

Matil tilted her head. She had expected a different kind of description.

"It's like moving your arms," he went on haltingly. "You don't really know how it feels until…you push yourself. But then you can tell just how much the world is trying to bring you down. The earth, the wind, the trees, they're all pulling at you, playing a game where they keep you out of the sky. And if you win – you have to *keep* winning – then you're strong. When you get to the ground and you're too tired to lift your wings, you know that tomorrow you'll be able to fly farther and faster. That's your prize for winning." He looked at the treetops that vaulted breathtakingly high over the forest. "Tomorrow, for a little longer, you'll break away from the dirt and beat the wind." His dark skin took on a red tinge, and he rubbed the back of his neck.

Dask's fake bushy mustache flashed into existence, disappeared, and reappeared. Matil held in a giggle.

"You're having too much fun with this," Dask said to Dyndal.

"*Oof!*" Khelya's Ranycht self fell to the ground and vanished while her Obrigi self reappeared on her hands and knees.

Matil reined in Dewdrop. "Are you—"

"I'm fine." Khelya staggered to her feet and looked nervously at Simmad, who sat front-facing on Olnar but had turned to watch with a concerned expression.

"Many apologies, dear Khelya," Dyndal said. "I will stop. I now am well prepared for the task."

Matil got Dewdrop moving again, but a short time later she noticed something different about the forest. At first she couldn't tell what, and then she saw them, high up in the trees. Threaded through the tree branches were long ropes knotted at intervals. Bundles of feathers had been tucked into each knot.

"Oh—" She pointed. "What's that rope for?"

Dask's wings drooped and he didn't look up. "Ask Sparkles."

"Me?" said Simmad. "Wh…I mean, I suppose I know a bit about Ranycht culture, but I—"

"You know where we are," he said. "Northwestern Nychtfal. Close to the border with Obrigi."

After a moment of scrunching his face in thought, Simmad lifted his head. "Is this where those Ranycht were attacked? That was ages ago, I was just going into university when it happened." He brought Olnar to a stop and followed the ropes with his eyes. "Those feathers…" he said slowly. "A memorial?"

Everyone else stopped with him.

Dask got down from Olnar. "There used to be a village here," he said.

Realization crawled up Matil's back. Were they talking about the Westfalinn Massacres? Were they standing where one had *happened?* She slid out of Dewdrop's saddle. Dewdrop bumped her head into Matil's side, and Matil absentmindedly patted between the beetle's antennae. There was still too much she didn't know about that day, but she had always been afraid to ask.

Simmad shook his head. "That- that's not right. Only…a few Ranycht died. Granted, my father and mother were terribly concerned that a war might start, but by next year everyone had forgotten about it. It really wasn't supported by most Sangriga."

Dask's fists clenched. "Liar. There's a reason we Ranycht call it the Massacres. Those feathers mark just one of the villages they slaughtered and burned."

Khelya looked ill.

"I know there's a bit of misinformation out there about it," Simmad said, "but I surely would have…would have known if…something so dreadful…" His voice thinned and petered out.

"Don't act innocent," Dask said. "You worked at a university. Haven't you ever seen someone change history?"

Simmad's face fell.

Dyndal focused intently on Dask with eyes the color of shadows on the forest floor. "Massacres, you said. Of what do you speak?"

Something dreadful deepened Dask's grim expression. "You were asleep. You slept through the worst day of- of

Ranycht history." His wings flared out slightly as he spoke. "You couldn't do a single thing to stop it because you didn't even know it was happening!"

Dyndal's leaf wings rippled. "*What* happened?"

"Sangriga, huge mobs of them, attacked Ranycht towns," Dask said. "Hunted my alva like animals. No war, no big dramatic fight, no one to protect us. Just killing. Then they went home and settled down to raise their kids. They didn't have to live with the consequences. We did."

Dyndal's face hardened.

Matil felt like she'd been slapped. She already knew everything he had said, but the way he had spoken, flatly, quickly, to cover up that intense feeling she had seen in his face…it made her want to comfort Dask – and it caused a rush of hot, dizzying anger to shoot through her. *They didn't have to live with the consequences.* Suddenly she had a hard time looking at Simmad and his wings of shimmering light. That anger…but there was something else, too. Terror.

Though her whirling emotions passed a moment later, they left behind a hauntingly familiar ache in the depths of her mind. It was a heavy, foreboding thing that struck again and again like a distant tolling bell.

Dyndal took a long look up at the feathers and then closed his glowing eyes. "You are strong, Dask."

A confused laugh burst out of Dask. "What makes ya say that?"

"You hold a burning coal deep within," Dyndal said, "a burden unjustly passed to you by others. And yet you do not let it control you." He opened his eyes. "Well, it may control your words, but not your actions. Your actions show us a heart that is not yet broken."

Dask was silent.

"And now I speak for myself." Dyndal knelt to look directly at Dask. "Before the great sleep, the world was falling under Myrkhar's sway. Things were happening in my time exactly like this hunting of Ranycht, and we could not stop them all. We had lost numbers as well as trust with the alva of Eventyr. Calo made the best choice he could. Shut the Elders away until a time when we were sought out. It meant that we could no longer do anything, but neither could the Saikyr."

Dask considered Dyndal's wispy form. "Let's say it was the best option. You believe in all-powerful Thosten, right? Tell me why *he* lets it happen."

Dyndal nodded. "In my youth, I thought that I could save everyone. When I discovered I could not…I was angry. With myself and with Thosten. Why did he make me a protector of alva, stronger than alva, yet not strong enough to protect them all? Surely I was his hand in Eventyr for carrying out justice. If I was not – if the Elders were not – then who was? Had he truly left us alone?" He stood and paced around. "I came to realize that he *had* made us strong enough, at the start. But we sought more power than he had gifted us with, and it was our desire for more that shattered us."

"Lord Dyndal," Simmad said, "are you referring to the Elders drinking from the Heart? You talk as if you were there, but you were born a long time afterward. Er…weren't you?"

"Correct! But does it matter? Would I not have drunk from the Heart myself? I know I would have. All of them did, save Calo, and he was created to be our leader so he is rather of a different sort."

"So," Dask said, "Thosten set everything up, and when it went bad he left it that way. Figures."

Khelya's brow was furrowed. "Dask," she said.

"Don't 'Dask' me. Where were *your* kind when the Massacres happened?" He waved his hands around at the trees. "No one is ever where they need to be, and innocent alva die because of it."

As Matil watched him, he met her eyes. His shoulders relaxed. She often thought that Dask's arguments were out of stubbornness, but he did ask questions that she hoped could be answered. And right now, she found herself entirely on his side. She was ashamed of her assumption that he didn't want real answers, that he attacked and asked hard questions just to be spiteful.

"Thosten gave us this forest," Dyndal said. "He gave us ourselves when he awakened the first Elders and the first alva." He gestured to all of them. "He gave us each other. That means he is not our puppet-master, and everything he has given is ours to do with as we please. Whether for good or evil. It is freedom."

"Freedom," Dask said. "That's funny. Last I heard, the Chivishi's full of nothing but rules. And if *we're* in charge of the forest, why do alva ask Thosten to take care of everything? Then there's that whole thing about good and evil." He ran a hand through his hair. "Why are alva like me supposed to be evil for not believing in all that junk? We get lumped in with alva who are actually evil, alva who actually deserve to go to a bad place after they die!"

Dyndal's misty body went from gold-tinged to silver, and his green eyes darkened. "It is as the Chivishi says. All of us deserve to go to a bad place after we die. All of us have the seed of evil planted in our hearts." His eyes brightened. "Yet there is love surrounding Eventyr. We can reach out of the darkness and take hold of this love that protects, provides, and brings home. This love that wants *us* to love as deeply as it does, and gives us the freedom to make it possible."

Dask looked off to the side. "Love, huh? Sure doesn't feel like it."

"Perhaps not," Dyndal said. "What does love feel like?"

He frowned. "Happiness." After a moment, his hand went toward his chest. His voice lowered. "Pain."

Dyndal gave Dask and the others a gentle smile. "Let us be where we need to be, my friends. To save the innocent." With weightless stride, he moved on ahead of the alva.

Matil placed a hand on a troubled Khelya's forearm. The two of them looked at Dask, who seemed lost in thought.

Simmad floated down from Olnar's saddle, paused, and then walked toward Dask. "I really didn't know how far it went," he said quietly. "The…the Massacres. I don't believe most of us did. But the fact that they happened…and that we were indifferent enough to never seek the truth…I… I'm so sorry."

"Wasn't your fault," Dask muttered.

* * *

That night they tied their beetles by a sheer dirt cliff, roots poking out of its side. Dask announced that he would search for food. Matil and Khelya looked at each other before quickly offering to go with him. The three stalked away from camp until Simmad's eager stream of questions to Dyndal could no longer be heard.

Khelya ducked under a fern. "You okay?"

"Hey," Dask said, looking back toward the camp. "Wanna know what I think? I think Simms has a colony of tiny alva living in his head, and they tell him what to say. I think at least five are on the job at any given time. It's the only explanation."

Matil would have laughed if not for the frantic undercurrent in his voice. "Dask," she said. She hesitated, afraid to ask her question but wanting to know. "Earlier…is that how…"

He glanced at her. "How my family died? Yeah."

"I'm sorry," she said.

Khelya seemed to be searching for words.

"Sangriga," said Dask. "Sangriga wear fancy clothes and build fancy houses. They act proper and dainty. They have

65

their Council, their king, and their temples. Civilized is what they call themselves. More civilized than any other kind of alva, especially Ranycht." He gave a cynical laugh. "On the inside, you know what they all are? They're *beasts* who wanna rip you apart for your meat and your money. Like their precious sun, they wanna burn you up and bleach your bones."

Matil felt numb listening to him, and she was relieved when he stopped. Khelya's face was white.

Oddly enough, irritation softened Dask's scowl. "That firefly makes me mad sometimes," he said. "That bookworm. 'Cause- 'cause he's not…he just makes it complicated. Used to be I could say things like that to myself and know they were true. But…that guy…" Rubbing his face, he sighed and turned to Matil and Khelya. For a moment he simply looked at them. "Thanks."

"For…what?" said Khelya.

He rolled his eyes. "For coming with me to see how I was doing. Now go back to the camp so I can concentrate on finding food."

A slight smile on her face, Khelya nudged Matil's shoulder. Matil took one last look at Dask before they left for the camp.

* * *

A voice called to Matil, guiding her. It was deep and resonated through her bones. It came from the Book, didn't it?

The Book…she saw the words on the page. "Hurach," she read out loud. "Sliva."

The night whirled around her as she curled over in pain. The voice told her to keep reading. Distant shouts tickled her ears. They were coming.

They were *here*. Light flashed and her foot slipped – she said the final words, but something was wrong. A sound like rushing water filled her head as the pain tore her in two, and then…

Matil saw faces and sounds from the past. Her life. Everything that had brought her to this moment. Tongues of flame rose around her and the smoke stung her eyes.

"Manners, can I ask ya something?" Etsel sat at his dinner table, looking up at her. The flames licked closer to him.

She could only watch. The rushing noise filled her head, but now it sounded more like fire than water.

"Where'd ya come from?" Etsel said.

More light seared her vision, striking her blind. There was heat…*too close*.

"Take your brother," someone said in another memory. "Go through the rosebush!"

Matil returned to Etsel's dinner table. She could see again, and there was no fire. The rushing sound faded to the background.

"I- I want them to die," came her younger voice. "I want to make sure it happens."

Etsel stared like he'd never seen her before. She felt a pang of regret. He didn't understand, either.

He fell away. Or was she the one falling? Falling into pure darkness. The deep voice of the Book flooded the darkness with its rage.

You pathetic child. The spell is ruined.

* * *

Matil wrenched her eyes open. Her heart pounded. The Book had said those words *after* she and Nychta split.

6

Spied Awake

The night-bell's brassy gong drew Brenna reluctantly away from sleep. Had she dreamed of her son, Amacht? Had she seen his face again? She let out a slow breath and opened her eyes. She couldn't remember.

The bell sounded two more times to signal the end of day and beginning of night. Brenna rolled onto her side to stretch her wings out, their light brown feathers rustling and the fine bones within them clicking. She felt a small presence in her arms and squeezed it – a soft toy aphid. It was a thin bandage for the constant ache in her heart. Eventually, throwing back her blankets, she held up the aphid and stared into its black button eyes. The aphid was her son's childhood toy, and holding it reminded her of holding him, of singing him to sleep for many, many mornings after they had gotten word that her husband was killed in the line of duty.

"Okay, Twig," she told the stoic toy. "I'm gettin' out of bed. I'm makin' breakfast. Then I'll head to the post office and see if there's sensitive intel to sneak a look at. You can bet your little antennae those Dominion dirtbags are getting ready for something big. I've gotta decide what to do about it."

That was a problem Brenna considered deeply as she went about her evening routine. She may have been a spy for hire, but she had her own operation now. Should she stay in Goska and see if she could turn the townspeople against a skeleton crew of occupying Skorgon? Strike out into the wilderness and look for the townships that had fled Nychta Olsta's advance? Or follow the Dominion leaders undercover and gather more information, maybe to sabotage their efforts?

For years, her role in life had been as a tiny, unnoticed gear in the machine of grander schemes. She'd done it for Amacht, to keep him safe. And look how that turned out. Guilt rose up in her as she started a fire in the stove. Amacht never really lived under his own name. He had accepted the life of a spy, but Brenna knew he hadn't enjoyed it like she did. He was too honest and, despite his shy nature, too proud. He'd told her a few times his dearest dream of opening a shop in a different town and living not two lives but one, as Amacht. Not as Nat or Stech or Bruen. Part of his dream was Brenna living with him as she got older and using her true name as well, not Brenna or Ulia or Alma.

Something always kept him from turning his dream into reality. A mission here, a mission there. News of events across Eventyr. He was torn. Part of him desired to be like the alva around them, ignorant and unconcerned, but the other part knew too many secrets. He knew too much about lies, corruption, and evil…and how to stop them. He had the barest taste of being able to change things, and it kept him hooked. He longed to be more than just a gear in the machine.

Brenna had encouraged him. She pressed a hand over her mouth while she cooked over the stove and tried not to drip tears into her steaming pan of rabbit meat and cabbage. Amacht. So different from her, but still too similar.

She struggled to get back to the questions she'd been asking herself. Stay, leave, or follow? She sat down to eat, not tasting her meal. Staying in town was folly, she decided. She knew her neighbors – better than they realized. They were like songbirds, living in noise and hurly-burly of their own creation, and fluttering away at the slightest outside disturbance. Whatever trouble she did stir up would be squashed in no time at all once the Dominion heard about it.

Leaving, though uncertain, was probably the safest option. Hide with other like-minded Ranycht and plan from deep in the forest. Brenna stood and picked up her empty plate. The idea didn't sit right with her. How could she plan when she had hardly anything to go on?

Before she left, she rumpled up the blankets on her bed, put a dirty teacup in the living room, and pulled out a few game pieces from the Climb set. It helped her tree house to look messier, a setting of the stage that she'd maintained since Amacht's death so her neighbors – and the Dominion – would think she was a helpless mother broken down with grief. Which she was, but being messy wasn't her style. Cleaning and working had helped her through some of the hardest times. Even with her heart-wound fresh and raw and her waking moments haunted by emptiness, she had to force herself to leave things untidy.

She stood outside her door on the balcony, a floppy dark hat pulled over her golden eyes and a black shawl with cutouts for her brown wings draping down to a drab blue skirt. Her graying hair ran out from underneath the hat in an uneven braid with strands of hair sticking out along its length. In her hand was a basket of wheatcakes and jam.

Following the Dominion would be extremely dangerous. The heaviness in her gut became lighter at the thought. No, too much danger was bad. She needed to keep herself safe. She couldn't die until she'd brought that wicked woman down from the sky – Nychta Olsta.

Brenna took off from the balcony and into the night, air streaming past her feathers. Memories came back from the time Olsta had shown up in Goska and proclaimed that she would bring new power to regular Ranycht who felt cheated by corruption in the Assembly of Magistrates that governed Nychtfal. Brenna had watched her, surprised. Olsta really resembled the girl Matil, though the leader of the Dominion had brown wings and pale lavender eyes hardened by life, while the wingless girl looked through wide, innocent eyes of sweet purple.

And when Brenna's surprise had worn off, she felt wrath growing inside of her. Standing outside the mayor's tree home, Olsta had looked smug and disdainful. Was there any remorse on that murderer's face for what she'd done? Brenna had slipped out of the crowd so she wouldn't do something stupid.

Olsta had put her alva in charge and left Goska soon after. That was only a few weeks ago.

Now, flying to the post office, Brenna wondered where Matil had gone. Last she'd heard, Matil, Dask, and the Obrigi were heading north to the land of Fainfal. Other information traders told her that Olsta was also moving toward Fainfal. Did it mean that Olsta was chasing them? Did they need help? Again Brenna was frustrated with the scarcity of information.

Two four-armed Skorgon soldiers stood on the entry balcony of the post office, their insect-like eyes staring glassily at Brenna as she entered. Another Skorgon buzzed through the air on a patrol.

Inside, the nervous young clerk was helping a bleary Ranycht. Two others waited their turn. The last alva in line worked for the Dominion – he was one of the townsfolk swayed by Nychta Olsta's promises of power. An old man sorted mail at a desk next to the counter and peered down through his eyeglasses at the addresses.

Brenna moseyed around the line. "Hello, Mina," she said to the clerk.

"Evenin', Miss Ulia," the young woman said in between counting her customer's payment twice.

"Nice night, Loger," Brenna said to the customer, who was a short man wearing a small pointed cap.

"Ulia." He lifted his cap and gave her a smile that turned into a yawn.

Brenna came to a stop across the counter from the old mail-sorter. "Good evening, Gunter." She set the basket of food on the counter. "I still can't believe you've never had cloudberry jam before." She gestured at the basket. "There. Try it, why don'tcha?"

Gunter looked over the top of his glasses at the basket, eyed her, and then scooted his stool closer to the counter. "You're a widow who just lost her son, but you still look after me," he said, pulling back the cloth covering the wheatcakes.

Brenna opened the jar of jam and handed him a tiny knife. "Oh, you know how much I enjoy your company."

Gunter smirked as he slathered a cake with jam. "Indeed I do, ma'am. Thank you." With the barest movements, he took two folded papers from his desk and slid them onto the counter, using the basket to shield the exchange from everyone else's eyes.

With her peripheral vision, Brenna observed the Dominion collaborator standing in line. She waited until he was looking the other direction to unfold the first piece of paper.

"Thank *you*," she said to Gunter. "For givin' me something to fill my days." Her eyes skimmed the writing. The Dominion was asking for supplies to be shipped west, toward the border and Dwell, the capital city. She'd seen similar communications recently. Just then, she noticed Mina finish helping Loger. The next alva in line moved up.

"I wasn't sure at first," Gunter said, "but I like this jam. Sweet and a little sour."

"Aw, that's all it gets?" Brenna moved the paper to the side and unfolded the other with one hand.

"Okay, I like it very much."

"*How* much?" she teased. Her eyes froze looking down at the second missive. *'Tyrlis.'*

"It's as fine as a spiderweb, ma'am," he said. "I'd eat it every other day."

'Recruit Ranycht for the Tyrlis invasion,' the letter said, its words louder in Brenna's mind than Gunter's voice. *'Send them to the encampment south of Loda's Brug. Move quickly, before the rebels gain more support in Nychtfal.'*

So this was Nychta's plan. An invasion on Tyrlis, home of the Sangriga. It was a huge undertaking. If an army of Ranycht attacked the land of light, the entire forest could get caught up in war. Brenna had always known it was possible, but it had been a long time since anyone gathered the strength and will…to break Eventyr's peace accords.

And why recruit Ranycht? Why not just use the Skorgon army that seemed to be growing week by week? How powerful was the Book of Myrkhar? When would the invasion begin?

Questions, questions. Brenna loved to answer questions.

She gently moved the papers back toward Gunter. "High praise for my humble jam," she said. "Thank you."

He took another crunching bite out of the wheatcake and carefully put the papers back.

The Dominion collaborator made it to the counter. Mina looked at the string-tied paper he set down. "One half-sgelding, sir," she said.

Brenna closed her hand around her basket's handle, paused, and then let go. "Be well, Gunter. I'll leave the food with you." She tipped her hat. "I'm thinkin' of taking a little trip."

Gunter adjusted his glasses while he studied her. He gave a nod. "So long, Ulia."

She smiled grimly and turned around. The Dominion man was heading for the door. "Excuse me," she said, hurrying toward him.

He was young and weedy, his eyes a reddish pink. "What do you want?"

"I'm…I'm interested in joining the Ranycht Dominion," she said meekly.

He crossed his arms with a delighted laugh. "It's good to see zeal for the cause is spreading. You're that widow from the east trees, aren't you?"

"Yes, that's me."

"You could do a lot of good in this town," he said. "If folks see a sweet older lady like you pulling for us, they'll think less about flying off with the rebels."

"Well…" Brenna tugged her shawl tighter around herself. "I wanna help the alva who are out makin' a difference on the front lines." She would come across a little strong with that line, but it was the quickest way to get out of here.

The man shifted his wings and thought for a moment. Brenna's scalp grew hot beneath her hat. Too much thinking was a bad sign. She should've taken it slow.

"I know the feeling," he finally said. "Here, follow me to the mayor's house. Captain Esher is in charge of Goska. He can assign you to one of the camps near Dwell or Loda's Brug and send you with a recommendation."

Relief flooded Brenna, but she didn't let go of all her tension. She still had to be on her guard. "Thank you. I've been so lost since my son died, and now…I need to get away. I've gotta have something to believe in."

"Wow." The collaborator smiled. "You're an inspiration, ma'am. It's fantastic that the Dominion can help a grieving mother. Ready to go?"

"You betcha," she said. She took one last look behind her. Mina watched discreetly from behind the counter. Gunter looked on with concern. Brenna winked at him and followed the young collaborator out the door. She would soon be a collaborator, too.

Her stomach…she felt it again. That tickle in her stomach, her heartbeat quickening. The anticipation, the imagination, the…danger.

Amacht would have understood.

7

Festive Foray

Matil stretched in her saddle and looked up at the bits of deep blue sky she saw through the tree canopy. The sun had just set and they would probably make camp soon. In the shadowy dusk, plants and trees curved around the travelers with a blanket-like warmth. She remembered back to the ethereal twilight in the Sangriga land of Tyrlis, the wide-open moonlit fields of Obrigi, and the strange nights of wild Fainfal that made her feel forever watched from the bushes. Out of them, she liked Nychtfal's evenings the best. They felt like home.

A day had passed since they'd come across the memorial. The group still traveled during daylight, avoiding nocturnal Ranycht. They were making good time, and Dask estimated only one more day until they reached Ecker's Brug and Dyndal's sister, Shora.

Just now Dask turned to the others. "Careful, guys," he said quietly. He pointed forward. Off in the distance, just visible through the forest, a large wooden sign was nailed to a tree. It read, *'Towne of Locka'*. A small cluster of round, twiggy Ranycht houses sat in the tree above the sign, and more houses peeked between the leaves of the next tree over. There were no Ranycht about, but the group shuffled off to the side and into a bush.

Dyndal rested his glowing eyes on the group. "'Tis time for you to practice being Ranycht. Before we take rest tonight, let us find a market or a well and talk with the villagers."

He activated their magic disguises with a sweep of his hand. Matil instantly felt a little weighed down as her disguise began to use her own magic.

"I will fly unseen beside you," the shimmering Elder said. "Let us have a delightful turn about town!" His form dispersed into nothingness.

The three smaller alva dismounted from their two beetles and everyone walked in the direction of the houses. Earlier, Dyndal had used some of Matil's and Dask's magic to enchant the eyes of Khelya and Simmad so that they could see in the dark like Ranycht. It was weak, but helped them get along well enough. Livi, Khelya's disguise, constantly squinted at the ground and carefully chose her steps. It was probably harder than it looked, considering Khelya's actual feet were nowhere to be seen. This was far from the first time she had been invisible, and she'd gotten better at walking without seeing herself. Simmad, too, had gotten good enough at turning down his wings that no light came from his back, where feathery brown wings now lay folded.

As they went, the still night gave way to melodies drifting through the bushes. Then, shouting and laughter came to Matil's sensitive ears.

"Sounds like a party," Volf-Dask said through his mustache. "I guess it's a festival night."

"Is that better or worse for us?" Geck-Simmad said.

Dask smiled, his ears angled toward the music. "Better."

At that, excitement quickened the group's steps and they soon came to a dirt road. There were Ranycht flying from the houses above toward the center of town, and then the group passed the first of the twig buildings on the ground. As the villagers, buildings, and dirt cross-streets grew more frequent, a rambling town took shape. The road opened up into a crowded square. Joyous sounds and greasy food smells surrounded the disguised alva. Tents littered the square and streets, and candles in every nook sparkled like stars.

A group of older women and their fluttering wings went chattering past Matil. Alva stood in lines at food carts and game stalls. A young girl hurried after some older children, her arms wrapped around a tiny, red-shelled beetle with its gawky black legs swinging as she ran.

Dask pulled Olnar's reins closer and patted the grumpy beetle's head. "I wanna hear some real Nychtfal music first. What about you guys?"

"The market!" Simmad said. "One of the best ways to learn about a culture is through its commercial goods!"

Khelya nodded toward him. "I'd like to go to the market. Ma—uh, Yuna?" Khelya's voice sounded like it came from the illusion's mouth.

"I'm not sure, but let's stay together," Matil said. "Just in case anything happens."

"We don't need to watch the musicians for very long," Dask said. "Once we're done with that, we could shop all we want."

"Well, all right," Simmad said. "Off we go to hear the traditional sounds of Ranycht culture!"

Invisible Dyndal spoke out of the air, causing them all to spook slightly. "Oh, how marvelous to be in the midst of jubilation!"

Dask snorted. "That was your plan all along, wasn't it?"

"No," he said, "but I am not disappointed."

The group began their stroll through the crowd. The paths were lined with candle-lit silhouette art. Dask pointed to some of the figures as folk heroes, like a man with scarf and rapier clearly visible called Pocken Prill, and a generous magistrate of generous girth known as Big Drang Gosser. Shops and stalls displayed all kinds of decorations and clothing, which Matil made note of for later. She closed her eyes for a brief moment, feeling like the breeze was carrying her through the festival's hubbub as her friends pointed out the things they saw.

"Looks like a music competition is in the works," Dask said. They had all arrived at a wide empty space bordered by busy Ranycht. "I recognize some of the troupes. You see a lotta shows when you live in the Brug."

Matil looked over the groups of alva unpacking and cleaning instruments. Among the musicians, Dask pointed out a man with a head of long gray hair and motley clothing. A few stout children were tuning up with him.

"That's Singing Steff," he said. "He's played music all over Nychtfal. The best there is. His band's made up of him and his four sons."

Disguised Simmad stretched his neck to see. "His sons seem so young to be performing."

"They only look like that. They're actually older than I am."

Khelya gaped. "You're kiddin'."

"Nah," Dask said. "I had a friend in the orphanage who was like them, alva whose bodies don't grow all the way. Sometimes he got hassled for his size, but he didn't let it stop him doing what he wanted, either. Last time we got together, he said he was a clerk for a lawyer. Obviously I couldn't tell him I was in a gang, so I just said I was a delivery guy."

He pointed out other musicians standing near the stage, tuning their instruments. A woman plucked strings stretched over a painted box, and beside her was a man famed for his yodeling, Dask told them. A few alva drew bows across stringed instruments of various sizes.

"*They're* here for the geisen competition," Dask said. "I've heard great music played on the geisen, but the competitions are always a bunch of boring complicated songs."

Singing Steff and his sons were on first. Men wearing hats with colorful chinstraps and women in flowing skirts filled the clearing. Everyone was so polished that Matil felt very grubby. But as soon as the lively music started, she forgot herself. The audience whooped at the opening notes of the vaguely familiar tune, and the dancers stepped and whirled. Matil and the others joined those clapping along with the beat. She thought she heard Dyndal clapping next to her though she couldn't see him.

The song ended to raucous applause and, now that Dask had his taste of music, the group agreed to go to the market before they left town. They all eagerly edged their way through the crowd.

* * *

Khelya frequently watched Ranycht fly straight at her only for them to swerve at the last moment – Dyndal's magic veil – but she didn't mind. In return, she got to see up close a place both familiar and foreign. Khelya had seen birdwing villages from the outside many times by now, but it was different to be a part of it. It reminded her of the fairs she went to as a child in Obrigi. Just a lot more musical. She didn't get the draw of music.

Khelya and her friends browsed stalls clumped around tree roots. There were clothes, games, and tools, as well as food smelling heartily of vegetables, meats, berries, nuts, and honey. The four of them each got something to eat, and Khelya's illusion even looked like it was eating while she nibbled on some squirrel-on-a-stick that turned invisible in her real hand. Everything in the market was small and cute to Khelya – a sentiment none of the Ranycht would likely appreciate.

Simmad held a gnarled pipe out to Khelya's Ranycht illusion. "Look, Kh—er, Livi." He lowered his voice. "See the carvings? The bold dabs of paint?"

"It sure is nice," she said.

"And *extremely* traditional!" He quickly stopped the light that was starting to glow from his fake wings. "Some time ago I read a Ranycht storybook dating back to the Age of Goec. The illustrations were faded but otherwise marvelously preserved, and I daresay the motifs on this pipe are exactly the ones in the book." He put the pipe back with care.

Khelya smiled to herself. Whenever Simmad was happy, she was happy.

"Oh, *wow*," Matil said.

"What?" said Dask. He and Khelya came over to look.

Matil, disguised as the darker-haired Yuna, was admiring a display of knives in different sizes, shapes, and colors. Some were more decorative and others more functional. The stall-keeper was speaking with other customers, but Khelya saw him look pleased when his spectacled eyes went over to the three of them. It was a…nice feeling, being seen as a Ranycht like everyone else.

"I wish they weren't so expensive." Matil's fingers went to the knife at her waist. "The Eletsol gave us good hunting knives, but I'd like one that's better to fight with."

"Which one's your favorite?" Dask said.

Matil pressed her lips together for a moment. "That one."

It was a slender and very sharp-looking blade, polished to brightness so that it picked up every glint from the candles around the stall. The grip was made of a rich brown wood with smooth metal fittings. Painted on the wood were three roses, their thorny stems extending down the length of the handle.

A tiny leaf with the price painted on it sat in front of the knife. Khelya didn't know Ranycht money, but it was a big number.

Matil shrugged with a smile. "Let's keep going."

The group moved on to another stall but were soon distracted by the sight of a large gathering in front of a mansion house. They drifted over, joining the back of the crowd. The mansion house was made of several round towers built near the ground. It was like a small fortress stuck halfway into the trunk of its tree. Was the tree a part of the mansion? It looked so different from the Sangriga's delicate tree-houses.

"What's going on?" Matil said to Dask.

Khelya couldn't get over Matil having wings – it didn't look quite right, but at the same time…it did. Which didn't make sense at all.

"I dunno," Dask said. "Maybe the mayor'll give a speech about the importance of whatever festival this is."

"Yoran's Night," Simmad said, "the celebration of a local legendary outlaw, Yoran, who was falsely accused by a corrupt mayor about a hundred years ago. He finally challenged the mayor to a game of Hamma, and whoever won would be mayor while the loser would be sent to prison. The mayor tried to cheat, but the alva of the town found out and helped Yoran win!"

Dask looked taken aback. "They taught you that in Tyrlis?"

Simmad gave an awkward smile. "I read it on one of those lanterns."

A balding man stepped out of the mansion house onto the porch.

"Everyone!" the man shouted. "Tonight is surely a night for remembering good times."

Hollers of assent piped through the gathering.

"But," he continued, "in just a few weeks, the mid-Vana sun will bring with it a day for remembering bad times."

Now the feathery crowd murmured sadly.

"On that day – the Day of Torches – we were visited by evil itself." The man took a step forward on the porch. "Most of you here knew an alva or four taken by the fires. For me it was my sister and her family, Thosten keep 'em."

Khelya looked at Simmad, making her illusion exchange an apprehensive glance with him.

"Bad enough that we were attacked," the man said. "To make matters worse, our very own *ee*-lected *oh*-fficials took a bribe to protect the attackers. A bribe that kept justice from being served." His fists clenched at his sides, and then he took a breath and relaxed them. "You good folks must have heard of the new power in Nychtfal, right?"

Echoes of "Yes," and "Mm-hm," came from the crowd.

"Then I think very little else needs to be said. Let me just welcome a representative of the Ranycht Dominion, the honorable Tren Yinder!"

The crowd applauded while another man stepped through the door onto the porch, flanked by two spiny, four-armed Skorgon. Khelya's arms stiffened in surprise. The bug-like alva's eyes – completely black in color – watched the crowd without blinking.

Matil grabbed Dask's arm.

"It's okay," he said, and then he whispered something that Khelya couldn't hear.

Matil nodded and let go, but she still looked terrified.

The man had said Ranycht Dominion, like the folks they'd fought off near the border. And who was this Tren Yinder guy with the Skorgon? He wore a simple black robe with a red sash, black hair cut at jaw-length, and his black wings were flecked with white. His expression was visible even from this far away; clear blue eyes opened as wide and friendly as his smile.

"Thank you, Mr. Vand, and thanks to all you hospitable folks." Though Yinder projected his voice, it had a gentle quality that set Khelya's teeth on edge. "I intend to speak very directly about things heavy on my heart. Things like frustration. Frustration and disappointment. I'm sure each alva in this crowd knows what they feel like, especially when it comes to our city-slicking politicians."

The crowd jeered.

"They open their wings like they're going to fly, but somehow they never take off. And their pockets are always fat while we wonder how in Eventyr we're supposed to pay our taxes. Let me now say something a little scary. Ready for it? This system is dead. All these mosquitoes and ticks feeding on our life-blood? We can get rid of them."

Dumbfounded and intensely interested expressions spread through the crowd.

Yinder put his hands on the porch railing. "We can change the way we live, starting from the top. Do you think our Grand Magistrate or our High Judge has ever been without a lavender-scented wing bath or a silver bowl to eat their Sangriga soup from? The Ranycht Dominion, in stark difference, is led by a Ranycht who's been through every trouble and pain that you have. A true Ranycht and a true common alva. Nychta Olsta. She can make you – each one of you – as good as the Grand Magistrate or the High Judge." He slapped the railing. "Nychta Olsta can bring the politicians down from their high nests and make them work like you've had to all your lives."

The crowd erupted with enthusiasm, and Khelya hoped no one noticed the four of them standing still in the back.

"But the most important issue at the moment…is the long-overdue justice we deserve for the Day of Torches. Doesn't it hurt to know that, right now, right over the border, Obrigi and Sangriga are sleeping? They sleep in *peace* while the unfairness makes us sick to our stomachs. Is anything about this situation right?"

The way Yinder spoke reminded Khelya of the alva she met after moving to the city as a youngster. Some alva were decent, some chuckled at her family's accents, and others, shopkeepers in large part, talked very particularly. They talked like they were trying to convince their customers they were someone they weren't. But those Obrigi were bad at hiding their laughter while they used "country" words, and it always made her mad to watch Pa and Ma go along like it was nothing.

Yinder seemed like those Obrigi shopkeepers, only better at faking.

"Nychta Olsta won't plead with us to be calm and let go of it," he said hotly, his voice lifting with the crowd's. "She knows what we want, because she wants the same! Like the moon, the Ranycht Dominion will rise against those who live in the sun. It will rise with our passion and anger. Can you imagine a world where no Ranycht is poor and orphaned, where the Obrigi labor to *our* profit, and where the Sangriga bow at our feet? That world is the Dominion's promise! Eventyr itself…*will belong to us!*"

As far as Khelya could tell, everyone else in the crowd was clapping, cheering, and stomping. Her heart thumped in her chest. Simmad cowered against her invisible side. Matil's face was stark with dread, and Dask's ears were twitching. Maybe they should…

On the porch, Yinder raised his hands. "Yes, yes," he said as the cheering quieted down. "I like what I hear." He gestured at a line of smiling alva to his right. "We have Ranycht right here who are happy to give you information about what *you* can do to help. Talk to them afterward, won't you? Right now I'll tell you all one thing that's easy to do. Be on the lookout for traitors, Ranycht who sell out their own alva. We know of two especially dangerous examples who are in hiding: Dask Rasker, a man of at least twenty years, with black wings, black hair, and green eyes; and a wingless girl of twenty years named Matil, with brown hair and purple eyes. They travel in the company of an Obrigi woman and a Sangriga man, and not only that, we've had reports of them using sorcery. You will be doing a great service by sharing your sightings of any of those individuals."

Dask moved closer to the others, his knuckles white around Olnar's reins. "Let's shop for something to, uh… commemorate this amazing night," he said.

They broke away from the crowd and came to the main square, which was emptier than it had been earlier. Some shopkeepers still tended their stalls and a few kids played together. But a lot of the town was listening to Yinder at the mansion house. A lot of them agreed with that faker about anger and revenge and taking over. Khelya remembered the white-hot energy of the crowd before her, seeming to scald her and pull back like a fist about to punch down hard.

Her heart raced. She'd seen those alva playing and celebrating just moments before. Now she knew they hated her kind.

8

Stealing Away

Matil's stomach turned at the thought of the speech. What had Nychta *done?* She leaned against Dewdrop's pack-covered shell. The four alva huddled near a big well in the center of the square.

And Tren Yinder's voice…Matil had heard it before. Where? In…*Goska*. He had been there, visiting the town where Matil and Dask found Brenna and Amacht. That was the plan, wasn't it? Yinder was trying to get everyone on Nychta's side.

Dask eyed each of the others. "Looks like the Dominion is a bigger deal than just some acornheads in Fainfal. And Nychta Olsta's involved."

"They all sounded so happy," Khelya said, a tremor in her voice.

"Before you met us," Dask said, "wouldn't you have been happy if you heard someone was gonna beat up the *Ranycht* and make them pay?"

She frowned indignantly. "I would not…have…" She kicked at the ground, audibly scuffing the cobblestones in the square with her invisible giant boot. "Okay, maybe."

"And you heard the first guy," he went on. "A lotta these townsfolk have connections to the Massacres. I don't blame them one bit for feeling like that." He looked at Simmad. "Bet you wish you were back home, huh?"

Simmad's Ranycht facade looked queasy. "The thought crossed my mind," he said softly. "But I'm glad I saw all that."

"We must go to Shora," the voice of Dyndal said. "I see now how little time we have."

Matil could feel her disguise wearing on her and making her tired. She nodded. "Let's find a place to camp."

"You!" came a shout across the square.

On Matil's right, Dask began to disappear.

"Don't you dare fade!" A tall man wearing spectacles was striding towards them. He was the stall-keeper from earlier, the one with the knives.

Dask made himself visible again. He looked as sick as Simmad had a moment ago. "Guys," he said. "You go ahead. I'll catch up, okay?"

"What's goin' on?" Khelya said.

The stall-keeper stopped with his hands on his hips, glowering at the group over his spectacles. "All of you, stay right there. And whoever has the knife, give it back."

A sinking feeling began in Matil's stomach.

Dask's mouth opened as if he were about to speak. After a moment, he shut his mouth and pulled a knife out of his satchel. It was the rose-painted knife Matil had admired.

"I…I'm sorry," he said. "My mother just passed away, and she loved roses. I thought this would mean a lot to my father. I'm sorry, I can't afford it."

Matil frowned.

The stall-keeper took the knife. "I suggest you leave town. I'll be telling the others about you."

"Sorry," Dask said again, his ears starting to droop.

"V-very sorry," Simmad added with a Ranycht-like accent.

The group went straight out of Locka. They didn't speak again until there were no more houses above them and the road was far behind.

"*Dask!*" Khelya finally said. "I thought you were different now! And aren't we tryin' to *not* draw attention to ourselves?"

"I know, I know. I'm an idiot. I'm sorry. I wasn't thinking straight." He ran a hand through his invisible hair, which made him look like he was polishing his disguise's bald head. "Matil?"

"Mm?" She didn't meet his eyes.

"I'm, uh…I'm really sorry for ruining things tonight," Dask said.

Disappointment filled Matil's mouth like the taste of rotten berry. She didn't know what to say to him.

"This looks like an excellent spot to rest," Dyndal called to them. His spirit appeared, standing atop two boulders leaning against one another. The boulders created a narrow but deep cave. The four alva went over to the entrance, where Dyndal flew down to them.

He waved his hand and their disguises fell away. Matil immediately felt less strain.

Dask and Simmad tied Dewdrop and Olnar to stalks of grass near the entrance. Simmad let his wings light up the rocky interior. He sat down against the wall, crumpling inward disconsolately. Khelya, no longer Livi, sat by him with her shoulders slumped. She untied her headband and tucked it in her rope belt. Matil stayed by Dewdrop, her hand resting on the beetle's shell as she tried to control her anger. Seeing Dask in his true appearance, avoiding her gaze, made it hurt more.

Dask grabbed his blankets from Olnar and went towards the back of the cave, but Dyndal stepped in front of him.

The Elder's smile was kinder, less playful than usual. "There is a wound you are neglecting to treat."

"What are you talkin' about?" Dask said.

Dyndal gestured at Matil. A moment later, Dask sighed, dropped the blankets, and slunk out of the cave past her. She hesitated, but joined him. They stepped around the corner from the entrance. Crickets chirped in the dark grass around them.

Dask's wings twitched. "I'm sorry I put us all in danger."

"That's not the only thing you did," Matil said.

He lifted his shoulders. "I mean, I tried taking something, yeah, but I gave up when I realized he noticed it. We were disguised, anyway. Does it matter?"

Everything went hot. "It should!" Matil's vehemence surprised herself, but she let it carry her. "Stealing is more than just the thing you take. It's- it's the thing you stole, the alva you stole from, and *you*. It's those around you, and it's the law. Don't any of those matter?"

Dask watched her with wide eyes. "I…I was wrong, okay? For what I did. I'm sorry."

She wanted to ignore what had happened so that she wouldn't need to say the thought looming tall in her mind. If only she could forget. Why weren't alva just…good? Why did Nychta exist?

"Dask." Matil swallowed past the lump in her throat. She would say it. "I can't trust you, can I?"

His expression darkened. "Of course you can trust me. Look, I've taken stuff for most of my life, but have I ever done *anything* to hurt you?"

"You have." She gave him an incredulous look. "Stealing. Lying. I thought that was in your past."

"Alva's pasts don't just disappear!" said Dask.

Matil's heart seized up.

"Because of who you are, you- you can't understand. Living life means you do things that aren't perfect." His voice took on a bitter tone. "So what do you know about living life? You're perfect."

Perfect? Dask's words struck Matil painfully for the second time.

They seemed to get to him as well, because both the sourness and the color drained from his face. "I didn't mean it," he said. "I'm so sorry, Matil, I'm sorry I stole something. I'm sorry I lied. I'm…"

A chuckle burst out of her before she could really think. The chuckle went on until it became breathless laughter, bubbling up miserably.

"Matil?"

She sank to the ground and her vision blurred. The air forcing itself through her throat turned into sobs. Tears spilled from her eyes.

Dask got down beside her. "Are you okay?" he said. "I won't steal again. I promise. Pluck my wings if I break it. Please don't cry, Matil. *Please.*"

Eventually her tears subsided and left her empty. She noticed that her hand was warm. In both of his hands, Dask held one of hers like it was made of thin glass. The contact brought her back to herself.

"You're right," she said tiredly.

He looked up, trying to read her face.

"Alva's pasts don't disappear." The statement gave her so much despair that she clutched Dask's hand. "I thought mine had, but it's coming back."

He stared at their hands for a moment. "Didn't you want it back, though?"

"I used to. I'm not sure if I still do."

"Why not?" he said.

"I don't like myself," Matil said. "If I'm not Nychta, I'm an object, a piece of garbage she threw out. If I *am* Nychta… then I'm even worse…than garbage."

His shoulders slumped and he gave no reply.

She very much wanted to trust him. "Are you actually sorry?"

"Of course," he said.

"Have you stolen anything else?"

He stood, unlinking their hands, and bent down to help Matil up. "No. I think from now on, we should…change. You should like yourself. You're an alva worth liking."

Matil's ears went down. She felt overwhelmed again – happiness, loss, pain – but she held it all in. Once Nychta was defeated, maybe things would become clear.

"And me," Dask said, "I won't steal anymore. Let's both be better."

Matil looked up at him. There *was* something different about him now – a new resolve. Her heart grew lighter. "That sounds good."

Dask gave her a half smile, and then they went back to the cave entrance in comfortable silence. He ducked inside, where the others were going over the happier parts of their visit to the festival. Matil took in a deep breath of the night air and patted the beetles' shiny heads on her way into the cave. She found Dask standing in front of the others.

Dask cleared his throat. "I'm sorry to you guys, too."

Khelya looked dubious.

"Stealing is part of—part of my past. But I didn't realize that it was. I didn't wanna realize it." He glanced at Matil before looking at the ground. "It's new for me to think… the law means anything, or to think of myself in someone else's place. And it's hard to go from old to new. I'm gonna do it, though. So I'm sorry for stealing." He fidgeted. "I'm really sorry."

"Okay," Khelya said. "As long as you don't do it again."

* * *

"Please don't eat any of the mint today," Father called.

"We won't, Mr. Olsta," Arla and Crell chorused back.

Father's twisting, scented garden was just what Matil imagined Fainfal would be like. "Want to play explorers?" she said. "Bechel can be an Eletsol trying to eat us."

Bechel crouched down obstinately, hugging a toy squirrel with buttons for eyes. "No!"

"Bel's adorable," Arla said, sighing. "I wish I had a younger brother instead of older brothers."

"Then I'll make *you* change his diaper next time." Matil twirled her finger by her head. "Bechel, are you sure you don't want to be a big Eletsol with a spear?"

"Ex-pore," Bechel said plaintively.

"I'll be the Eletsol," Crell said. "Okay, Bechel? I'll be a scary Eletsol and you can be an explorer with your sister."

The little red-eyed boy jumped up and grabbed Matil's hand. With his other hand, he carried the toy squirrel by its tail.

She smiled down at him. "Say 'thank you for letting me explore' to Crell."

"Tang you," Bechel mumbled.

Everything around her disappeared in a peaceful haze. His small voice echoed on.

9

Ray of Sunshine

The Ambermeet's thick, honey-coloured walls filled with sunlight, and Lyria, standing far beneath it on the ground, wondered how this beautiful building could hold so much filth. There had been triumphs, too, she remembered. Every time something good had happened during her junior Councilwoman days, she'd nearly shot off into the clouds.

"Hello, Lyria," a young woman said. "Isn't it such a pretty day?"

Lyria turned to see Lady Annest Ren, round face beaming, standing beside Commander Dalen. Annest was Lord Councilman Owynth's daughter. In fact, she was also one of the few junior Councilwomen who didn't make Lyria feel like pulling off her own head and chucking it over a cliff. Annest was short and shared her father's rich, golden hair, in counterpoint to Dalen's frosty blond.

A pretty day? "Rain may be more of a blessing," Lyria said. "The crops need water."

"Mm, true, true. Did you hear about the shortage in Farien? I've been trying to get Father to donate food and the like. He's very cautious with finances of late." Annest turned her face to the sky and breathed in. "But just looking at that glorious blue gives me hope that if we do what we can, it'll all turn out."

Lyria began to feel the niggling irritation that came from being around an optimist.

Dalen grinned at his betrothed. His military buttons and badges gleamed across his sturdy chest. "I can understand your father's position. We're all being careful with our money."

"All of us?" Lyria raised her eyes meaningfully to the Ambermeet. "Many spend even more freely out of a sense of impending doom."

"…Fair point," he said.

She turned to Annest. "It's a pleasant enough day. I wish you both well." Off she went. Thank Calo she had got out of—

"Hold, Lyria," Annest called. "Do you have time for a meal?"

Anxiety jumped in her stomach. She turned and smiled tightly at them. "Oh, I couldn't possibly. Too much to do."

"You work all the time," Dalen said. "Please sit with us an hour or two, your company would make Ann really happy."

A few more excuses later, Lyria found herself sitting across from Dalen and Annest on the balcony of an inn. She filled her mouth with the various dishes on the table so she wouldn't have to talk much, but a question did soon occur to her. Everyone in the Council already knew she wasn't the type to dance about, so she decided on a straightforward approach.

"You two go on seeking me out with no purpose in mind," Lyria said. "Why?"

Dalen's eyebrows drew together. "One doesn't need a purpose aside from hunger to have a meal with friends."

An edge entered her voice. "We're not close enough to be considered friends, surely." She felt a pang of regret. "Or…I mean to say…we don't often share meals."

"I suppose we ought to, in order to become better friends," he said. "We're allies, after all."

"Allies?" Based on agreements, Lyria politically supported certain members of the Council while they supported her. Despite strategizing from time to time with the commander and Annest, she didn't recall making any such agreements with them.

"What he means," Annest said, "is that you share our convictions. Precious few around here sincerely do. Sometimes it's enough to make one wonder."

Where did convictions get an alva? Dashed hopes and poor sleep. Yet a sense of curiosity tickled Lyria, and she shushed those thoughts to better listen to Annest. "And what does one wonder?"

"If – oh, I don't know – if anything will improve, or if it'll keep sliding downwards," Annest said. "But just because there are only a few of us doesn't mean we can't make a difference. I'm quite excited for the future. Lately I've written bills to present regarding funds distribution. Have you seen the accounting? I reckon it's been languishing for ages. Honestly, how could anyone stand for it? The distribution favors particular parties and individuals within the Council *and without*. Some rich milliner in Wyrsan is receiving tax money because a Council member's mother likes his hats. Urgh." Her wings and expression brightened. "But my bills will bring attention to the matter and perhaps put it back in order. Speaking of, Lyria, would it be a bother for you to work them over with me? Of course, I won't press."

Lyria sighed into her spoon before sipping some soup, and then set it back in the bowl. "I'll have a look."

"Fantastic!" Annest said. "Thank you, truly."

"It's strange, isn't it, Lyria?" Dalen said. "There were rumblings from Nychtfal not long past. But it's since become quiet."

Annest patted her mouth with her napkin. "That's a relief."

"A relief?" Lyria said. "It's when your enemies are quiet that you can't tell where they are."

The young woman frowned at her dumplings. "Right."

Dalen nodded. "I see it as the birdwings planning or distracted by something. They know their military isn't up to invading the Accord. They need Nychta Olsta's Skorgon, and she hasn't been seen in weeks." He waved his spoon. "Troubling developments aside, I'm pleased with the state of our forces. Even with peacetime reduction of our numbers, inspections and drills have gone off trim as a topiary. It's clear that our Sun Accord is not yet, as the poets are fond of saying, a faded bloom." He grinned.

"'Yet' being the key word," Lyria said. She popped a spoonful of mashed pea in her mouth.

"'Yet' only becomes 'now' when we give up, Councilwoman," said Dalen.

She arched an eyebrow and swallowed her food. "Running a nation is a far sight more complicated than simple perseverance."

Dalen chuckled. "You're right, of course. Although…I can see why the junior Council members call you a badger."

Lyria pressed her lips together. What a lovely image she kept in the Council. Fitting, too, since most of the time she felt like a badger.

Annest nudged Dalen, saw Lyria looking at her, and smiled nervously. "*I* don't call you a badger."

"Very good," Lyria said. "I'll take you off my To Eat list."

Dalen and Annest paused, then exploded with merriment. As Lyria watched them laugh, she couldn't help smiling. Light fell across the abandoned halls inside of her. The woman living alone in that dark castle peeked her head around the corner and felt the light's warmth on her face. She remembered…oh, but it was no use. She retreated from the light. The lessons of the past were not meant to be repeated.

"Commander," Lyria said, "I understand that the army is moving into Obrigi."

"Most of the army, anyway," Dalen said. "We're about to march out and take up positions along the Nychtfal border. After I've gone the length of it I'll report back to the capital, and then I'm set to wed this chirpy little robin." He shared a happy glance with Annest, the wings on both of them glowing brightly.

Lyria smiled slightly. "That is one thing I won't spoil with my words. Congratulations."

"You should congratulate us at the wedding," Annest said. "You *will* be there, won't you? We'll have that famed Nervoda chef – can't remember his name – and he'll prepare wonderful dishes from all over Eventyr!"

"Can't very well turn down such a feast, can I? But, with our money woes, is it wise to…"

"To be slightly extravagant?" Dalen said. "Don't worry about us, Councilwoman, and don't ever lose hope. This airing out of our army is the start of a new spirit in the land. Others will follow. You'll see. By the time our wedding rolls up, things will have really changed."

Dalen's enthusiasm was hard to resist, and it made Lyria that much more determined to keep him from being crushed under a mountain of hope. "So…Nider's got himself involved in the army."

A shadow came over Dalen's brow. "Yes, he's put himself and his minions by my side to 'oversee military operations in an advisory role, providing a civilian's perspective.' Lord Owynth says it's a compromise to keep peace in the Council. However, I fear that Nider's advice will eventually become orders."

"Well, I think it's a decent idea," Annest said. "Councilman Nider can help you better understand how the army and its actions impact the rest of us."

"It may be so," he said, "but—"

She laid a hand on his arm. "Father's looking out for you, Dalen. He is the Lord Councilman, after all, and I *don't* believe he would make an unwise decision."

Lyria listened with unease. Dalen began to reply, but her thoughts turned to the day she had lost faith in Owynth. The Council's decision regarding the Massacres…Owynth's decision. At the time she hadn't been as strong and had only *felt* its wrongness. Later, she *knew*.

"…hope you're right," Dalen finished saying.

"It will be fine," Annest said.

"All the same," Lyria said, "be cautious. Be alert."

They finished their meal, Dalen and Annest chatting about lighter topics. Lyria stood, picked up her staff, and considered the iron triangle at its top that pointed downward. Upon becoming a full Councilwoman many years ago, she was allowed to choose a staff of office. She'd taken this one because it looked the least silly and like it might be quite painful when applied with force. The staff maker showed his disappointment that she chose the plainest, but told her that the design came from metal triangles that judges used to wear, meaning 'discernment'. She'd liked it even more.

Her fingers closed around the comforting, worn wood of its length. "I see what you mean," she said, "us being allies.

War and politics are very much alike." She hesitated and then pressed on, feeling that for once she couldn't keep her thoughts to herself. "Both are detestable games of power, which we must nevertheless play for the sake of those who can't."

Annest nodded intently, but it was Dalen whose entire bearing changed. Lyria saw her words settle on him like a weight. After a moment he seemed to work through them, shoulders squaring and a light entering his eyes.

"Thank you for eating with us," he said. "Let's fight together for a long time."

One side of Lyria's mouth lifted in a smile. "Let's."

10

The Big City

The morning of the second day since the festival, the group came across a worn dirt road carved through the undergrowth.

Dask turned suddenly, hands shielding the sides of his face. "Let's do the disguises now. We're getting close. Can't have anyone from the gangs recognizing me." He looked up at Khelya. "Or the very tall woman."

Dyndal clicked his tongue. "That is not the way to ask, young one. Think of the politeness with which Matil conducts her—"

"Please," said Dask flatly.

Dyndal bent down to Matil and whispered, "He is improving." The Elder waved his hands over the four alva to disguise them and then made himself invisible.

The four 'Ranycht' followed the dirt road – Yuna, Volf, Livi, and Geck. Soon, houses and hanging farms filled the trees. Buildings clustered on the ground along the road.

This area was quiet with most alva having settled down to sleep for the day, but Matil's sensitive ears picked up distant clatters and shouts.

The dirt road eventually turned onto a wider stone-paved road where a few alva wearily drove their animals and carts. The city was clearly beginning to form around the group, swaying walkways strung through branches over their heads like cobwebs. The buildings they passed were of rich, dark colors; wooden browns and the reds of awnings and brick were framed by the black of metal fences, window grates, chimneys, and unlit braziers. As the establishments and streams of passersby grew denser, the group walked steadily upward. The city seemed to be built on a great rise. Running beside the streets were deep gutters that carried away spurts of soapy, dirty water. The buildings were now so close together that they became a maze of walls, and many small streets joined the broad main street.

Tall trees stood out among the buildings, small windows in the trunks showing that alva lived and worked inside of them. Ahead, the city's blocky mass filled the forest from floor to canopy, obscuring the trees within.

Marking the city's bounds was a stone wall three stories tall with battlements. Buildings even taller stood behind the wall. A grand gate of stark metal tracery was wide open to let through steady currents of Ranycht, pack insects and other beasts of burden, Nervoda with white skin, wagons, and—Matil startled when she saw three clear-winged, four-armed, bug-like alva wearing ragged clothes and carrying huge knapsacks. The group entered the press and were swept toward the city, keeping a tight grip on Dewdrop's and Olnar's reins. Dyndal's magic veil kept the sea of alva from bumping into their fake wings and invisible Khelya.

Voices, feathers, smells, and motion swarmed Matil's senses. The buildings were stacked and stuck together like a puzzle, having been built from every direction, and their architecture was a stew of new and old. Roundish wooden houses wedged cozily between box-like and well-established structures of stone. Matil looked backward. Somewhere along the way they'd entered the gate, and now they were quite far in. Dask tugged them into a slower side street. On the sidewalk they pressed together near a wall.

Matil's heart fluttered when she turned to look again at the main thoroughfare. She knew this place. Etsel. Her dreams had shown her Ecker's Brug, the time she had spent there after running away from Crell. Dreams, dreams, not just dreams…The city's fast pace made her dizzy. She rubbed her arms, remembering how cold and hungry she had been. So hungry.

"Whaddaya think?" Dask said. She was taken aback by his new face. He stood beside her and gave the pulsing streets a smirk. "They say the Brug makes you into one of two kinds of alva: someone too small to be noticed by it, or someone big enough to own a piece of it."

The city's heat returned, and Matil regained her presence of mind. She noticed that Dask's accent had gotten stronger. "I've never seen so many alva at one time," she said. "Not even in Corwyna."

"It's…impressive," Khelya said. Her brown hand reached out and felt the stone wall.

Dask pointed at her in exasperation. "If *only* you looked like yourself right now. I'd give my feathers to see an Obrigi call Ecker's Brug impressive."

"It's frightening and splendid all at once," Simmad said in a daze. "I feel as though I'm dreaming."

Looking as pleased as Olnar did after catching a caterpillar, Dask shuffled his wings. "So where to, imaginary friend? Got directions for us?"

"Something has changed about this city," Dyndal said out of the air behind them. "I do not know what." He paused. "Ah, now I see. It is only a small thing after all."

Dask's ears turned toward the voice. "What changed?"

"*Everything.*"

He dropped his broad face into his hands. "Talrach. Then you don't know where your sister is? Isn't that the whole reason we woke you up?"

"Not the whole reason," Dyndal said defensively. "Like the secret trails through the forest, one step must come before another. Waking me was integral to unlocking the magical seal of the Hibernation. And I narrowed our search. I *know* it is in this city. The south side, when I was here last."

"Okay, okay." Dask looked up and down the street. "Let's find a place we can eat and plan."

"Yo," said a gravelly and astonished voice. "You hear 'im, too?"

Everyone turned around.

An extremely grimy man sat against the wall. "Hey. Hey. You know, I've hoid voices, but I never hoid voices uddah alva could hear." He jerked his chin up at them. "You guys loo-loo, too?"

"A little," Dyndal's disembodied voice said. "I am Dyndal. Do you want me to help you?"

The man's unfocused magenta eyes brightened. "Dyndal? *That* Dyndal? Sure ting!" He shook a hat, clinking the few coins inside. "Any help I can get, ya know? But…do you mean somedin' else?" Then he slid sideways with his eyes closed and mouth open.

Dask stepped back. "Did he die?"

Dyndal snickered. "I have only put him to sleep. And when he wakes," the sleeping man's face glowed briefly, "the voices he hears will not trouble him anymore."

* * *

Aside from the main roads, the city streets weren't all that active. Not until nighttime would the entire city wake. Dask took the group along a few streets and up a ramp, peering into alleyways until he found a tall and narrow alley, empty but for several crates stacked along one wall. They took a few crates from the stack to make a table, on which they unpacked leftover chunks of fruits and berries. The two beetles huddled together.

"South side of the city. Any other clues?" Dask snapped his teeth down on a splinter of apple.

"Is that not all you need to know?" said Dyndal.

He swallowed before continuing. "You said yourself that Ecker's Brug has changed a lot since your time. Kerl told me once about a landslide that happened when he was a kid. It wrecked the north side of the city and everyone moved down. So the old south side is now the north side. I'll bet it moved before that, too, up and down and side to side."

"Oh." Dyndal sounded demoralized.

"*Ha!*" Simmad burst out. "I knew I remembered something! At Icto Lan, one of our greatest treasures is a poem thought to be very early Hibernation, perhaps even *contemporary* with the era's beginning. The poem's got heaps of holes in it, but parts are still legible, if not intelligible." He grinned. "Did you hear that, those words sound…legible, intelligi…ahem, well, the poem mentions two Elders in particular, Shora and Calo. It says that Shora was laid to rest with justice and the forest swallowed Calo up."

"Justice," Dask said. "Well, *that* narrows it down. There—"

"Sarcasm doesn't help, Dask," Khelya said.

"I'm not being sarcastic. Out of the oldest buildings in Ecker's Brug, I know two that have to do with justice. One is the High Court building."

Khelya gave him a surprised look. "Oh."

"I should have asked about courthouses first thing," Dyndal said. "Shora adores them."

"She was there when the High Court was built, if I recall correctly," Simmad said. "However, it was not the very first courthouse she established. That would be…"

"Ecker's Hall?" Dask said.

Simmad smiled. "Ecker's Hall."

Dask pointed at him. "We just had a mind moment and I'm not sure how I feel about it. Are we gonna try Ecker's Hall first?"

"Yes." Dyndal sounded pleased. "Thank you, alva."

Glancing around the streets, Dask said, "We should go fast. Olnar and Dewdrop can move around fine until sunset, when traffic starts up. It'll be like the gate back there, but everywhere. And much worse."

Again he took the lead down the winding plank streets and narrow walkways that connected each level. The daytime sky was not visible here, where they traveled under layers and layers of buildings. The city here in the lower levels was dark for the most part, but shops signaled their openness by lighting candles, dim braziers warmed cool areas, and ventilation spaces let in gloomy natural light.

Dask also pointed out locations along their route. "Down that street, you'll find the best sweetbreads in the Brug," he said. "*The* best. But you have to be careful walking out, 'cause there's a palm reader across the street who'll convince you to go in his shop to look at crystals."

"Is it near where you lived?" Matil asked. She wondered where Etsel's place was, too.

"Nah. My flat's all the way across town." Dask slowed down. "It's not really *my* flat anymore, since I haven't been around to pay rent. Everyone over there would turn me in for the bounty in a heartbeat, anyway. I didn't leave anything valuable there, but I guess it's a little strange being in the Brug and not going home." He looked at Matil. "Strange and nice. I'm glad home isn't still in the same building as Hock the Lock or Tizzy or…" he shuddered, "Ned."

Dask quickened his pace, bringing them up ramps and stairs and then down, back to the cobblestones. Where they were now, the streets and structures were quiet and venerable.

They entered a large plaza with beautiful stone buildings up to three stories tall. Because of the city above, it was like a great room with a ceiling of plaster resting on the buildings. Three Ranycht wearing creamy linen robes and floppy black hats flew from one place to another, focused on their business. Other than them, it was empty.

Dask pointed across the plaza. "The old courthouse."

In the plaza's center was a tree trunk larger than a mansion, flowing smoothly into the ceiling. The wood's color was light, almost ashen, and alva in austere dress had been carved into it at intervals. After Dask tied Dewdrop and Olnar to a hitching post, the group cautiously approached the building. *'Ecker's Hall,'* it said in cracked, blocky script over the door.

Khelya squeaked. "It ain't made of wood?"

Her illusion was touching the courthouse wall. Matil followed suit, also surprised at how cold and hard the rough bark of the tree felt. Now that they stood close, she saw that some bits of the wood glittered.

"It's rock," Dask said. "Now how do we find the place?"

"Simmad holds my velanach," Dyndal's voice said. "It will guide him to the velana stone."

They all looked at Simmad.

His eyebrows shot up and his hand went to his vest pocket. "I-I do feel something. An odd tickling sensation! Perhaps like what you felt in Fainfal, Miss Matil. If so, the stone is certainly close by."

Dask jumped up the steps of Ecker's Hall and lugged open one of the tall doors, holding it for the others to go in.

"No…" Simmad said, walking forward. "It's pulling me round that way." He pointed to the side of the building.

Following his directions, the group meandered to the right of the doors and walked beside the round wall. Almost at the back of the huge courthouse, Simmad told them to stop. Matil saw the faint shape of a tall, narrow oval set in the wall, close to her height and smoothly integrated with the stone tree trunk.

Simmad reached toward the oval.

Dask stepped between him and the wall. "Wait," he whispered.

Two robed men strolled down the stairs of another courthouse behind Ecker's Hall.

"Well, I'm done-zo," the stout one said. He stretched his arms. "How'd a case about a lost carrot even wind up in the Upper Courts?"

The skinnier one groaned. "Stop talkin' about it. I never wanna hear the phrase 'vegetable precedence' again." He paused. "I'm curious about something. Whaddaya think about the villages that seceded from Nychtfal? Almost three whole towns! Crazy, right? They really musta lost their feathers."

"Huh. Seems like it makes sense to me. I mean, this Nychta Olsta character came outta nowhere. How can we trust her?"

Matil's ears pricked up.

"For real, Yacks?" said the skinnier man. "Okay, sure, she's got big talk. But she's also got, oh, I dunno, *an army* to back it up! We don't really have no choice in the matter. It's go along or get stomped."

"C'mon," Yacks said. "It's too early to tell what'll happen."

"Hey, bug army aside, don't you hear what her alva are sayin'? They're gonna put Ranycht in charge of the whole forest. That's what I call a *goal*. If only we knew where those breakaways got to. I hear they're in the south."

Yacks studiously picked something off his robe. "I wouldn't know. Haven't asked around."

"Lemme know if you find anything out." The man and Yacks parted ways. "I'm the first one you'll tell, right?" When he was out of earshot, he added, "Big fat earthworm." He stopped to stare at Matil and her disguised companions. "Who're you?"

Dask flashed a smarmy grin under his mustache. "Oh, we're out-of-towners," he said in a nasal tone. "Seein' the sights. I gotta say – just have to say – this is a *real nice* hunk of rock you got here." He slapped the courthouse wall. "Ha! Looks exactly like wood!"

The man's eyes glazed over and he passed by the group, ruffling his wings. "Yeah, yeah. Enjoy yourselves. Don't get in the way of the legal proceedings."

Once he was gone, Dask relaxed his wild expression.

"Pfft," burst out of Simmad's mouth.

"That was entertaining," said Dyndal's disembodied voice.

"Glad you enjoyed the show." Dask waved toward the stone embedded in the wall. "Go for it, Simms."

Simmad stood up straight and laid his palm against the stone oval. The symbols for *velana* slowly appeared on the wall's surface. He jumped back as a square section of the ground before the stone seemed to fall away with a loud grinding noise. When the grinding stopped, they saw a stairwell leading beneath the courthouse.

Matil, Khelya, and Simmad stared. Dask stroked his chin, trying hard to look unimpressed.

"Let us enter," Dyndal said.

11

The Weighting Game

Each of them descended into the black-as-ink stairwell. As soon as Khelya's head was clear of the entrance, it shut behind them with a thump that Matil could feel through her feet. She whipped around. Cold, musty air filled her nose.

"What was—" Simmad spluttered and tripped down a stair. "Dask, your wings are in my face."

Dask folded his wings up. "The door kinda surprised me by closing on its own, okay?"

"It closed?" Simmad said. "*We're trapped?*"

Dyndal appeared out of the darkness and held up a glowing silver orb. "Peace, Master Long-Ears. Shora will have the ability to open it." He put on a cheery smile. "Onward, then. We must wake her."

"Could we take off our disguises, just for now?" Khelya said.

Dyndal passed his hand over the four alva, revealing their true appearances. "Ask my sister to make the disguises visible again before you leave this place."

Ask my sister? Matil stared up at Dyndal's translucent face. "Aren't you staying with us?"

He smiled again, but it didn't reach his eyes. "I will return to sleep. The velanachs sustain but one Heilar." A thought seemed to occur to him. "Recall that Kanay's spirit was awakened upon my own waking. Before the Hibernation, I bound her with my magic. She should not have appeared at all. However, I believe the Book-bearer somehow manipulated my binding to draw Kanay to me when the velanach was used, allowing her to invade my sanctuary. I would hazard a guess that the same will happen with the Saikyr prisoners bound by my sister and Falgar. Shora would fain hear such news. Be sure to tell her!" His smile widened and he led the way down the stairs.

The stairwell continued onward, cramped and quiet. Matil found herself worrying that the stairs would go on forever into an abyss. Finally, she set down her foot, relieved when the next step was a flat stone floor. She looked up.

The small passage opened into a lofty hall lined on both sides with larger-than-life statues made of porous white stone. As the group walked, Dyndal's silver orb and Simmad's golden wings cast eerie shadows, deepening the carvings' furrows. They passed many distinguished-looking Ranycht in tall hats, several Sangriga, two towering Obrigi, an ant

Skorgon, and a few alva with animal features such as tufted ears and clawed fingers. At the foot of each statue was placed a name plaque shaped like a downward-pointing triangle. According to the plaques, they were overwhelmingly judges and magistrates, and a number of them had titles such as 'Evenhand' or 'the Thorough'.

"This one looks familiar," Dyndal said, pointing to a bespectacled Sangriga woman named Judge Haiwyn Tang. "Ah yes, she held me in contempt for lack of gravity in her courtroom. But you four know me – drifting into the air is something I do quite respectfully." A Ranycht man caught his sight. "And there is the founder of this city." The man was tall and skinny, even up to his ears, like he'd been stretched. A string of a beard hung from his drooping face. According to his nameplate, he was High Judge Ecker.

Then Dyndal saw another Ranycht, a man with thick muscles. The Elder's laughter echoed through the hall. "Ardisker the Gentle! Of course I remember you. He was the only alva ever to wallop me in the face. It almost hurt, too. Even if he were not friends with my sister, she would have made this statue for that accomplishment alone."

Simmad listened to Dyndal with a rapturous expression and went on to read each plaque carefully.

Khelya wandered to one of the two Obrigi and then eagerly called Matil over. She spoke in subdued tones that seemed to suit this place. "Velbert Vashen. One of the smartest Obrigi ever, an' close friends with Falgar."

Matil looked up – and up – at the statue. The Obrigi man's arms were filled with scrolls, and his mouth lifted to one side in a satisfied manner.

Khelya grinned. "Learned about 'im in First School. He's been my favorite since then."

"Favorite what?" Dask said. He'd stayed in the center of the hall the entire time, glancing around at the statues. "Favorite history alva?"

"Is there somethin' wrong with having a favorite history alva?" said Khelya.

"No, I guess not. Except that it's as creepy as these statues are." He rubbed his arms. "C'mon, guys. Get your wings flapping."

Simmad shook his head. "Examining all of these would take weeks. At least give me an hour."

"Dask is correct," Dyndal said. "We do not have much time. And some of these statues are certain to give me nightmares! Come, Simmad."

They continued through the solemn hall until they reached the end. There, stark and astonishing, they found a woman lying deathly still on a low stone bed, her eyes closed. She had small, pointed ears and was nearly as tall as Khelya, but more slender, with ice-pale skin, sharp, otherworldly features, and black hair in a long plait. Her hands were folded on her stomach and she wore a simple but fine gray robe. A flickering silver glow surrounded her, keeping the darkness at bay. Two measuring scales, one set at each end of the bed, stood like watchmen over the woman. But the plates on both scales rested with one higher than the other – the scales were tipped. Silver weights of different sizes sat on the floor along the length of the bed.

"Mu gevi," Dyndal said quietly. "Halsedys."

Khelya and Simmad gazed at the woman in wonder.

They had found the Elder Shora. The hope it gave Matil was tinged with melancholy. Dyndal's body slept protected by alva who cared about him. His sister rested alone beneath a city that didn't know she was there.

"Look at the wall," Dask said.

Words were carved into the wall behind the bed. Matil stepped closer to make out the writing, but tried to keep her distance from the silent body.

'For food my feet led me across the boundary,' it read, *'where I was punished for my trespass. What led my feet and why? What binds me?'*

Dyndal groaned. "My warm feelings for you are now cold, sister. You never fail in contriving ways to make my head hurt."

Taking in the words on the wall, Simmad slowly pulled soft gloves from his pocket. He put them on and bent to pick up a weight.

"Do you know what it means?" Matil said.

Dask reached out for one of the weights and Simmad smacked away his hand.

"Ow!" He looked up at Simmad in disbelief. "Yeesh."

"Don't touch the artifacts without taking precautions." Simmad formed a small ball of light in his left hand and examined each weight in turn.

The others watched him, no one wanting to be smacked. Matil noticed that the weights were all different shapes; some were animals and others were objects. Each weight was inscribed with the amount it weighed.

"It's a riddle," Simmad said at last.

"Obviously." Dask went to look at some nearby statues.

"Perhaps we choose weights according to the riddle and place them on the scales." Simmad scratched his goatee. "Will it wake Lady Shora if we get it right?"

"That is its purpose," Dyndal said. "For me, the velanach was the frog—"

Simmad opened his mouth.

"*Toad* pendant. Sorry. The song that the Eletsol sang unlocked the velanach's power to wake me. The same applies here. One of these weights is the velanach, and the riddle's solution will cause Shora to awaken."

"Guys?" Dask said. "This is only a guess, but if we get the riddle wrong, I think we'll all die. Except Dyndal. He'll survive since he's not actually here. Good for him."

Everyone turned to Dask, who looked back with genuinely frightened eyes.

"What's wrong?" Matil said.

"Did you notice these little holes in the statues?" He gestured frantically at the statue beside him. "Something is gonna come out of those. I don't know what, and I don't want to find out, either."

Khelya gaped. "How in the whole of Eventyr can we solve that riddle in one try?"

"One chance," Simmad said shakily. "Well, let's not touch the scales until we've gone over every option. Lord Dyndal, y-you must have a pretty good idea of the answer."

"I had forgotten she mentioned a trap." The Elder gave a shamefaced smile. "Shora trusts me. I feel bad now."

"Why would you feel bad?" Dask said with a touch of panic.

"Because the answer is…not obvious."

"But you can solve it," Dask stated.

"Ye—not exactly." Dyndal scratched his ghostly nose. "No. Nothing comes to mind."

Wings carrying Dask upward, he threw a punch straight through Dyndal's misty head and landed a few steps away.

Dyndal turned to stare at him. "Why?"

Dask heaved a breath. "We're gonna die, but I feel a little better about it."

He crossed his arms, raised a finger, and then uncrossed his arms with a laugh. "Second alva to wallop me in the face! Although, were I awake, you would not be bold enough to hit me."

Simmad's eyebrows drew together tightly. "The riddle mentions feet, and that might just mean the scale next to the Lady's feet. But there's also a scale near her head, perhaps representing her mind. In which case, I should think the mind led the feet."

"Yes, it is beginning to make sense," Dyndal said. "And you see that the scales are unbalanced." He held up his hands at the same height. "The scales at both ends must come into balance…and weigh the same, I should think. Shora often says that the body and the mind are equally important."

"How do we determine which weights to use?" Simmad looked at the bases of each weight, reading the number that showed how heavy they were. "There are many combinations that could result in an equal outcome. And some of the weights are the same value as another, but look much larger or smaller! Is there a solution at all?"

Dask had been looking at the weights. "It's not entirely about the numbers, Sparkles. We're under a courthouse, where judges make judgments. We have to be judges here."

"Judges?" Simmad asked.

"I mean…eh, let's start with the easy parts. She already gave us the answer to 'why'. Her feet crossed the boundary for food, so we could put food at the feet. I think that's her starter weight for us."

"Which food?" Khelya said. "There's a rabbit weight and a pile of berries."

A different weight caught Matil's eye and she got a closer look. "Here's one of a plate and fork, with some kind of meat on it."

"What does everyone think of the dinner plate?" Dask said.

Simmad rubbed the side of his face with his sleeve, making sure to keep his gloves spotless. "It does seem like the one most strongly associated with food. Let's take it for now."

"Good. Moving on." Dask went back over the weights. "She crossed a boundary, somewhere she shouldn't have gone, and was punished. How are alva usually punished for things like that?" He held up a weight that depicted a pile of metal links. "Chains," he said. "As in locked up, hobbled, restrained. This one seems pretty likely. I also thought of being fined or having the offending limbs, uh, removed. Didn't see a weight with coins or anything better than chains."

Simmad pulled the weight from Dask with one hand and whacked his arm with the other.

"*Ouch*." Dask clutched his arm and glared at Simmad.

The Sangriga regarded the weight. "It's a possibility. Do we know if it would have been a common punishment?"

"You've probably never been caught where you shouldn't be, huh?" Dask said.

Dyndal's huge leaf wings seemed to wilt. "Caught," he said. "Now I recall what Shora did when I read her secret journal."

They waited for him to continue, but he was content to stop there.

"What did she do?" Simmad said. "It might give us the answer."

Dyndal began to shift from one foot to the other. "Ah, it- it is not likely that it would."

"It's all right," Matil said. "We're still curious."

Simmad grinned. "Extremely curious!"

"I've never heard this legend before," Khelya said eagerly.

Dyndal cringed. "I will only tell you if you promise never to speak of it again."

"Don't worry." Dask rolled his eyes. "It'll remain buried here with us."

He took a deep breath. "She…knocked me over the head, chained me up, and hung me by the feet from a tree for four days."

Khelya clapped a hand over her mouth, trying to compose herself.

"Chains," Dask said triumphantly to Simmad, who appeared dumbfounded.

"I could not abide someone seeing me in such a state," Dyndal continued, "so I cleverly pretended to be a terrifying wolf-bat. No one knew it was Dyndal."

"*Oh*," said Simmad. "Is that where the tale of the iron cocoon came from?"

"Cocoon?" the Elder said. "No, no. I was a *wolf-bat*. Grrr! Eeetch, eeetch! Terrifying, yes?"

Matil gave him an encouraging smile. If she said anything out loud, she would fall over laughing.

"All right, then!" Simmad displayed the chain weight. "The chains bound her."

Khelya glanced between the two sets of scales. "Which part of her? Mind or feet?"

Simmad lowered the weight, newly puzzled. "Good question."

"Dyndal said Shora thinks both the mind and body are important," Matil said. "And the riddle goes, 'What binds *me?*' Maybe the chains bind her feet, and something else binds her mind."

Dask snapped his fingers. "So if the second question has to do with both scales, then the first question probably does, too!"

"That accounts for all four of the necessary weights!" Simmad shook Dask's hand vigorously. "I think we've done it!"

Dask pulled his hand away. "We only have two weights picked out, buddy. Let's keep going. What binds her mind?"

"How can we know?" Khelya said. "None of these make sense. There's a book, a pair of dice, a hawk, a rucksack, a house…"

Dask pointed at the weights. "What about the rucksack?"

"What about it?" she said. "Is there anything aside from the fact that it don't make sense?"

"No, it- it does. See the strap?" Dask said. "It's a heavy load that you carry."

Everyone from Matil to Dyndal looked at him in confusion.

"Well," Dask said, "sometimes…if you do something wrong, you, uh, you feel guilty, right? It's possible, anyway. To feel guilt. And guilt is…"

Matil looked down. "Heavy."

Dyndal's eyes washed over with deep, dark green as he stared at the weight. "Very heavy."

Simmad nodded. "Then that's three weights we've got! Next is…'What led my feet?'" He crouched down beside the weights. "What would represent the mind leading the feet? A map?" Setting his gloved finger on the map weight, he turned to Matil and the others.

"What're the numbers on our weights?" Khelya said.

Simmad gathered the three they had chosen and examined them. "Thirty-six on the dinner plate, fifty on the chains, and sixty-seven on the—"

"Nineteen," she said. "That should be our last weight."

Everyone goggled at Khelya.

"You…know mathematics," Simmad said.

Khelya looked back at them uncertainly. "Lots of Obrigi learn numbers."

"Apologies," Simmad said. "I haven't met very many Obrigi. But I'm impressed. You would do well in university."

"*University?*" Khelya said. "No, no, I could never match up to them Sangriga."

Simmad chuckled. "Believe me, you'd more than match up."

"R…really?" she smiled bashfully. "So- so, um, the dinner plate and chains add up to eighty-six, and the rucksack on the other side, if it's sixty-seven, leaves nineteen. Which weight says nineteen on it?"

Simmad looked through the twenty-five remaining weights and set some aside. "These five are nineteens."

The five weights were a goblet, a bolt of cloth, a hawk, a spider, and a tulip.

"Five?" Dask said. "Is this lady for real? Look, I know I said we have to make some judgments, but this is ridi—"

"At last, something that I know," Dyndal said. "Shora once told me that desire has the spirit of a hawk, hunting for food and swooping down when it is found. Choose the hawk."

Dask shrugged.

"Then…" Simmad put the four chosen weights beside each other. "The hawk as the mind's desire led her feet. She crossed the boundary for food. Now chains bind her feet and a heavy burden binds her mind."

Everyone checked over the combination of weights and considered switching weights out or trying new combinations. They mulled over it until their brains were numb. In the end they hadn't switched out anything. Both sides added up to eighty-six, and Dyndal looked more sure than he had since they'd entered the underground hall. Simmad placed two of the weights on the scale by Shora's feet. Smoothly and without a sound, the plates became even with one another. He let out a relieved puff of breath. He walked to the other end of the bed and hesitated with the last two weights, the rucksack and the hawk.

"One chance," Dask repeated. "It's been an honor, you guys." His voice sounded sarcastic, but his expression was sober.

Khelya squeezed her eyes shut and said, "Please let it work," before opening them to stare intently at the scales. "It's the right answer. It's gonna work."

"Sure." Dask went to stand by Matil.

They were trapped, with this riddle the only way out. It was worth Matil running through the combination again in her head. Her heart stuttered in her chest, but she couldn't tell if it was because of the tension or from the hushed way Dask now wound his fingers through hers.

Hands shaking, Simmad placed the heavier weight on the higher plate of the scale and the lighter one on the lower plate. The plates leveled with each other. The lined-up statues and the words on the wall gleamed out of the dark.

An echo dripped from the old stone walls, whispering in Matil's ears. "*Let justice remain unchanged,*" it sighed, "*writ forever on rock. Let the rot of corruption be removed. Let us remember that, no matter how different, how rich or how poor, each soul is the work of one hand.*" The quiet rush of words steeled Matil with certainty.

Dyndal looked down at himself. His nebulous body was fading, his orange hair losing its essence. "Stay alive," he said. "Stay strong, my friends."

A new phantom appeared facing him. Like an hourglass, one form siphoned away while the other grew in solidity. The other was a woman with strikingly dark hair and shining, pupil-less eyes of stormy gray. Shora.

"Telviyof?" came her faint voice.

"Gevi," Dyndal said. Then he vanished.

12

Elder Sister

Shora bowed her head. After a moment, the transparent Elder straightened. Though shorter than Khelya, Shora loomed over the other alva. Her dark gray robe hung motionless on her slender frame and the robe's severe collar came halfway up the cloudy white skin of her neck. Around her sharp cheekbones and wide-spaced, unfathomable eyes fell locks of her black hair that were not bound in her braid. "Greetings, alva." In spite of her words, she didn't sound welcoming. "You woke us?"

Khelya took a deep breath, eyes flicking up to Shora and down to the ground. Simmad nervously wrung his gloved hands.

Dask grabbed Simmad's arm before he could start bowing. "We did."

"Then I thank you," she said. "What is the situation?"

"We- we need your help," Matil said. She stepped forward and explained everything that had happened with as much brevity as she could muster. It was even more nerve-wracking than the time she spoke in front of the Corwyna Council; Shora's silvery eyes simmered almost impatiently. The Elder's expression deviated from stern only once, when the Book of Myrkhar was first mentioned.

"It is no book, alva," Shora said vehemently. "It is a putrid bundle of parchment that has claimed more lives than plague."

When Matil was done talking, Shora concluded, "Then we have little time in which to find Falgar. Bring the tulip weight. It is my velanach."

Simmad pulled a reasonably clean handkerchief from another of his pockets and wrapped the delicate weight in it. He put the parcel and his gloves back in his tunic pockets.

"Good," Shora said. "And if what Dyndal supposes is true, we must now be on our guard. A certain Saikyr may soon show himself."

Her vaporous figure stepped down the hall past them with a graceful, long-limbed stride, her robe rippling only slightly as she moved. Matil watched in surprise. Shora had wings folded on her back. They looked like moth wings – long, pale brown, and silky.

"Stay close," Shora ordered, looking over her shoulder at the four alva.

Matil and the others began to follow, and then something silent, invisible, and ominous flowed through the room. It felt like a brood of vicious creatures had entered, pressing up against the alva. Matil had the feeling that if she moved, if anyone moved, they would die. The others seemed frozen by the same fear. Someone's nonchalant, disembodied humming danced around them.

Shora scanned the hall ahead of her. She pivoted back toward the alva in a defensive half-crouch. A long metal pole formed in her hand and its sharp, curved blade poured into place at the top, embedded with a sapphire. The entire glaive gleamed like it was bathed in moonlight. "Igsun," she said in a ringing voice.

Khelya gasped while Simmad made a choking noise. Igsun was one of the Saikyr, Matil remembered. He'd been a trickster and a schemer in some of the stories Khelya had told her. She and Dask drew their knives.

In the space between the alva and Shora's bed, the stone floor cracked and a tall apparition appeared facing them, floating in the stuffy air. The strong, gray-and-white wings of an owl extended from his back. He wore a sleek black tunic over scarlet trousers and fine shoes with a low heel. His ears were long like a Sangriga's and veins stood out sharply underneath his pale skin. Black hair was swept away from his haughty face in jagged disorder. He looked down at the alva with dark crimson eyes that, like the other Elders, lacked pupils. Then his attention settled keenly on Shora.

"You guessed right," he said pleasantly. "Sister, I—"

"Leave," Shora said, narrowing her eyes.

Igsun smiled and tilted his head. "I was not finished talking. Ahem. Sister, I have missed you dearly. I dreamed of our reunion, and, to be honest, the surroundings were better in the dream. Expensive paintings, fine wine, soft chairs, and the like." He wiggled his fingers around at the stone hall. "Your austere taste eternally baffles me."

"I am not your sister," Shora said. "There is no familiarity between us."

The sound of a shoe clicked on the floor just before Igsun took a small step forward. The effect made Matil feel off-balance, and she wondered if something was wrong with her eyes.

"You began it," Igsun said. "You told me to call you my sister. Why should I stop?"

Shora, too, stepped forward. Now she stood with the alva. "At that time you were different."

"Was I?" His smile grew to show sharp, yellow teeth. "If I recall correctly, you are the one who changed. After you became attached to the cripple. Do you remember?"

Shora's taut expression didn't waver. "I remember a *boy* telling me that he planned to drink from the Heart. With its power he would heal Olen's wounds, but only if I did not wed Olen."

A snarl flashed across Igsun's face, transforming him into something savage, but it was gone as soon as Matil had seen it. He put on a hurt look. "It took courage beyond measure to say that, you know. It should not be spoken of carelessly."

"A foundational law should not be broken," Shora said.

"Single-minded, are you not?" He smirked. "Your husband...dear Olen...he was more understanding. I wonder what he will do if he wakes. Will he be able to last in the Sanctum, alone and weak?"

She lifted her chin. "He will never be alone."

"The definition of 'alone' rather fits him," Igsun said. "Forsaken by all others…cut off from the outside. Poor friend. Might he not look upon the Heart and thirst?"

Piercing white surged in Shora's eyes.

"Or…" The corners of Igsun's mouth curled up. "Do you have a way to keep him company? A way to find the Heart through him?"

"For what are you playing?" Shora spat. "Time? Information? End your meaningless babble and *leave now*." Her wings spread out, revealing dark eyespots and swirling patterns.

"I have all the information I need, sweet Shora." Igsun glanced at the alva. His eyes turned into pools of brighter red.

Shora darted out and stabbed her glaive straight through his chest.

He gave her a dry look. "That hurts a bit." He eased himself off of the glaive and turned to walk slowly towards the back wall. "I know you very well, Shora. And I know it is because of your love for him that I no longer had a place in your heart."

"No." Shora's voice quieted. "It was because you took Thosten out of your heart and put *yourself* in his place."

"Do you truly believe you have not put another in Thosten's place?" Igsun said, stopping beside the weights lined up on the floor. He bent down and picked up the weight that looked like a goblet. "Does not a delicate flower grow in your own heart?"

Shora stood perfectly still between Igsun and the alva and said nothing. Igsun chuckled as he looked at the weight. The chuckle turned into a laugh that grew louder and louder.

The weights on the floor exploded up and out at the alva. Shora whipped her glaive from one side to another, forming a shimmering pane. The weights hit the pane and fell to the stone floor.

By the time she dispelled her shield, Igsun was gone. Dark gray clouded Shora's eyes, but her expression was unreadable.

"We shall go," she finally said. She turned away from her body lying on the stone bed and gave a respectful bow to the statues along the walls. "Mu ramtuv ieni." After that, no hesitation slowed her march down the hall.

Matil, Dask, Khelya, and Simmad followed, perplexed and jumping at shadows. Climbing the stairs was less mysterious but more difficult than descending them.

When they reached the top, Dask said, "Hold it. Dyndal gave us magic disguises and protection. It's not exactly a good idea for the four of us to be ourselves in Nychtfal. So uh, Shora, can you do the magic stuff?"

Shora looked at him with keen eyes.

He shrank back a little and coughed. "Please?"

"I have many questions about Eventyr," she said. "About you. Are you criminals?"

"It…depends on who you ask," Dask said.

Matil nudged him. Somehow it felt wrong to talk vaguely to Shora. "We were captured by the Sangriga Council and escaped, the Book-bearer put out a bounty for us, and Dask stole something but gave it back. Other than that, we're not actually criminals."

"You didn't have to explain," Dask whispered. He spoke up. "That part doesn't matter as much as the fact that Khelya's an Obrigi, Simmad's a Sangriga, and Matil has no wings. No way we can walk around like normal alva."

"Are Obrigi and Sangriga no longer welcome in Ecker's Brug?" Shora said.

Dask laughed. "To say they're no longer welcome is honey-coating things."

A scowl darkened her brow. "Just before the Hibernation I had sorted it out for the fifth – and I hoped last – time." She waved her hazy-looking hand at the alva, returning their disguises, and then waved at the door. It rolled open in response. She faded until she was a mere ripple, only noticeable if you knew she was there. The alva climbed out of the door and it closed behind them once again.

After they retrieved Dewdrop and Olnar from the hitching post, Shora gave a sharp instruction to follow her rippling presence. She led them through the streets. Drowsy alva bought sausages on a stick or the bread-wrapped sausages called gotenskamp from the street vendors who were still open. The buildings became larger, with more intricate and angular designs. When they emerged into another plaza, they stopped before an imposing building made of dark stone, seven stories tall with each level featuring many ornate pillars. Alva flew in and out of doors on every level. Bearing the weight of the city above the building were several stone arches in a line, like the ribs of a huge animal.

"It has been a long time," Shora said. There were faint glimmers in the air where her eyes would be.

Dask tapped on Matil and Khelya at the same time. "This is the High Court of Nychtfal. Home of the Big Seven, or the Seven Screwballs, whatever you wanna call the guys who pretend to make decisions about the law." He indicated several tall wooden walls curving around the plaza. "Those are the voting boards, where we stick a voting tack to pick the candidates that we like best. Sometimes we're voting for magistrates who'll go on to join the Assembly in Dwell and be in charge of Nychtfal. But most days it's little councils and offices we're voting on. Each citizen gets only one tack per board. And—oh, look. The fixers are out early."

A few Ranycht in dark clothes were flitting by the boards. Each one stuck a tack in it while the guards watched diligently. Matil saw one of them pull out two extra tacks. The guard tapped the three-tack Ranycht on the shoulder, and there was a quick exchange of something between their hands. Then the extra tacks went up on the board.

"Those guys really like who they're voting for," Dask said with a smirk.

"Would that I could catch them and show them what justice means," Shora said. "Go ahead, deprive some poor farmer of his sovereign right! Pathetic."

Dask shook his head. "Votes don't mean a seed. Politics is just a competition between gangsters, demon-summoners, and rich quillheads to see who wins the government. And even then, they're all holding hands behind the boards."

Matil looked at the boards in disbelief and then at Khelya and Simmad.

"I'm not surprised," Simmad said. "It's the same in Tyrlis…minus the voting bit."

Shora's eyes shimmered into visibility again. "It looks as though I have my work set before me now. I will return, Ecker's Brug." She lowered her voice to a dangerous whisper. "Wait for me."

Dask rubbed his arms. "Ooh, she's scary. That gave me toadbumps."

They took a moment to plan their next destination, which Shora described as a mountain in the west. Khelya and Simmad tried to pinpoint exactly where she meant and they determined that it was a place known as Green Mountain in northern Obrigi, the area where Khelya's family lived.

The sky-light coming in from ventilation shafts had grown dim. It was probably close to dusk by now. Dask began leading the group toward the western gate of Ecker's Brug, turn after turn after turn. Whenever he saw a street clogged with alva, animals, and wagons, he took them down a much narrower street over which houses teetered. They walked right through the residents' yards and a couple of fungus gardens, stepped around children playing street games, and filed one by one past elderly Ranycht with stark white wings. Smells of the evening breakfast wafted through open windows: potatoes, meat, bread, and herbs.

Finally Dask was forced to take them onto the main street that led out of town. The ground traffic barely moved while a steady current of Ranycht flew overhead. But Matil found it interesting to pick out conversations from the hubbub. All the noise could be overwhelming if she didn't focus on something.

"New here?" said a man with the scratchiest voice Matil had ever heard. "From the country?"

The reply came from what sounded like a very young man. "Yes, sir."

"Drafted?"

"Yes, sir. Last week."

"Yeah, I rememba my time in the army. No fun. But you're in for a treat, kid. Betcha anything you'll be stationed by the border. I hear there's war just around the corner, and if that's so, you'll get a chance to take out some of those flighty lighties and jumbo dumbos."

Matil realized what he meant, and she reached out blindly to put a hand on Khelya's invisible arm. Khelya's attention was elsewhere, though, on the buildings and walkways around them. Simmad, too, was entranced by the city's sights. The men Matil had overheard moved on in the opposite direction.

War. Would it happen? The Ranycht and Nychta's Skorgon fighting the Obrigi and Sangriga. She looked at her friends again and tried to relax. More conversations vied for her ear, but one just behind her seemed to drown out the competition.

"…He's very smart, my son-in-law," a female voice said. "I told you he's a doctor, right? But I really don't know about what he's done. I really don't know. Taking his family and joining those rebels."

Matil thought back to the old courthouse where the two men had mentioned 'breakaways'.

"Oh, I hear you," said a second woman. "This whole business is a mess. Alva going to war, alva in hiding, and that scary witch telling our government what to do. What are we supposed to think of it all?"

The first woman sighed. "I just hope my son-in-law can find the right herbs for little Nych down there. Poor, sickly boy."

"Did you hear them?" Dask said in a low voice. "Talking about rebels? That lawyer said they might be in the south." He lowered his voice further. "If it's true, they're probably east of Lowen. That's where I'd go if I were them. Barely anyone out there."

"You think so?" Matil said. If there were alva who wanted to rebel against *her*…then Matil and her friends weren't alone.

Past nightfall, outside of the city, they were far enough away from the outskirts to make camp on the side of a gully. Shora revealed herself and removed their disguises. She offered to keep watch as Dyndal had, asking that they set out her tulip weight and Dyndal's toad pendant. She considered them with foggy gray eyes before sitting straight and alert.

13

New Walls and Old Wounds

Council tea parties had potential – potential to be vastly boring or interesting to a dangerous degree. Lyria's attention drifted about the room's conversations as she poured herself a cup of blackberry leaf tea in the corner of the room. What she heard was the typical simpering small talk that started out such gatherings.

And then a welcome voice spoke softly in her ear.

"Hello, Lyria," Annest said. She stood at the cart beside Lyria, dropping a spoonful of sugar into her own tea.

Lyria lifted her head. "Councilwoman Annest. How are you?"

"Quite well," the younger woman said with a restrained smile. "And you?"

"Better than you, I imagine," Lyria said. "Can't be easy, staying here with the commander away at the border."

Annest tasted her tea and then added a bit more sugar. "Oh, I'm used to it. I need to be used to it or else I've no business marrying him. I—" She lowered her voice further. "I just keep overhearing…awful things. From the other Council members. To think that our alva would *try* making his job harder than it already is. And why? Because they don't agree with him?"

"Learn this lesson well." Lyria glanced about at the Council members immersed in various conversations. "No one on the Council is 'our alva'. No one is loyal to some notion of 'our side' or to 'the great Accord'. We're all in it for what others can give us or for the preservation of what is most valuable to us. Look at it like that and you will understand more and more. You may even discover *whose* alva some of us really are."

"But, Lyria…when you say 'us', surely you don't speak of yourself."

She gave Annest a serious look. "If you wanted to discern my true motives, all you've got to go on are my words and your observations. Those are rarely enough. You don't know who I am or why I do what I do, therefore you cannot trust me."

Annest's chin stuck out a little stubbornly. "So how does one get to know another, to the point where one could trust her own discernment?"

Lyria drank her tea while she thought. "An alva's money is often a good place to start. Look into where they get it and how they spend it. It can prove revealing."

A cheeky smile grew on Annest's face. "You know, I think spying on my friends' finances is what I've been missing all these years."

"Annest, dear," came the voice of Lord Owynth across the room.

"Ah, then I will leave you to mingle." Annest bowed her head to Lyria. "Thank you, Lyria, really. Perhaps I can't trust you, but I certainly am fond of you." She threaded her way through the other party guests.

"Take ca—" Lyria stopped. Fond? She chuckled. Silly girl.

After she had finished her tea and pretended that she understood a discussion comparing different wines and meads, she chanced into speaking with Cilian, an older Council member usually found in company with Nider.

"Well, I don't have any love for the Ranycht," Cilian said, "but treating with them is *the* most efficient way to deal with their threat. We make a few reparations, placate their anger, and ping! War averted, how do you like that?"

Lyria thought that "ping" was an overestimation. "It's an idea."

"A guttering good idea!" Cilian took an aggressive sip of his tea.

"How much do you expect these reparations to cost?" a woman said.

Lyria startled to see that Councilwoman Branneth had snuck into the conversation. She tipped her head in greeting.

Cilian stroked his greying moustache. "A considerable amount from the royal treasury would be in order. The king's household is, to put it politely, overfed."

"I can't imagine him parting easily from the crown's wealth," Lyria said.

"But you know the king," Branneth added. "It's anyone's guess what he'll do on a given day. He's a bit…" She crossed her eyes and tilted her head.

Lyria resisted the impulse to snort. Branneth and her faces. Memories shuffled through her mind – those long childhood carriage rides to Corwyna when they would make fun of Council members like Owynth and Count Delian, Nider's father.

"A bit?" Cilian said. "Oh, he's more than a bit. How many wives have mysteriously disappeared now? Four?"

Lyria polished the triangle on her staff with the edge of her sleeve. "Only three, Councilman. Give your monarch some credit."

A smile was evident in Branneth's eyes, but she remained turned to the side with a restrained expression.

Just as well. Lyria scrubbed harder at her staff.

"Monarch." Cilian heaved a sigh. "Paper box of a monarchy, I say. Haven't you ever thought that he doesn't cut as kingly a figure as, for example, Lorbryn or Nider?"

Branneth looked concerned. "One must watch one's words."

"It's the powerful one must watch. The king may be king today, but who will rule tomorrow? I'll stand where the sun is shining, thank you very much. If you girls look closely, you'll find that it's getting bright in the Ambermeet…" Cilian tapped the side of his nose. "And cloudy over the palace."

* * *

The wall was a stark wooden line through the wilderness. Ranycht guards patrolled its top and a few made rounds above with their wings sweeping and metal weapons catching the dying gleam of day. On the other side was Obrigi, the land where Shora said they would find the Elder Falgar. They had marched from Ecker's Brug westward through Nychtfal to reach this place.

The group – out of disguise – crouched in verdant undergrowth at the edge of the cleared land beside the wall. Matil squeezed between Khelya and the ghostly form of Shora. Dewdrop simply nosed in right through Shora, who didn't appear to notice.

"That's it," Dask said, pointing through the leaves. "I heard some alva calling it the Fortification. Matil, Khelya, and I saw it when it was being built a few weeks ago."

"Is there a way to get past?" Matil said.

Shora aimed a critical gaze at the wall. "We will consider options as my strength returns. For now, flying is impossible for Matil and Khelya."

"Hm." Fading slightly, Dask wandered away from them.

"You'll find a way, Lady Shora," Simmad said. "Won't you?"

"With a little time, yes," she replied.

Matil looked for Dask through the undergrowth, but couldn't see him.

Khelya, meanwhile, seemed to be measuring the wall with her fingers. "It's tall," she said dispiritedly.

"That's why we'll go underneath it." Dask appeared behind them. "Follow me. I found what I was looking for."

He led them parallel to the wall for a couple of lengths. He scuffed at the ground near a fallen branch. A large, dirt-covered mat slid back, and below it was a sloping tunnel framed with wooden beams.

"Smugglers' tunnel," Dask said. "Looks like an old one from before the Fortification."

"Smugglers," Shora repeated drily.

He looked down at the tunnel and then at her. "You got a problem with us using this thing?"

"No," she said. "I suppose that we shall become smugglers in a moment."

Simmad eyed the sky. "Shouldn't we wait for nighttime?"

"We go now," Shora said. "Twilight and dawn are good times for crossing the border between the land of night and the land of day."

"She gets it." Dask raised an eyebrow. "Were you a smuggler?"

"What a good jest. Smuggler?" She mirrored his raised eyebrow. "I gave smugglers their just reward."

Each one of them, Dask first, Khelya last, and the beetles at their sides, slid into the dirt tunnel. Matil could see the others ahead with her dim Ranycht vision. Though the tunnel was wide, Khelya had to bend and sometimes crawl to fit under its low ceiling.

Matil couldn't stop worrying that right above them was a wall decked out in guards. But the upward slope at the end came into sight, allaying her fears.

Dask moved the tunnel cover, climbed up, and then lowered himself again. "That's a problem."

Khelya tried to look past the others. "What's—"

"Shh!"

"What's the problem?" she said in a quieter voice.

"I see a lotta lights up here," he whispered. "I think it's a camp. There are Obrigi and Sangriga moving around."

"Should we go back?" Simmad said.

"No…we'll need to be very careful," Dask said, "but we can make it."

Matil peeked out of the hole. Only a thin line of grass shielded the tunnel mouth from the light of nearby lantern-posts. Tents of different kinds were established beyond the lanterns, both the large, identical tents she had seen in an Obrigi military camp before, and smaller tents decorated with flags and colorful emblems. Obrigi carried boxes from one place to another and sorted through their contents. Sangriga floated above.

Matil looked at Dask. "What do you mean?"

"We'll sneak past," he said.

A sigh from Khelya rose from lower in the tunnel. "More sneakin'?"

They all held hands while Matil and Dask – Matil had moved to the back of their line – faded. The gathering night helped her to step into invisibility. Khelya soon faded as well, making a face before she disappeared. Simmad and Shora's spirit were the only ones still visible.

"You're supposed to *take* the magic, Mr. Simmad," said Khelya.

"It's a bit…" He scrunched his nose and mouth together, going red from exertion. His wings were gone, but nothing else was. "It's too dark! I can't use magic without light."

"It is shadow," Shora said. "Think of it as shadow cast by your light. They are equally parts of this world."

"But there's too much," Simmad said. "I'm- I'm afraid that it'll take over and that I won't get the light back."

"Reconciling opposite elements is indeed difficult. Allow me to complete the illusion for you." Shora walked along their line with her hand outstretched, causing Simmad to vanish, and then dissolved herself away.

"Okay, everyone," Dask said. "Move slowly, as quickly as possible. Does that make sense?"

"No," came four replies.

"Great," he said. "Let's go."

Khelya's unseen hand tugged Matil up to the surface. At that moment, a Sangriga and a much taller Obrigi stepped out of a nearby tent. They both wore gold-and-white surcoats emblazoned with a symbol that looked like a closed eye inside of the sun. The chain of hidden alva came to an awkward stop.

"…and begin loading up supplies," said the Sangriga. "I suspect we will pull out as soon as word of the commander's death reaches Corwyna. You are dismissed, Quartermaster."

"Yes, sir," the Obrigi said.

He brushed by the grass as he left and it wobbled from side to side, touching Matil's ear. Prickles ran up her arms.

The Sangriga examined a scroll in the light of a lantern and then flew away. The group started going again, away from the camp. At a safe distance, they stopped fading.

"That was an army camp." Simmad's voice wavered. "Right at the border!"

"Probably not much longer, though," Dask said. "That Sangriga told the Obrigi to start packing up. That might be a bad idea for them, considering what's going on in Nychtfal."

Khelya spoke quietly. "Do you think they'll attack? Will the Ranycht invade us?"

"No one can answer that question for certain," Shora said.

Dask chuckled. "I bet *I* could. But I don't wanna."

Matil squeezed Khelya's hand, and Khelya squeezed back.

* * *

They chose to continue traveling through the night while the Obrigi farmers slept. The land of Obrigi was just as Matil remembered it: expansive fields of grass waved over the traveler's heads, lonely trees stood far apart from each other, and hills sloped gently in the moonlight.

Matil's and Dask's sensitive ears made it easy to avoid large and loud Obrigi going home for the night. The travelers only used the roads when they needed to cross a stream or river, and then they hurried over the gigantic bridges. Khelya knew exactly where in Obrigi to find Green

Mountain, and Dask and Shora kept them on course; Shora was an excellent navigator, yet, according to her, Eventyr had changed a lot since the Hibernation began. Dask looked very pleased with himself when he made a correction that she accepted.

Khelya and Simmad told stories to Matil and Shora as they traveled, many of them about the Elders. Some had to do with historical events or the lives of famous alva, to which Shora listened closely. Others were folk tales they'd grown up with, like the tallest Obrigi that ever lived, and the Sangriga who turned into a butterfly. Dask added some of his own from childhood, telling them somberly, or raucously in the case of stories he'd heard or lived through later in Ecker's Brug.

During the tales of Elders, Shora broke in with brusque comments on what really happened. Dask would then whisper to Matil what really, *really* happened. His jokes were funnier than they'd been when she first met him. Part of it was that they weren't as mean-spirited. And maybe another part was that she liked just walking beside Dask and listening to him talk.

While the night turned to early morning, the group skirted a town full of willowy, Sangriga-style buildings.

"That's Vyng Lan," Simmad explained as they looked down on it from a hill. "An old university town, quite like Icto Lan. My aunt worked here for a long time."

Khelya looked back. "Sometimes I snuck out here to try an' get a peek of the university building – heard it's really somethin' else – but it's all tucked away. I even asked to get work moving supplies into town. No luck. I wish Obrigi could go an' look, even if we can't study there."

"They don't let Obrigi go in?" Matil said. "Why not?"

She sighed. "We're not capable of reachin' their knowledge level, and our presence would only distract."

"Is that what they told you?" Dask whistled. "The Sangriga aren't even trying anymore."

"Dask!" Khelya said with a nervous look at Simmad.

Simmad stared at the town disappearing behind them, his eyebrows pinched together. "I- I know it was unusual that they'd let a commoner like me study in Icto Lan. But an Obrigi can't even set foot inside Vyng Lan? This is their land, isn't it?"

Shora silenced everyone after the light of a watchman's wings flared up near the town. They stayed quiet until they stopped for the day.

Matil felt something like kinship with Shora in their common focus on the hunt for Falgar. Waking him would bring them closer to knowing if the Elders could really fight the Book of Myrkhar. The Book, Nychta, and her childhood friend Crell were always on the edge of Matil's thoughts.

Too often memories of that night hung over her; the night she discovered who she was. The knowledge had not been worth Amacht's life. In the worst ways, Matil and Nychta were truly the same. Amacht had come to save Matil, and Nychta had killed him. They were both responsible. And then Khelya would rest a hand on Matil's head, or Simmad would turn to her excitedly, having thought of something new to say. Her insides would seem at odds with the outside world. At times she still wondered who she was.

That afternoon, she woke up to see Shora keeping watch, her form silver and wavering in the shade. Shora sat the same way every time, straight as a pillar.

Matil thought back to Mr. Korsen's ability to "read" alva. The Elders might have it, too, if they could grant it to others. Having just been asleep tinged everything with a sense of unreality, so she didn't think for too long before creeping out of her blankets and over to the stick Shora sat on.

"Lady Shora," she whispered. "Can you…see who I am?"

Shora looked at her. "I can, to some extent."

"Then…"

There was a flicker of a smile on Shora's face. "I see a companion I am glad to have. Someone who has shouldered the burden of waking the Elders, though she plainly carries a heavy burden of her own."

Matil lowered her head, humbled and at the same time trying to hide her disappointment. It didn't seem like Shora was using special powers to gain insight. "Thank you. But… aren't I too…"

"We all have wounds, Matil. When you live as long as I have, you get to be one very large scar. It is beyond our power to protect ourselves from life. Instead we must protect the heart."

"The heart?" she said.

"Your heart is delicate and diseased." Shora placed her hand over her own heart. "It fills you with doubt and fear."

Matil bit her lip. No wonder she felt weak.

"That is the way of every heart," the Elder said. "Mine as well. Still, the reason you and I are here together is that we have fought the illness. And we must continue to do so." She looked up at the leaves of the young tree above their camp. "A baleful cloud does hang over you, for you were born through a sorcerous ritual. But mere sorcery will not destroy you unless you let it. Guard your heart, don't give up, and hold to right. If you fight to the end…you will find healing. As is said in the Chivishi, all will be well." Her faint hand pushed Matil's shoulder. "Now sleep, so you have no regrets later."

* * *

"Mother, I'm tired." Matil yawned widely as an example.

"Are you?" Mother spoke with a kind voice, kneading out dough at the table. Sunlight came in through a chink in the window curtains. "Sleep if you're tired. Come over here so I can give you a kiss."

"But Father and Bechel are already asleep," Matil said. "You should go to bed when I do."

"The mayor's feast is tonight, olrin. There are going to be so many alva, and there has to be bread for all of them."

She pouted. "Then let's wake up and make the bread early. Really early."

Mother chuckled and used her wrist to brush a few strands of hair out of her eyes. "Go ahead. I'll be done soon anyway. Wake up early and help me bake the dough in the evening."

Matil sneezed suddenly. She was lying on her bed, covers pulled up. A strange gray blanket covered the ceiling. She coughed. Why did it smell like a fireplace? When she stood up, she realized that the gray blanket was smoke. Panic seized her, and she stumbled out of her room.

"Father! *Father! Mother! Bechel, where are you?*"

The hallway was empty except for a layer of smoke clinging above like mold. Windows lined the hallway's right side. Sunlight still beamed through the curtains, but it was thick and harsh, as if it wanted to burst through the—

Glass shattered, the sound driving painfully into Matil's ears. Someone had knocked in a window and torn the curtains. Laughter filtered in from outside. A moment later, the window closest to her exploded. She saw a blacksmith's hammer, and then the thing that held it. The thing was a monster made of pure light, staring in at her. Matil's heart pounded, trapped in her frozen chest. Her breathing came more and more shallowly.

The monster's hand darted past the window's glass teeth to clutch the air in front of her face. She screamed, though the smoke in her nose and throat burned. At last she could move again, and she ran through the tunnel, eyes unable to stay open in the crumbling world of fire and sun that chased her.

The monster's voice stayed with her. "Why are your wings dark?" it sang. "Because you bathe in mud!"

She tripped and got back up. Her face felt raw.

"Why do you wake at night? So Myrkhar can eat your souls…"

She put her hands over her ears and could still hear everything. Crashing, laughing, screaming, blazing.

"Why is—"

Silence swallowed all sound. Cool air swept by, soothing the memory of heat. Matil opened her eyes cautiously and found that there was nothing around her but a black night sky bejeweled with stars. Her body floated in such a way that her limbs had no need to strain.

Two of the stars were particularly bright. They gave her a peaceful feeling. Even in this lonely place, maybe someone was watching over her.

All will be well.

14

Sun Down

Yaric, Lyria's oft-hooded agent, had arrived late. It was just past midnight.

"You've news from the front, then?" Lyria said. She beckoned Yaric toward the living room. "I'll bring out some tea."

He stayed in the hallway, fidgeting. "It's one news *item*, ma'am. Just…the one. It's, er, to do with…you talked about 'im warmly. I know you 'ad hopes…"

Lyria froze where she was. Surely his tone of voice didn't need to be so heavy-hearted. "That's ridiculous, Yaric," she said a little desperately, "You know I'm not the type to have hopes."

His expression didn't change.

"Get on with it, then," she said. "Speak."

"It…was told to me like this: 'Commander Dalen's been assassinated. They found a Ranycht nearby an' executed 'im for the crime. His Lordship Haiwyl Song is now acting Military Commander of the Sun Accord.' That's all."

For a moment, Lyria's mouth moved in an absentminded attempt to speak. "Dalen?" she finally said.

"I'm sorry, ma'am. Terribly sorry." He shook his head. "Doesn't feel right, does it? Seems like the Ranycht might've been accused to cover up for one of the commander's enemies at home."

Lyria came back to herself. "Perhaps. Thank you, Yaric, I…I'll see you at our next meeting time." She dropped a few coins into his reluctant hand.

"Be safe," he said.

"I suppose I must." She added another coin. "Buy your children a treat."

"Thank you, ma'am." Yaric bowed, pulled up the hood of his cloak, and left, his wings barely visible behind him.

Lyria floated up to her bedroom to lie down. It couldn't be true. She remembered talking with Dalen and Annest. She had heard their plans and seen the life in their eyes. Dalen wasn't meant to die. Was his death…a failure on her part? She should have looked out for him more. Maybe she could have kept him safe.

And, though she hated herself for it, her thoughts turned towards what would happen in the Ambermeet now that such an important player had been lost. Haiwyl was an honorable man, but hardly one to speak for himself. He had no stomach for politics and thus would remain a mere piece on the game board.

Lyria fell into a deep sleep and didn't wake until late in the morning. The rest of the day she spent in gloom, thinking, planning, and attending to duties that couldn't be put off. Conflicting thoughts plagued her mind. The next night's sleep was restless and rife with strange dreams. As she descended the stairs the following day, someone rapped on her front door. It was a small man floating regally over the threshold and wearing a gold-and-white servant's tunic.

"Lady Annest Ren wishes you to join her for tea with several close friends," he said. "What may I tell Her Ladyship?"

Lyria's heart sank. "Tell her I will attend."

In her closet she kept two white mourning dresses. One was for wearing whenever someone she knew died, especially if they had been important in the Council. She replaced the dress every so often to keep up with the fashions and it was considered very tasteful by other funeral-goers. The second dress was older and bereft of all ornament. A simple thing, closer to what the lower classes used. It was what she'd worn after her father's death. It was the one she chose now.

A short time later, Lyria sat in a drawing room in the midst of five young, gaudy noblewomen and Annest, and she wondered how it had come to this.

"I can't, Annie," said one named Elwen, her face dripping prettily. "I can't believe it. It's exactly like a tragic romance. I mean, the love you and Dalen shared was beautiful."

Shanlyn sniffed. "You'll find someone else someday. You will."

"Until then," Cara said, "you've got us. We understand you. Last night when *I* heard about Dalen, I cried so hard I couldn't sleep."

"When I heard, I felt this terrible despair." Forrie dabbed at her eyes. "I nearly fainted."

Elwen gave Forrie a *look*. "I know," she said. "It's *awful*. I mean, I haven't eaten a bite since I heard. I doubt I'll eat anything after this tea."

Shanlyn apparently didn't want to be left out and opened her mouth, but Medwys, the last of Annest's friends at the tea, spoke first, laying a gentle hand on Annest's wrist.

"Remember him for his good aspects," Medwys said, "and move on when the mourning has ended." She tilted her head and looked up, like she was on stage. "Even though he was a soldier, he had a kind heart. Maybe it was for the best that he died almost as a martyr, before his sword could destroy more lives, and before his heart could at last be sullied and broken by war. I think – I really do – that he will be happiest if you live on to find a man of peace and intelligence rather than another…military officer. Wherever Dalen is, he must know *now* what is good for you."

The other women sighed in agreement, and then each one tried to top Medwys's speech. Lyria was at once impressed and distressed at how Annest could sit there meekly while they jabbered and postured and implied. Even for Lyria, it took everything she had to keep her mouth shut so she didn't spoil the gathering.

And then— "Ladies," Annest said, standing up from her couch. "You've all been gracious to me in this bleak time. Thank you."

The guests looked at each other in confusion, but responded with smiles.

"I hope your families remain well," she went on, "and I wish you the best."

They realized what she was angling for and stood uneasily.

"We haven't even finished our tea," Elwen said. "Don't you want someone to keep you company?"

Annest gave them all the saddest look Lyria had ever seen. "I'm sorry, I must rest. Farewell, my old friends. Roth?"

The small servant man, Roth, brought the guests' shawls and other effects and escorted them out of the mansion. Lyria looked back at the door as it closed behind her. The five younger women clumped together and spoke briefly before dispersing to fly home. The street was bright and the day was warm, but the world felt cold.

"Councilwoman," said Roth, suddenly at Lyria's side. "Her Ladyship has further business with you."

Of course! Lyria knew the tea party wouldn't have been the only reason she was called out. Perhaps Annest had plans in light of Dalen's death, and perhaps Lord Owynth was in on them. She followed Roth inside to the tea table, where Annest had returned to her couch.

For the first time today, Lyria saw her without sparkling noblewomen sitting around her like decorative jewels. Her hair hung loose and her eyes were like dark grottoes. On her lap, she pressed shaking hands together.

Lyria sat across from Annest. The other teacups had been cleared off the table, but hers remained. "You have business with me?" she said softly, pouring herself a new cupful.

"Yes…well, sort of. I'd like to talk, if you have time." Annest took a deep breath. "I'm sorry I asked you to come, Lyria. It was selfish of me." Her mouth curled into a smile, a tight mockery of her old cheer. "I knew what would happen. What they'd say and how hollow they'd sound. I didn't want to believe it. So I brought you here as moral support."

Lyria couldn't stop a certain widening of the eyes that said, *You've not thought it through all the way, have you?*

"Moral support is what my friends used to be," Annest continued. "From the instant I met Dalen, he was helping me grow up to use my own brain, and it got harder and harder to fit in with their group. Even though I'd hoped they'd still be a comfort, I lost faith in them ages ago. No, today…*you* were my true hope. You always cared about Dalen's work, the things close to his heart. You would see through anything those women said. And you can't know how thankful I am that you came."

Lyria cleared her throat, at a loss for words. "Of…of course. You're very welcome." Was that the reason Annest called her back? It was a little more personal than she'd expected. But as long as Lyria didn't get all soggy like Annest's friends, she'd be safe. Keep it simple. "I, erm, I miss Dalen already. You must be devastated."

Annest lowered her head. "They said he was assassinated by a Ranycht." She looked up, eyes bright with tears. "Tell me, Lyria. Do you believe them?"

Should Lyria be straightforward in return? She scrutinized Annest and then leaned forward. "I don't. Not for a second. Then again, I'm paranoid."

"You're not paranoid," Annest said. "You're realistic. I wish I had the heart to tell myself the truth the way you do."

"Truth is a poor friend in Corwyna." Lyria set down her cup. "Be glad you aren't like me."

"Maybe so. But I can't help looking at my own friends and thinking that, however poor, truth is a better friend still. If I asked them what I asked you, they would laugh, say they don't know what I'm talking about, and change the subject. Do you know what that is? It's darkness disguised as light. I no longer desire it."

It was almost disconcerting to hear the sunny Annest speak in this manner. But, like a breeze on a hot day, it refreshed Lyria. "It's easy to mistake," she said. "Real light is so rare."

"Rare and valuable," Annest said. "From now on I won't settle for anything less. And I know that you don't settle, either, so please tell me. What have you found?"

Lyria wiped her mouth with her napkin, sorting out in her mind what she could share. "There were those who opposed Dalen's causes, but few who could carry out this deed. I've suspected them of similar plots in the past."

"Who are they?"

"Greffyr, Rianna, Adoc, and…" Lyria wrinkled her nose and looked down.

"Councilman Nider?" Annest said.

"Yes, although…" Lyria began, "I'm reluctant to include him. When the other Council members accuse me of bias against the fellow, I'm afraid they're quite right. I look at him and see a rat stuck in a dress." An unladylike snort made her look back up.

The snort turned into a laugh until Annest was giggling a bit madly. "Sorry," she said, covering her mouth but still giggling. "I think I needed," she snorted again, "a laugh."

Lyria restrained a smile. "You see where I may not be the best judge of his intentions."

"Don't let the others tell you such rot. I've done my own research in the past. What he did to you was inexcusable."

Lyria's cup hovered above its saucer for a moment before she lifted it all the way. "Research?"

Annest ducked her head shyly. "Do you remember when my father first introduced us before my initiation ceremony?"

"Yes…"

"You were in such possession of yourself," Annest said. "I decided right off that I wanted to be like you."

Lyria choked on her tea.

"Are you all right?"

"Fine." Lyria cleared her throat. "I'm fine. Continue."

"Anyway, I learned about your past efforts in the Council and asked around. Not many alva appreciated your presence, but those who did were the dearest to me of the Council members, including my father. I trusted them. And when I learned of the Commoners Riot, I was even more intrigued."

Lyria winced.

"Even I could tell it didn't go the way it should have gone," Annest said. "Someone interfered. What I learned pointed towards Nider, but I couldn't fathom him being responsible for the disaster. He's always been moderate and well-spoken, hasn't he?" Her blue eyes were as hard as river rock. "As I woke up this morning, a veil lifted. Many things became clear that I'd refused to see before. I recalled especially what I knew about the Riot, and once more I pieced it together in my mind. Lyria, I now believe that Nider's mercenaries kept your Common Council out of the Ambermeet and let in those who would tear it apart."

Each time Lyria thought of that day, it brought a new flood of shame. How could she have trusted him? "Nider himself has now confirmed it," she said. "And I am grateful for your consideration and regard. The information itself makes no difference."

"It *could* make a difference. I finally know what we're up against, and perhaps we can reach others as well. The Corwyna Council is not too far gone. The Common Council could have its day in the sun. We simply need to fight harder than before."

Done with her tea, Lyria sat back on the couch. "Your father wouldn't want us to fight."

"When we've won some leeway, Father will understand." Annest's chin trembled. "Even if he—even though he's not all I thought he was."

A catch rose in Lyria's throat, but she pushed it down. Now the young woman would really regret spending time with a doomy-gloomer over her happy friends. "Remember your own words and keep them close, Annest. They are a lesson. The best one I've ever learned, as well as the worst. Remember: Alva are never all you think they are."

And…here came the tears. Lyria wondered if she should switch couches to pat Annest's arm like a normal alva. She wouldn't apologize for saying what she did, but she could have got it across better. The girl was in pain.

"M-maybe not," Annest said, wiping her face with a napkin, "but they're not as bad as you think they are. You and I will work together. We'll fix the Council, and then you'll see."

After considering possible responses, Lyria chose instead to sit beside Annest. They sat in silence until the light falling through the windows turned brazen, signalling the day's end.

"I'm sorry for keeping you," Annest said at last. "You should go."

Lyria knew how it felt to be alone at times like these. "Are you certain? However long you'd like me to stay is exactly how long I will stay."

She nodded. "Father will arrive home soon. He's looked after me since the news came in."

They walked to the front door together.

"I can't thank you enough," Annest said, looking down. "Before you go, I must ask. If you have no faith in alva, why do you continue on as a Council member?" She met Lyria's eyes. "Why don't you leave and not bother with it anymore?"

With a dry laugh, Lyria shook her head. "I don't know. I suppose…foolish though it is, I…I do have faith. Faith in alva, faith in the Elders, faith in Thosten. Something or other of those, I'm sure. It won't leave me alone. I'm forever nagged by this ridiculous, impossible…hope. That tomorrow might be better than today – and that I can help bring it about. Silly, isn't it?" She felt a bit flustered; rarely did she admit such things to herself, much less another alva. Another Council member possibly full of agendas and secrets.

"Silly? Then perhaps I'm the silliest one of all." Annest smiled. "See you tomorrow at the Ambermeet, Lyria."

Alarm bells went off in Lyria's mind. "Annest, with all that's happened…isn't it too early for you to attend meetings again?"

"At this time more than ever, I need to show my strength. Dalen may be…" She trailed off with a sigh. "But I'm not. And I will see you – and the culprit – tomorrow."

"So be it," Lyria said. "If things look different in the morning, feel no shame in staying home."

"Of course," Annest said. "You're a good friend."

Something closed tight around Lyria's heart and stomach.

"And thank you," she added. "For telling me the truth today."

Lyria edged out the door. "Good…goodbye."

She began to float away from the mansion. As soon as she heard the door shut, she sped up recklessly, not daring to think until she was safe behind her own locked doors. Once there, her mind picked up where her wings left off and raced in spirals through Annest's words. Lyria had seen similar tactics before. It was a way to artificially strengthen bonds with someone so that one could rely on them for favors and alliances. Or a way to extract information from the naive. Annest had been quite wrong. Lyria *was* paranoid and she needed to stay paranoid. She couldn't become attached and trusting. She mustn't let it happen again.

She must not be…

You're a good friend.

15

A Royal Mistake

Lyria found a rather disturbing surprise when she entered the Ambermeet the next morning. She tried not to stare. The rest of the Council members filed in, also very obviously trying not to stare. Owynth called the Council to order, and then the herald stepped into the sun mosaic on the floor.

"The Council presents the Lord of Drendel Palace," the herald announced in a louder voice than usual, "the Great Light, Sovereign of the Sun Accord, and ruler over us all… His Luminance, King Arwyl Aury, fourth of that name!"

Everyone bowed toward the butterfly-winged throne that nearly always sat empty, where King Arwyl now reclined. His flowing blond hair was braided on one side and streaked with purple dye on the other. Expensive jewels dotted his long ears. The voluminous robe he wore was purple, edged with gold. His purple shoes were completely round on the bottom, clearly not made for walking. Either his wings or his servants carried him where he wanted to go, but at the present his feet lay upon an extravagantly cushioned footstool. A strange smile, one that was part childish pleasure and part patronizing indulgence, graced his thin countenance. Dark blue eyes gazed out from the intricate swirls of black makeup decorating the top half of his face.

"Greetings," the king said. "It has been a while."

Owynth's normally curly golden beard was limp today. "Welcome, Your Majesty," he said lifelessly. "May the sun rise forever on your reign."

"May it. Yes, may it, indeed." King Arwyl looked around. "Well, are you starting the Council or not?"

Owynth gestured to the herald. "Council Herald, report."

The herald unrolled his scroll and, in a grave manner, made the announcement. Few of the Council members reacted with surprise, since news of Dalen's death had already spread. Lyria studied faces anyway, especially those of the alva she'd mentioned to Annest. Each one showed varying levels of the appropriate concern, Nider showing the most – shaking his head and making sad remarks to his neighbors. That likely meant he was the culprit. And what could anyone do about it? Lyria remembered what she'd said to Dalen about war and politics being similar. She had neglected to mention just how easily they could become one and the same.

"Ah," sighed King Arwyl. "Tsk-tsk. That is the reason I came here." He turned to Owynth. "Let me do something."

He waved his hand as though drawing an explanation in the air. "A Council thing. Quickish."

"Er, yes, Your Majesty," Owynth said. "Please grant us… your wisdom."

A satisfied smile spread across King Arwyl's pale lips. "My dears, I have been informed of the terribly high costs of war, and, taken with the death of our premier general, it does not paint a pretty picture. What's the point in it? That is why, by royal decree, I hereby reverse the lamentable decision you alva made to put our men right on the border. Tell them all to return to Corwyna and their various bases round Tyrlis."

Lyria turned her head ever so slightly to see Nider out of the corner of her eye. His eyes were closed and his face at rest like he was listening to a pleasant symphony. That one glance did it. She kept her face blank with some effort, but she wasn't sure whether the torrent of bad thoughts running through her head was gibberish or advanced cursing.

"Your Highness," Annest said, bringing all attention to her. She floated from her seat to the centre of the hall.

Lyria clutched her staff and willed Annest to go back. Simply interrupting the king was grounds for punishment. Saying anything further that wasn't effusive praise could be considered treasonous. But Annest was clever. Perhaps she would apologize. It might be part of her plan, and maybe she wouldn't do anything too—

"I disagree."

Sinking a little in her chair, Lyria watched the calamity unfold.

"With the highest respect," Annest said, voice shaking, "I argue that your course of action is severe, first-degree owl pelletry. What else can you have up there in that royal head of yours besides *leavings*—"

"*Order!*" Owynth's eyes blazed with light as he sent out a pulse of energy and slammed the butt of his staff on the ground. "Sit *down*, Councilwoman!"

Lyria had never seen him burst like that before. She could say the same of Annest. King Arwyl's dark eyes fixated on the young woman, who shouted over her father.

"You mock the commitment of our soldiers and destroy their sacrifices if you send them out, only to bring them back!" Annest's wings flared up. "You'd have us just...fly away in willful ignorance. Our army exists to protect the alva of this land, Your Majesty, the families of the men who fight. They're not servants for you alone to order about! Great king, we debate in this hall. Why does *your* word suffer no opposition? Aren't you merely an alva like the rest of us? I'd wager you've never given a thought to anyone outside of Corwyna. Probably not even outside your precious palace!"

She took a deep breath. By that point, everyone, even Owynth, had gone deathly silent. "Commander Dalen didn't die for nothing," she continued. "He died because he did his job. Because he wanted to keep safe those who can't fight for themselves, including *you*, Arwyl Aury. And if you hold to this Stal-cursed decree, you stunt that purpose, which yet outlives the commander." She stood straight up, red-faced but unflinching. "Please reconsider."

Owynth turned to give the king a deep bow. "She is grieving, she means none of it. Commander Dalen was her betrothed. I beg that you don't take her words to heart."

Annest clenched her fists. "I mean all of it."

"I will have her escorted from the Ambermeet, Your Highness." The entire lengths of Owynth's ears had also turned red. "Worry not. Guards?"

"No," King Arwyl said, waving his hand.

Owynth cringed. "I promise you she will be disciplined, but her outburst has been distraction enough. We must not waste your time, my king."

"Hold…" He narrowed his eyes at Annest. "Her betrothed is dead, you say? Then there will be no unnecessary bother."

A haze of doom lowered over Lyria's vision. Her fingers hurt from digging into her staff.

"Were this woman anyone else," the king said, speaking to the entire hall, "I would see her beheaded in a trice. However, I am known and loved for my appreciation of beauty, and before me I behold a wonder. A shame, indeed, should I waste such a share of the sun's glory as has seen fit to grace Eventyr."

Owynth's eyebrows rose.

"What sort of ruler would I be if I did not immediately prepare for a wedding?" King Arwyl laughed, a rich and delighted sound. "The Sangriga shall be pleased with their new queen! Guards, take her to the White Mansion and make her comfortable. Then set Drendel Palace to stirring.

Tell them what miracle has occurred here this day, and give the orders for a wedding party to rival all that have gone before!"

Annest's mouth fell open. Lyria closed her eyes.

* * *

It was the stupidest action of Annest's life, surpassing the time she set the music room on fire. At least the latter had been of scientific interest to her child self. This particular escapade taught her nothing she didn't already know, muddled her chances of making a difference, and made her wish the music room fire had eaten her up. Any frustration she'd had with Lyria in the past for being overly cautious went out the window. Not to mention that after the wedding happened, a season later she'd disappear from public life and, sooner or later, the king would get another queen. That was his pattern. No one knew why and no one wanted to know, either. Only, now that Annest had become the unlucky bride, she felt more than a touch concerned.

She was preoccupied to the point that her new room remained a background blur of gold, white, pillows, and canopies. Following the king's announcement, she'd been shuffled out of the Ambermeet and placed in the White Mansion. She couldn't leave, so she attempted to dredge up a plan of escape. It was not going well.

Dalen could have gone through it with her, poking holes in it and making all kinds of common-sense suggestions until she had an airtight strategy. She imagined what he would say to her various threads of thought.

"Good manoeuvre there, but leave room for flexibility. Keep in mind, 'You can't count on alva or the weather, only animals.' General Suncloak said that. Did you know he led a few badger hunts, Ann, did you? I almost wish there were still more badgers about, so I could try my—oh right, let's get back to plotting. Hmm, would Roth have connections with the staff here? There could be some servants eager to rescue a fair lady from—"

Someone knocked, startling Annest out of her thoughts. She dried her eyes and went to open the door. Her father stood outside between the stoic door guards, followed by her family's most trusted servant, Roth. The lines etching Owynth's face were deep. His kind eyes drooped. She felt a rush of affection for him that melted away her anger about the way he had acted in the Ambermeet. He was only trying to keep her safe. Maybe they could discuss ways to get out of the whole situation.

Over his shoulder, Roth caught her eye and blinked twice. Annest blinked twice in answer, completing the sign that they would talk later. She wondered what news he had for her.

"Can I…" Owynth began.

"Yes, yes, do come in," Annest said. "I must see my dear father again before I marry." She closed the door firmly behind him.

"How…how do you feel, Annest?" He stood in the centre of the room without a drop of determination or will in his face.

Her heart sank. It couldn't be. "Not good," she said in a despondent voice. "I'm an idiot."

He closed his eyes. "This is a hard time. The king's decision came right after Dalen. I should have insisted you put off Council business till the mourning period was over." The anguish twisting his expression told her everything. "My poor daughter."

"Father, it *doesn't* have to end here."

"What are you on about?" Owynth stepped closer to her entreatingly. "Nothing's going to end. It's a new beginning."

Distressed, Annest shook her head. "Aren't you afraid? The king was born the day you got a place on the Council. You've watched him his entire life and you know very well that you won't see me after the wedding. Besides, isn't it strange that the king would show up just after Dalen died? It feels…scripted, like a play."

"Stop troubling yourself." He patted her arms up and down as if to reassure himself she was still there. "I'll put everything in order. Remember, it can only work if you're at your most respectful around the king – nothing like that performance today. At any rate, it looks like my donations to the Sun Temple finally paid off." His nervous chuckles trailed off into an atmosphere of unease. "Ann, about today…I agree with your sentiments, but I warn you that expressing your own thoughts with such strength will divide more than it unites."

"I'd rather have division that truly unites than unity that divides," Annest said. "And the latter is what we've got right now. The Accord is crumbling from within, Father."

Some of the old steel flashed in Owynth's eyes. "It was crumbling for a long time before I took office, Annest. I've slowed it as best I could. Think about your situation. The method you used today was…clearly not effective."

Annest coughed, turning a bit red.

"But I have seen you do incredible things in the Council for your young age," he continued. "If you take at least some of my advice going forward, you will do great things wherever you are. You'll also probably avoid making a powerful king upset. So please tell me you will consider my words. Losing you would destroy me."

Tears welled up in Annest's eyes. She hugged her father. "I will," she whispered. "I'll consider them. But if I go first, you mustn't let it destroy you."

Owynth held her tightly. "Don't talk like that. I love you too much, do you hear me? I love you, dearest butterfly."

"…I love you, too, Father."

They spoke for a bit longer, but Annest could hardly pay attention. She wracked her brain for any kind of escape that wouldn't end in her death. Before Owynth departed, Annest asked if Roth could stay behind for a goodbye.

"I don't see why not," her father said with a smile. He left the room.

Roth entered shortly thereafter, closed the door, and bowed his head to Annest. "My lady," he said. "You leave tonight."

* * *

Lyria sat ensconced in a large, mauve-coloured armchair with her knees drawn up and feet on the cushion. What a mess this day had become. Well, it was her fault for getting caught up in the optimism of youth. She should have warned Annest against fighting. All that rot about faith…urgh.

A few timid knocks at the door prodded her out of the chair. Apparently she went slowly enough that the visitor started knocking again and didn't stop until the door was opened.

The visitor was a servant, a boy, who held his fist in the air. He hastily put it at his side. "Good afternoon, Lady—er, Councilwoman Lyria. Councilman Muwyn has sent me to pick up the book you promised him."

Lyria understood right away and invited the boy inside. "It's not a book, young man, it's a well-regarded treatise," she chided before the thick door closed, bringing them into full privacy.

The boy looked around. "Are there…"

"No servants. No one else lives here."

He drew himself up. "I bring a message from a friend."

Lyria's gaze bore into the boy, whose wings guttered in discomfort. What did he mean by 'friend'? She didn't have friends. He likely wouldn't know, either. The usual procedure when communicating in secret was to send it through a series of bearers, each with different instructions and no knowledge of the sender. "Continue."

"The message is as follows: 'The white bird needs wings, and the outer wall must fall tonight. Please help.' End message."

Lyria nodded once. "Dismissed. Oh, hold on." She hurried through her living room to the bookshelves, took a small scroll entitled *'Bio-Political Ruminations on the Stomach Juices of Mice, by Teacher Rynth'*, and handed it to the boy. "This is your cover," she said. "Bring it back in a week, or keep it, I don't care. Repeat the message one more time for me, would you?"

The boy did as she asked and then left, eyeing the scroll.

"White bird, wings…" Lyria floated up to alight on the second-floor banister. White was important. Who was the white bird? Who would call himself a friend?

Annest. Stuck in the *White* Mansion. That meaning made sense. She wanted to escape and was asking Lyria to do something. Outer wall could be a literal phrase. But bringing down the walls of the Mansion by *tonight?* Instead, perhaps it meant the outer defenses. The guards? Ah.

Annest had the inside of the Mansion under control. Lyria had to clear a way on the outside. Or she was completely wrong and the message really meant, 'Have Councilman Whitewing's bodyguard assassinated.' Lyria was confident in her first interpretation. In that case, the message was preposterously treasonous. All risk and no reward. A proper Council member would not accept.

Very good thing for Annest, then, that Lyria wasn't proper.

She looked out the window. Almost dusk, the time of the usual meeting. She threw on a cloak and slid her leftmost bookshelf – the one holding hollow books – to the side, revealing a cramped passageway lit only by her wings. After descending through the passageway, she opened a trapdoor by her head. It let her out beside a mass of gurgling stone pipes, amongst which she hid herself.

As soon as the sky took on an edge of darkness, Yaric darted in beside her. "Evenin', ma'am."

"Good evening," she replied. "I had a number of tasks for you tonight, but one has risen above the rest. You know, of course, what the White Mansion is."

"Yeah, 'course I know it." He raised his eyebrows. "You ain't tellin' me…"

"I am." Daylight sank beneath the trees while Lyria explained what was necessary.

Yaric leaned against a pipe and scratched his forehead with his thumbnail. "We'll 'ave our hands full, ma'am."

"But we must do it." She looked at the ground. "*I* must do it, anyway. For a friend."

16

Poetic Justice

A faint, gray-blue peak became visible against the darkening sky.

Matil shaded her eyes to look up at it between tree branches. "Is that the mountain?"

"Green Mountain," Dask said. "Doesn't look green from here."

The corners of Shora's pale lips turned up slightly. "Falgar's resting place."

Khelya glanced at the peak. "My family's home is less than a day from the mountain," she said hesitantly. "They live on the other side, just outside Tarn City."

"Maybe you could…" Matil was just as hesitant. "Maybe there would be time for you to visit them."

Khelya tucked her thumbs in her belt and hung her head. "Naw, we should keep goin'. That letter I sent my family was good enough, I s'pose. Hope so, anyway." Dreaminess came over her face. "I can't believe we're gonna meet Falgar."

"It's terribly exciting," Simmad said. "It feels like we've entered the legends."

Khelya sighed. "The ancient days. When the Obrigi built cities."

Shora spread her moth-like wings and flew atop a long tree root. "The alva we left behind a thousand years ago would not speak so highly of the ancient days." She watched Khelya, Dask, and Simmad help Matil climb over the root. The beetles only needed a little tugging for them to scuttle up. The group arrived on the other side panting, with clothes covered in bark splinters.

Simmad held Olnar steady. "What do you mean, Lady Shora?"

She began to walk onward as the alva mounted their beetles. "Before the Hibernation, for hundreds of years, we honed methods of protecting alva. Ways of keeping them away from the Saikyr's corruption. We succeeded with a few generations and failed with others. As time went on, more alva parted from us to follow after Myrkhar's promises. We worked harder, providing structure, safety, and sustenance for our loyal ones. Providing everything and controlling everything. All that we required of them was to stay away from the Saikyr. Away from sorcery and theft and murder. I did not think their burden too heavy."

Dask chuckled. "But they wanted all that help without strings attached, and they got mad that you wouldn't give it to them."

Shora studied him. "In a sense. When we finally saw that our efforts had created our problem, it was too late. Besides

Dyndal's steadfast Eletsol and a few others, the alva wanted nothing more to do with us. Myrkhar was close to finding the Heart. We could no longer fight on our own and succeed. And so with one last great trap, we imprisoned Myrkhar, sealed the Saikyr, and fell into the Hibernation. Calo believed we would awaken one day. I did not. I had little faith that alva would seek us out after roundly rejecting us."

"But here we are," Simmad said. "And we'd like the old days to return."

"Can't believe alva back then didn't want you around," Khelya said.

Dask rolled his eyes. "I can. Speak for yourselves about the old days."

Khelya swatted him lightly. "You sound like those ancient alva."

"Not quite." Shora gestured to Dask. "I admire each of you. Though some may wish for our past and some may not, you are all fighting Myrkhar and the Saikyr. You have an inner desire to do what is right. The Hibernation seemed folly to me, yet it gave you alva what we had feared to allow – responsibility. You have worked out for yourselves reasons to turn your extraordinary powers to good. I am thus gladly proven wrong."

Matil frowned. "Extraordinary powers?" she said. Alva weren't powerful. That was why Nychta had gone to the Book. It was why Matil and her friends were waking the Elders.

"Time and again I have seen your kind change the tide of the war," Shora said, "for good and for evil. I believe it will occur in this age as well. May we Heilar use this second chance wisely." She looked at each of them walking and riding beside her. "Khelya, Matil, Dask, Simmad. As you require our aid, we require yours."

* * *

The night's journey went on and Green Mountain became a huge black silhouette on the horizon. By morning, trees could be seen coating the mountainside. The group slept until sunset and then continued. Their path began to slope upward, feathered with bending grass. Far out in the field stood a cozy Obrigi building with dark red stag beetles surrounding and crawling over it. Later on, Shora took the lead, and the group combed the foot of the mountain for the stone that would mark Falgar's resting place. The ground became rockier. Nearing midnight, Simmad, who held the tulip weight, announced that he felt the velanach leading him.

The object of their search was higher up on the mountain, an elongated stone nestled among several boulders on the gravelly slope. Simmad rested his fingers on the stone and the word *velana* appeared across its surface.

The alva jumped back as the boulders scraped against each other. But instead of falling, the stones were rising. The rocks and pebbles from the ground arranged themselves into twisting columns, and the boulders parted, opening a chasm. Shora drifted inside.

Khelya looked in dubiously. "The door's gonna close on us again, isn't it?"

Shora shook her head. "Falgar did not secure his resting place as thoroughly as I did."

Giving the columns a wary look and clutching Dewdrop's reins, Matil stepped forward with the others. The cave mouth stayed in place.

Unlike Shora's straight and narrow stairwell, Falgar's tunnel wandered, wending farther downward until it opened into an echoey cavern. The expansive ceiling was studded with purple crystals. Greenish light emanated from moss that grew in patches across the rough walls. The group stood on a vast projection of stone floor curving out into a lake.

The water was still and dark, except where moss shone under the surface. Reflections created wavy patterns on the ceiling. Extending into the lake from the floor's edge was a stone dock, and chained to the dock was a handsome longboat. The craft's lines swooped, its wood planks were hearty, and it was painted with deep, glinting colors. Everything was in good shape, no rust and no rot. At Shora's gesture, the group crossed the ground and edged out onto the dock.

A beast lay in the boat. He looked like a Kyndelin halfway through transformation; gray fur on his face and neck, long snout, and magnificent curving horns, mixed with a man's build and dark skinned hands. His clothes were a practical jacket and trousers of purple trimmed with red, embellished by subtle flourishes of gold thread.

"Hal, Falgar," Shora whispered. "Mu bavosh."

Khelya rubbed her eyes and sniffed. "He's...real."

"He'd better be," Dask said.

"Soon you will all meet him." Shora's eyes were soft, like gray feather down. "Falgar and his wife, Chalena, raised my siblings and me after our parents fell in battle. He is one of the First Generation. We are the Second."

The boat's chain wrapped around a stone pillar with a hollowed top. Sticking straight up out of the top was a smooth cylinder. Matil went closer. The cylinder was made of gold-veined marble.

"Is that Falgar's…waking-up thing?" Khelya said.

Shora tilted her head. "Take it out."

Simmad quickly pulled a cloth from his pocket and gave it to Khelya. With one cloth-covered hand, she took the cylinder down from the pillar and held it for everyone to see. The whole thing was almost the length of the Obrigi's forearm. Along the sides of the cylinder were a gem-encrusted clasp and hinges.

Some unearthly, high-pitched noise came from Simmad's throat. "An ancient scroll case! *Ancient!* Pre-Hibernation! It's—"

"Gaudy," Shora said. "Do you hear me, Falgar? Whether you call it style or art, it is gaudy." She pursed her lips. "Well? Open it."

Khelya delicately twisted the clasp with two fingers, Simmad wincing the entire time, and opened the case. A small cloth scroll and a metal flute lay inside. Simmad hastily pulled on his soft gloves to unroll the scroll himself. All four of them peered closer while Shora held her hand above, causing silver light to fall on the scroll. There were only three lines of writing near the top of the cloth.

'Salty, boiling, strong-flavored soup;
the hands that made it,
that chopped the seasons—'

"Is it a poem?" Simmad said.

"It seems to be." Shora ran a finger over the blank lines below the verse. "The flute is his velanach and this poem, once finished, will awaken him. I must write the rest."

Dask looked skeptically at the scroll. "And how long will that take?"

"Till midday, at the least," she said. "Perhaps longer."

"Guess we'll be here for a while," he said. "We'd better get topside and set up camp."

The Elder nodded. "Let us go."

The group and their beetles went up through the tunnel and placed their sleeping blankets in the mouth of the cave. They tied Dewdrop and Olnar to some tall, concealing weeds while Simmad set up Falgar's scroll on a flat rock near the beetles, laying the poem out so that Shora could study it. Morning light began to appear between the pine trees on the mountainside. After a dinner of root slices, dried meat, mint leaves, and pine nuts, the alva settled into their blankets and fell asleep.

* * *

Matil's left shoulder hurt, especially when she flexed her wings. But now she was safe in Etsel's hideout. Looking around, she padded across the rough wood floor. In her hand was a pouch of money. Not big, but satisfyingly heavy. She tried not to dwell on Magistrate Gerig's triumphant sneer as he had grabbed the putrid amulet from her hand.

"Hey, Manners. I guess you was plannin' to sleep in."

Matil twisted, tripped, and sprawled on the floor. Etsel sat on a chair in the corner. He walked up and nudged the fallen money pouch with his stockinged foot.

"Looks like a decent haul," he said.

"I-it's mine." Matil cringed at her shoulder pain as she snatched the pouch and hopped up. "I didn't steal it."

He studied her with concern. "What's wrong? Didja get in a fight?"

It was best not to mention her escape from those thugs. "Just pulled something when I was flying."

Etsel shook his head but grabbed a metal plate from the pile on the table. "Where? On your back? Turn around." He held the cold plate to where she pointed. After the plate grew warm, he got a new one and said, "Who paid ya?"

Matil closed her eyes. "Does it matter?"

"Sure, it matters. If you're gonna live here, and if I'm gonna spend my time worryin' about you, it matters."

She held back tears, glad that he couldn't see her face. "I'm not helping a gang. I promise."

"Yeah, but who *are* ya helping? Oh, no." He slapped the plate on the table. "Don't tell me it's the mud-drinkers."

"Etsel." She turned and gave him a pleading look. "I need to help them so they'll help me."

"Cultists. They're chanty-incanty cultists! Just as bad as the gangs, too, if ya take out the stupid sorcery! Whaddaya thinkin', huh?" He scowled at the money in her hands. "We get by fine, don't we? Tell me if there's a problem. We can fix it. You and me."

"No, we can't. We're too weak."

His mouth hung open. "Is this about…"

She stared at him, hoping that he could finally understand.

"Listen," he said, "I'll take you to Dwell myself. We can talk to the magistrates and make sure something's done. Maybe there are others like you who'll go with us! The magistrates can't ignore a protesting crowd."

"They can and they will," Matil said quietly. "You've done so much for me, Etsel, but it's…not enough."

His ears drooped and he plunked down on his sleeping mat. "Can't ya forget the whole thing? Put it in the past, where it belongs? No good comes from keeping those thoughts inside all the time."

"The dreams won't let me forget. I came to this city to do something, and if I don't, I think I'll go crazy." Matil lifted her own sleeping mat to put the money in a hole she had made. She didn't need to hide it from Etsel anymore. "I can leave, if you want. I think I can make it on my own now."

He got under his blanket, muttering to himself, and faced the wall. "You barely have any real fightin' experience," he tossed back. "And you- you haven't learned my best recipes yet. So stay right here, got it? This is your home."

Matil watched him. How could her heart be wonderfully warm and, at the same time, freezing cold? "Thanks, Etsel."

"Don't forget to stretch that shoulder," he said, and then he pulled his covers over his ears.

* * *

Outside the cave, the sky brimmed with stars. The night was new and Matil had been lying awake for some time.

A different world opened itself to her whenever she woke up thinking about a dream. Before learning she was Nychta, she had clutched the memories close when she received them. Now, she preferred to leave them alone and instead contemplate the present and the future. But sometimes she couldn't help brushing by her old life.

She'd known Etsel was dead since the night Amacht died, because, in both her and Nychta's minds, Amacht's body had briefly turned into Etsel's. For a while, his death was the one thing she knew about him. Every dream that brought her back to the city gave her more information, though, and…caused her to miss him more. She didn't say much about him to the others. They had mostly heard bits about her family. The happy, thornless memories that Matil could hold onto without fearing pain.

Was there a way to stop the dreams? Was it possible to learn exactly what she wanted and nothing else? She shook her head to clear it and sat up. The other three alva still slept, and there was Shora near the beetles, her transparent head low over the scroll.

Dask lifted himself up, one eye squeezed shut. Black hair spiked around his head like an impressive headdress. "Good evening," he said across their camp to Matil.

At the sound of his voice, Simmad stirred. "Shhhhhhh… I'll be there in a…" His eyes shot open. "The poem!" One moment he was lying down, the next he'd tossed away his blanket and scrambled to the rock. "Shora! Lady Shora, how is it—"

The Elder hissed sharply. "I am nearly done."

Dask yawned. "You said you'd be done by now."

"This poem is not a simple country jig, young Dask." Shora didn't even look away from the scroll. "It must be a worthy continuation of Falgar's own writing."

He stared at her, taken aback. "What's she got against country jigs?"

Khelya woke later, when the aroma of stewing meat, potatoes, carrots, and dill leaves filled the air. After the alva had filled themselves, Shora rose from the rock with cold grace.

"I require your assistance, Scholar Simmad," she said. "Write down the words I dictate."

Dask rubbed his hands together. "Finally! Let's hear it."

Simmad pulled a wrapped charcoal stick and a scrap of paper from one of his pockets. "I am ready, my lady."

Shora hum-coughed to clear her throat and began to recite the completed poem.

"Salty, boiling, strong-flavored soup;
the hands that stirred it,
that chopped the seasons—

"How alva eat soup in a group:
they gather round the
pot and all squeeze in."

"Wrinkled, drying, and dying leaves;
Thrual is bringing
a very cold wind.

"Sparrows that fly away to grieve
the just-gone Briden
who grievously sinned."

Matil crinkled her brow. Maybe she needed to think about it on a deeper level.

Dask scratched the pointed tip of one ear. "That's… kinda…"

"The syllables match exactly," Shora said. "And I can compose a second one in the event that it does not prove worthy."

"A second one?" Simmad said. "Er, how many chances do we have this time?"

"Ah. Yes, you would not know. Falgar will give us many chances. I was the only Elder to add the security of a trap. I thought it necessary, and the others agreed."

"Bloodthirsty," Dask muttered.

"You made it through, did you not?" she said. "The puzzle was meant to ensure the worthiness of those who sought to wake me."

Matil looked up at her. "But Dyndal didn't even know the answer to your riddle, and none of us could have figured it out on our own."

Shora laid her spectral hand on Matil's shoulder. "There are many reasons why alva find each other. One is to solve riddles together that they could never understand by themselves."

Dask crossed his arms with a huff and a snap of his wings.

"What're we waitin' on?" Khelya said. "Let's try the poem!"

They took the beetles to keep them safe and went down through the winding tunnel into the mossy cavern. Simmad held up the poem beside Falgar's boat while Shora read it out loud. Her words echoed across the water.

The group waited. Matil could see Dask pressing his lips together as he struggled to not make a comment. Khelya frowned in confusion.

Shora looked at Falgar lying in the boat. "It seems my old bavosh does not approve my writing."

"If…if we really are allowed to use multiple poems," Simmad said, "might I try my hand at one?"

Matil perked up. "Can I help?"

Shora looked at them coolly. "You may as well, but I shall give the final word on what we bring down here."

As they walked back to the surface, Matil fretted about the extra time a new poem would take…and then she had an idea.

"Khelya," she said. "While we're writing another poem, would you like to visit your family?"

Khelya pondered it. "Yeah, I won't be much help with a poem."

"Um…" Matil always forgot that her friend didn't take to art. "That's not what I was thinking."

They all agreed that Khelya could go. Once at their camp, the Obrigi threw a few things in her pack.

"It's time," she said nervously. "Been long enough that I don't know how they'll react to me."

Dask jumped high enough with a wing-flap to pat her on the shoulder. "Don't sweat it. If they can't handle the new and improved Khel, that's their problem. Have them call you Khel, too."

"I ain't doin' that."

"Why not? It makes you sound tough." He snickered.

Khelya bent down to hug Matil.

"We'll miss you." Matil felt anxious for her friend. "I hope it goes well."

"Watch yourself, tree-legs," Dask said.

"Look after Matil, birdface," Khelya said.

Simmad beamed. "Have a terrific visit!"

"And ensure your safe return," Shora said.

"I'll do my best, Lady Shora." Khelya hitched up the pack at her side. "See ya." She set off through the grass in the moonlight, occasionally looking back until she had passed behind a faraway tree trunk.

Soon, the other alva sat at the flat rock and huddled around the ancient scroll, Matil and Dask tossing out suggestions while Simmad held up a small light orb and scrawled on a scrap of paper. Shora paced around the camp edgily, once in a while leaning over them to see their work.

"I think we need to remember that it's a poem," Matil said, "not a key."

Shora raised an eyebrow. "You misunderstand. It *is* a key."

"But…" Simmad coughed. "Respectfully speaking, Falgar would look at it as a piece of art, wouldn't he?"

"Mayhap it is so," she ground out through her teeth.

Shora later relented by giving them advice about what Falgar was like, and they worked long into the night.

17

Homecoming

The sun had already come up when Khelya finally slowed her pace, panting. She watched her old home from the road. Nothing about it had changed – not the dry creek bed nearby, the dust that tinted everything the same light brown, the thick-boned architecture, nor the smoke that rose from the smithy building.

She'd moved away just two seasons before, but it seemed like years. Rushing back were those times when she would climb onto the low roof to watch clouds, scale trees with her brothers to collect firewood, and sit inside while Ma taught her to sew. Memories appeared in her mind, all the early mornings that she looked up at the house in the dim, blue light before making the trip into town close behind her brothers and waiting in the cold outside the school hall before the doors opened. She didn't miss that tradition.

A scream like a whistle turned Khelya around right away. Brown eyes glared at her, and a brown braid draped over the girl's shoulder.

"Khelya Dylsen, where have you been?" the girl shouted.

Khelya was relieved to recognize her younger sister, who had gotten taller since they last saw each other. They were about the same height now. "Marya! Keep your voice down!"

Marya eyed her sourly. "Why should I, huh? You're the one who burnt down a farm an' ran away."

Khelya covered her eyes with one hand. Something told her that her homecoming would be even more awkward than she'd imagined. "*Skorgon* burnt it down."

"Skorgon?" Marya's voice got shrill again. "Skorgon! You've seen 'em? Can I see one? Did they come all the way to Obrigi just to set your house on fire?"

"No, I'll…tell you later. I should see Pa an' Ma first."

"Mmm." Marya shook her head. "They're mad at you."

"I'm sure," Khelya said sadly. "Still gotta let 'em know I'm doin' all right."

She trailed behind Marya as they approached the house. However familiar the Obrigi world was, it disoriented her after living with other kinds of alva for so long. She felt small. Marya tugged the door open. It swung on its hinges without a sound, like it'd been fitted yesterday. The well-oiled door gave Khelya a greater sense of peace. Maybe things would be okay.

"Pa, we got a visitor," Marya called through the house as they went down the hallway. The two of them walked into the plain, but comfortable sitting room.

"Yeah?" Pa's grunt was the same as it always had been. "Who?" Heavy steps moved toward them from the kitchen, and then big shoes came into Khelya's shyly lowered view.

She felt out the floorboards with her boot's worn toe. "H-hey…I'm back. Just for a visit." She reached up to scratch under her headband but put her arm down, deciding against it.

"Why?" Pa said. "Is there a reason you'd come back?"

She looked up, stung. "Pa."

His thick-muscled, stocky build that used to make her feel safe now made him seem like a cold, intimidating statue, especially with his stone-still expression.

"You think we wanna see your face 'round here?" he said. "We've seen it plenty in the bounty notices."

Right, she was still an outlaw. Thiffen. "Pa, listen," she said. "I was helpin' a friend. That's why the Skorgon burned my farm down. And it's why there's a reward out for me."

"Not a very big one," Marya said, disappointed.

Pa raised a thick gray eyebrow at Khelya. "That doesn't sound like a friend to me."

"I don't think you'd say that if you knew her. I wouldn't give her up for the world." Khelya brightened. "We're makin' a big difference, too! You won't believe it. You know the Elders? Well, don't tell anybody—"

"Elders," he said. "Elders again. I won't hear any more about no 'friend' *or* the Stal-cursed Elders!"

Marya giggled. "Stal's an Elder!"

"Get to your chores, Marya," Pa said.

She sniffed in offense and kissed Khelya on the cheek before bolting out of the room.

Pa put his hands on his waist. "Can't believe I wasted five tayuls of good money on you. Lookit you slouchin', too."

Khelya straightened her back self-consciously. Talking to little folks all the time didn't help her posture. "I'm sorry, Pa," she said. "I'm really sorry about the farm – I'll pay you back when I can – and for leavin' without notice. We were in danger. The Book of Myrkhar was stolen, and—"

"There's no excuses for chasin' bedtales, and that's what it sounds like you've been up to for the past season instead of workin'! I knew you were a loafer, but I didn't think it was this bad."

Khelya glared at him. "Won't you just *listen*, Pa? I'm your daughter! If I told you the Elders are wakin' up, shouldn't you consider I might be tellin' the truth?"

"Porridge an' gravy!" a familiar voice proclaimed. "Just like old times, huh? I wondered how long it'd take for her to come crawlin' home."

The front door shut and Khelya leaned into the hall to see. Two young men were hanging their coats on the wall. It was burly Lon, one of her older brothers, with her skinny younger brother Ston behind him.

"Shut up, Lon," Pa said loudly.

"Khelya, that true?" Ston said as they ambled over. His voice hadn't gone deep yet, but, Thosten bless him, he was trying. "The Elders are fixin' to wake up?"

She grinned. "Yeah, and I've met two of 'em! Uh, don't tell anyone else. They're not all the way back yet. How's it been around here?"

"Ooh," Lon said, "where'd Miss Grumpy go? She's been swapped out with Miss Crazy." He laughed.

Khelya's fists shot up. "Laugh when it's actually *funny*, Lon!"

Lon opened his mouth mockingly. "Uh-oh, Miss Grumpy never left!"

"For the love of dirt," Pa grumbled. He stalked out of the room, and a moment later the door to his smithy slammed.

The front door opened again.

"Coats!" Someone new spoke from the door. "I see the boys are back. Howdy, boys!"

"Howdy, Ma," Lon and Ston said.

"Howdy," Khelya chimed in.

"Kh—" A big woman with brown hair in a bun rushed into the sitting room. Her eyes glistened with tears.

Khelya's shyness returned. "Hey, Ma, I…I know I shoulda gotten here quicker."

"Why?" Ma said in a threateningly low voice. "You'd've come back earlier if you really cared to." She turned and marched into the kitchen.

"You too? Ma!"

Lon and Ston chuckled.

Khelya shook a fist at them, then followed Ma. "I'm sorry," she said. "I told Pa sorry, too."

Ma ignored her, pulling off cloth sacks slung across her body and laying them on the kitchen counter.

Khelya's heart hurt. The kitchen brought out the most homesickness. She'd designed the kitchen in her burned-down house after this one to remind her of the good times she'd had cooking with Ma. "You got my letter, right?"

"Not that there was much to get." Ma whipped a carrot sliver out of a sack. "'Don't fuss, am well,'" she recited, waving around the orange spear. "'Sorry about everything. I'll explain later. Love y'all. Khelya.' Real thoughtful! Is she even my daughter? Is she? That's what I thought after reading that- that *military dispatch*."

"Huh," Khelya said under her breath. "Dask was right, I should've wrote more." She spoke up. "But I really couldn't get to you before now. I'm on an important mission. It has to do with the Elders."

"Elders?" Ma said. "You still believe in 'em?"

Khelya scowled. "I believe what the Chivishi says. *And* I've seen live Elders. Their spirits, anyway."

Ma looked concerned. "It's not like you to tell fibs. What'd your pa say?"

"He hates me again," Khelya said with forced cheer. "Surprise."

"He doesn't hate you. Whenever we visited your farm a while back, we found it in ruins. We thought you'd died, girl. That old man's eyes turned wet."

Now Khelya was silent. She opened a cupboard and traced a finger along the familiar brown edges of a stack of plates.

"With the taxes so high nowadays, we all worry about your future," Ma said, heaving a sack of potato chunks into a lower cupboard. "How'll *you* survive when your ma n' pa can hardly afford food? It's why we keep on arguin'."

The faces of Matil, Dask, Simmad, and the Elders ran through Khelya's head. She set her jaw. "Then don't worry anymore. I finally know what I have to do."

Ma folded a bag as she regarded Khelya. "We need to have a long talk."

"Yeah. Let's talk. Then I'll head back." However much she missed her family, there were reasons she'd left.

"Stay," Ma said. "Just for lunch."

"But Pa wouldn't…"

"Stay. Please."

* * *

He was right, he was right. Etsel was right. Matil was wrong.

As she flew, her wings dragged and she switched directions mechanically. Wooden walls, poles, and bridges swooped into view just soon enough for her to avoid them. Voices called through the streets, pointing out where she was to the others. When would she lose them?

Then she was trapped, cornered like last time. How many? Five, six, seven? More? They were men with sharp, stained knives and eyes in every color of poison.

"Thief," someone growled, but it seemed to come from all of them at once.

A softer voice drifted over from a pair of dusty yellow eyes. "Let's take her to the boss. Maybe we can use her skills."

"Too late. She went and made us mad."

Yellow-eyes raised his voice. "But—"

"Get lost if ya can't handle it!" one of them shouted at him.

Boof! Something exploded. Dust puffed into the air. *Boof, boof!* The alley was filled with shouts and white powdery flour.

Matil sneezed, clutching her dagger. What was going on? Tall bodies loomed out of the mist, and she struck, near-blind, with tears in her eyes.

"I'm here," Etsel said from her side. "We can handle 'em."

She swung at him without thinking, and he grabbed her arm.

"Whoa! Get the bad guys, not me!"

They fought wings-to-wings while thugs emerged from the clouds of flour. Matil stabbed and ducked. She didn't know where they would show up next. Her heart hammered wildly.

And then she noticed that nobody stood by her. "*Etsel!*"

He responded from the mist. "It's okay, it's okay, I'm—"

She followed his voice in time to watch him stab an attacker and beat him down. But when Etsel faced her, the air behind him rippled and a half-faded form became visible.

As Matil screamed for Etsel to watch out, she flew past him and grabbed hold of the thug, driving him backward. A few dagger-strokes and he was motionless.

She turned around. Her breath caught in her throat. "Etsel!"

He'd fallen to the ground, face-down. A knife was stuck in his back and his shirt was soaked with blood.

Matil dropped to her knees beside him. His back shook as he tried to breathe. Her hands felt numb, but after two attempts she pulled the blade out, covered the wound with her hand, and turned him over. The clouds of flour were settling around them like snow. Dead and wounded littered the alleyway.

Etsel's chest heaved. "It's, uh, pretty hard to survive stab wounds like these. Unless you're a doctor and didn't tell me." Between groans, he kept up a flickering grin.

"How did I fail this time?" Matil said quietly. Her voice began to rise. "Etsel, what did I do? I trained so hard. *Why couldn't I stop him?*" She tried to hold in her sobs. "I'm sorry, I shouldn't have come out tonight. You can't go. Please. I need your help, I still need you. Don't go, I won't survive!"

"Don't…lose your head, Manners. Lose your head and you'll have a molt of a time finding it again. So don't, okay?" With difficulty, Etsel moved to see her better. A content smile spread across his face. "Glad we met, Nychta. Thank you." He gave a whisper of a laugh. "See…I got manners, t…" His head rolled to the side.

"No!" Matil gripped his shoulder desperately. "Please, Etsel, stay here. Stay alive. Stay with me!"

A scraping footstep drew her attention. It was the man with yellow eyes, standing at the entrance to the alleyway. He looked sick seeing the remnants of the deadly fight, but he edged toward Matil. "I'm sorry, kid. I don't wanna hurt you. Lemme know if- if I can help."

She stared at him through her tears. Fire and ice shook hands inside of her, their purposes finally aligned. They burned her head and chilled her veins. Her dagger had fallen somewhere, so she picked up the first weapon that came to hand – the knife that killed Etsel.

Air rushed past her.

She was moving.

The man's dusty yellow eyes flashed wide in shock, and then they lost all life. Matil stumbled back from his body, the bright red knife heavy in her fingers. She threw it away with a whimper. Her lips formed an apology, but nothing came out.

She opened her wings and flew.

* * *

Matil jolted awake. It was bright out, near midday. Dask, Simmad, and she had fallen asleep slumped over the rock. Where was Shora?

When her heart had slowed down enough, she could hear a soft tune. She looked for the source of the sound and noticed a bush branch where Shora perched, afternoon sunlight sifting through her. The Elder was staring at the golden clouds marbling the sky and…humming. At first the tune sounded sad, but then it sounded happy. Whichever one it was, Shora's voice was warm and her song brought peace to Matil's mind.

"I know it's a little late to say this," came Dask's hoarse whisper, "but they're really coming back. Hm. They're not what I pictured when I was a kid."

Matil looked at him. "The Elders?"

"Yeah." He chuckled. "Kerl's gonna fly over the moon when he finds out."

"Kerl," she repeated. "I wonder how he's doing."

"Probably the same as ever." He rubbed the back of his

neck. "Once in a while, especially now with Khelya visiting her folks, I worry about him. All the times I asked how old he was, he just said a hundred and two. I bet he's in his hundred-forties by now."

"Let's go see him soon," Matil said brightly.

Dask smiled at her, and her heart started to hum along with Shora.

He suddenly tapped the rock, looking at the Sangriga snoring between them. "We should put Simmad in his bed and get more rest and put that poetry junk away and... um...and get more rest."

"Wait," Matil said. This felt like the right time. "The man who taught me to fight. Etsel."

Dask squinted and then nodded.

She took a steadying breath. "He lived in Ecker's Brug, like you. He's part of the reason I got away from Nychta when she captured me. I think both of us saw him, like he was a vision from the past."

"Vision from the past?" Dask searched her eyes. "I dunno whether to be happy that mind-twisty stuff saved you, or angry that you have to put up with it. Hm. So Etsel's from the Brug, huh? I guess we ran in different crowds, but we mighta crossed paths once. We should look him up when we're in town again."

Matil shook her head. It got harder to talk. "Today, I- I dreamed about him. He's gone. And I...saw how he died."

Sadness weighed down Dask's expression. "You okay?"

She swallowed. "I hope you get to visit Kerl again."

They were silent while Shora's quiet song came to an end. Even Simmad's snores had stopped.

"You're awake, aren't ya?" Dask said.

Simmad sat up, causing Matil to jump a little. His hair wisped up on one side of his head. "Sorry." He glanced at them guiltily. "I wasn't sure whether to interrupt or not."

"No problem, Simms. Get that scroll rolled up."

They put everything away and Dask called up to Shora, saying they were going to bed for real now. Before Matil and Dask went to opposite sides of the camp, he caught her hand and pressed it.

"Sleep well," he said.

And she did.

18

Leavetaking

Khelya tugged her pack onto her shoulder and tied her cloth headband tight. She stood in the sitting room, feeling real good after a huge, hearty Obrigi meal. "Where's Lon?" Her older brother had gotten up halfway through lunch. Pa hadn't come at all.

"He left," Ston said. "But I'm here!"

"So'm I!" Marya skipped around the room.

"Tch." Khelya had to smile. "Y'all aren't as annoying as when I lived with you."

"Did I hear Lon's name?" Ma swept into the sitting room with a pile of laundry and sat down to fold it. "Good Calo. Chooses his friends over his sister."

Khelya's heart got heavy. With the way things were going in Eventyr, she might never see any of her family after this visit. She looked at the wall over the fireplace, covered in chips of rock, bits of wood, and pieces of metal. Generations of her family were listed on those labetas, each one bearing the message, "A day's work, done well." And right there, by the corner of the mantelpiece, was her telvogir's simple brown stone. *'Kenner,'* it said. *'Labet.'*

She sniffled. "Well, Ma, tell Ardy an' Lon bye for me. Make sure they don't go teachin' these ones any more curse words, okay?"

"Aw," Ston and Marya whined, but they eagerly hugged Khelya goodbye.

"Look after each other," she added. "Keep your eyes open. Things're goin' bad in Nychtfal and…there could be a war."

Ma folded a dishcloth without looking up. "An' you're just gonna throw yourself in the thick of it, I guess." She pulled another cloth into her lap and paused. "'Fore you leave…try makin' things right with your Pa."

"He hasn't come outta that smithy since he yelled at me." Khelya gripped the strap of her pack. "Why should I go in?"

"You know what he's like," Ma said.

"Yeah. I do."

Ma set aside the laundry and stood up to hold Khelya's hands. "Please, just try."

The smithy door handle was warm as usual. Khelya opened it, but not even its well-maintained hinges could soothe her agitation. Heat wafted in her face as she stepped into the dim smithy. Pa was at his work table, sorting through metal pins. A brown cloth lay on the table as well. Her headband had started out its life as one of those rags.

"I'm s'posed to make things right with you," Khelya said.

He looked up at her and dried his sweating forehead with the cloth. "So, how're you gonna make things right?"

She cleared her throat. "Guess I'll start by explainin' better. The reason I'm out in the forest and not on my farm is 'cause something's happening to Eventyr. I *saw* the Skorgon. They burned my house up tryin' to take my friend, Matil. An' then Matil heard that they'll get the Saikyr's help. *Myrkhar's* help! I can't go back to farmin' now when I know that I can—that I can try to stop 'em." Khelya fidgeted. She could never find a way to finish with the wallop she hoped for.

Behind her, the door opened and Ma came in softly.

"First Heilar, now Saikyr," Pa said. "When do you plan to grow up?"

"I- I *am* grown up! It's why I moved out—"

"Maybe you weren't ready!" He shook his head. "Back then, I just knew it. I knew it whenever you started bringin' home blueprints with all those designs mashed together. We never should've let you see your telvogir so much. He turned you strange."

Ma gasped. "Arden, you don't mean that."

"That was just for fun, Pa." Khelya's chin trembled. "Telvogir taught me what it might've been like when we had the Blessing."

"The Blessing?" Pa said. "You talkin' about those made-up humans?"

"Elders," Khelya said.

He snorted. "Oh, then at *least* you ain't seen no humans."

"Well—" She stopped herself from mentioning Mr. Korsen. It wouldn't help right now.

"And just 'cause our grandpas believed that heap," he went on, "you believe it, too?"

She wanted to scream. "Not *just* because of Telvogir! I've talked to the Elders, like in the stories!"

"See?" Pa said to Ma. "She ain't a proper Obrigi anymore. Heard so many bedtales she thinks she's in one."

She wouldn't cry, she *wouldn't* cry. Instead, she tore off her headband, threw it on the table, and yelled, "Why in Eventyr did I ever wanna be like you?" Then she stormed through the smithy's outside-leading door. The yard was so happy and sunny that she angrily scuffed the dirt up as she walked.

"Khelya," Ma called. "Khelya, hold up!"

She stopped and turned. "What? You want me to go back and say I'm sorry?"

Ma put her hands on her hips. After a pause, she said, "You wait here," and started back toward the house.

Khelya watched in dismay. Would Ma pull out the paddle for talking back to Pa? Or would she bring Pa and his belt? The options ranged from bad to worse. But Khelya didn't like the prospect of leaving without a word, either.

The front door popped open and Ma strode out with her hand clenched. She stood before Khelya. "Behave yourself out there," she said. "Make some money so your pa doesn't feel like a failure. There'll always be a place for you here, girly, but if you need anything from us, you have to go by your pa's rules."

Khelya sighed. "Yes, ma'am."

"Good." Ma opened her hand to show a smooth, brown rock. "This is yours."

It was Telvogir's labeta. She took it slowly, stunned. "R-really?"

"You two were alike," Ma said with uncommon gentleness. "You lit up his days and he lit up yours. Keep it."

"I'm sorry for everything." Khelya looked up at her. "You know I love you and…and Pa, right?"

"Right," said Ma. "But don't ever stop sayin' it. Get over here."

They embraced as Ston and Marya ran out to see Khelya off.

* * *

Lyria scanned the forest, waiting in the sweet-smelling twilight breeze. Because she had difficulty dimming her wings for a long time, she stood with her back right up to the base of a tree from which she could see the top of the wooden Fortification over the tall grass.

A few nights ago, she had set Annest's escape in motion and nearly left it at that. Annest hadn't asked for anything more. She warranted a goodbye, however, so Lyria invented some business in Obrigi that required her presence and travelled all the way to the border with Nychtfal. Annest would arrive here just before nightfall this evening or tomorrow, if all was well.

The meeting place was Annest's ticket out of Accord territory. Through the dimness, Lyria eyed the clump of clover that hid a tunnel entrance. The tunnel was new, having been built by smugglers or an espionage-minded Council member. If she'd had the resources, she would have built it herself. The guards here were incredibly easy to bribe.

Out of the corner of her eye, Lyria saw the timid glow of someone else's light-dampened wings. She whistled two notes, heard a whistle in reply, but didn't show herself until the other Sangriga came into view. It was Annest, dressed in a long, dark cloak.

"Lyria?" Annest said when she got close. "What are you doing here? The danger…"

"I have alva in place. And don't mention danger, or I'll start regretting. What about you? Are you all in one piece?"

"I am." She tugged at her cloak's hood. "I wish we could have worked together in the Council. Things might've been different. I ruined it all."

"You certainly did," Lyria said. "But you're getting another opportunity. Don't make mistakes this time round."

"Yes, ma'am," Annest said with a glimmer of good spirits. "This is jolly decent of you. You've taken risks upon risks—"

"Stop there," she groused. "You sent me a code that meant, 'Help me or I'll die. Thanks!' What else could I do?"

Annest looked at her blankly. "I did what?"

"You sent me a message. Or did you?"

The two women stared at each other.

"Could it have been…Owynth?" Lyria said.

"*Father*," Annest said joyfully. "*That's* what Roth meant! Great sun in the sky, Father fooled me. How could I have thought he'd leave me there? Oh, Lyria, I almost feel like… the world's not as dark anymore. I've caused you and Father so much trouble, yet here you are."

So Ownyth had done the right thing after all. Lyria could never tell with him, but at least he would fly close to the sun to protect his daughter. She passed Annest a small pack of supplies. "Sometimes alva go mad and you have to help them clean up after. Sometimes *you* go mad and need another's help. And if we don't help each other, there will be no help for any of us." She paused, surprised at what had just come out of her mouth.

"I suppose," Annest said.

"Then…thank me and pass on the favor to someone who needs it."

She smiled. "Thank you, Lyria."

Lyria let herself smile as well. "It's time for you to leave."

"Oh, crumbs, that's right. Where shall I go?"

"Those rebels in Nychtfal are likely your best chance," Lyria said. "My source has sent word that they allow allies, Ranycht or otherwise, to join. You will have to convince them you are an ally."

Annest nodded quickly. "I'll take that chance."

"There's a tunnel entrance under the clover," Lyria pointed. "It goes below the border. I've arranged for a guide to take you to the rebels, but in the event you two fail to meet at the end of the tunnel, move away from the Fortification and wait on the near side of the stream. If you are still not contacted, your final option is to travel alone." She held out a scrap of paper. "This map has their encampment's general location marked down. There, in the southwest, somewhere between these towns. You will need to travel unseen as best as you can, so move during the day and keep those wings dark. Is this…will you be all right?"

"I will," she said with a heavy breath, like she was trying to convince herself.

Lyria's heart, dull for so many years, suddenly felt sharp pain. "Be careful, Annest. Colthal."

"You too. Colthal, Lyria." Then she crept away and disappeared into the clover patch as the sky darkened.

The Fortification was quiet again. Lyria swallowed past the lump in her throat before she, too, took to the night and disappeared.

* * *

A ray of moonlight fell into the cave mouth where Matil set a splinter down neatly beside Dask's messy line of splinters. He called this game Tallies, and it was more complicated than it looked. The three alva were playing quietly and competitively while Shora watched in agony; Dask had demanded a rule that the ancient and wise Elder could not interfere to help someone win. At this point, Simmad was edging Dask out and Matil would put Dask in third after this move.

A steady crunching noise in the distance made her prick up her ears. Those were footfalls. Heavy footfalls. "Is it…"

Dask pointed at Simmad and then above them.

"What?" Simmad said.

"Check who it is," he said.

Simmad looked alarmed. "Is someone approaching?" he whispered.

Dask shook his head at Matil. "Sangriga's ears are so long, but they can barely hear."

"I have very good hearing. Ranycht just hear better." Simmad stood on his tiptoes to see over the rocks, and then floated when that method didn't give him enough height. "Hello! I see golden hair. Is that our friend?"

He left and came back with a worn-out Khelya. Shora raised a hand in greeting.

"Howdy," Khelya said.

"Did it go all right?" Dask said.

"How is your family?" Matil gave her a hug around the legs. She stopped. Something was different about Khelya. She looked a little down, but that wasn't it. Oh! She wasn't wearing her headband.

Khelya shrugged. "They're fine. It was good to see 'em again."

They all sat for her to guzzle water, recover from walking for so long, and, in between gulps, tell them about what happened. It had been a decent trip, she said, better than she'd expected. The family was worried, but happy to see her. She even got to take her telvogir's labeta with her.

"Where's that rag you wear around your head?" said Dask.

Khelya slid the labeta into her pocket, becoming downcast again. "It's gone." She patted her pack. "My ma sent me away with some real Obrigi food in real Obrigi serving sizes! Can't wait to try it later."

Dask made a face. "Obrigi food."

"Shush up. What about you?" She went on. "Is the poem done?"

Simmad pulled the paper from his pocket and looked down at it. "Er…yes."

"Can I see?" Khelya sat down beside him.

He held the paper out to her. "You know," he said to the others, "there, erm…there is one line that's bothering me."

Dask glared at him. "There were a lot of lines that bothered you. I think we've worked on it enough."

"Really, though," Simmad said. "It's one that I've noticed over and over again but couldn't pin down until just now."

"Which one?" Matil said.

"*'Take it, eat it, and cast its spell,'*" he read. "It doesn't feel right."

Matil tilted her head. "Yeah…"

"Fine, Mr. Expert Poet," Dask said. "What can we use instead of 'spell'? Fell?"

Simmad's eyebrows lowered. "Dwell?"

"Well," Khelya said.

Dask turned to her. "Hm?"

"*'Take it, eat it, and…something well.'*" Her eyes moved over the paper. "Take it, eat it…work with it? No. Use it?" Khelya lowered her head and shoved the paper back at Simmad. "I dunno."

"*'Use it well,'*" Simmad said. "I like it!"

"Okay," Dask admitted, "that's better than what we had."

"Let's write it down," Matil said excitedly.

Khelya looked up at them in surprise, her cheeks red.

Simmad took out his charcoal and added the changed line.

"It is done, for now," Shora said. "Let us see what Falgar thinks."

The Elder, four alva, and two beetles walked the tunnel and stepped into the dark cavern. Matil's eyes were again drawn to the patches of luminescence and undulating reflections on the ceiling. They approached the boat as before. The empty scroll case sat upright in the pillar where they had left it.

Shora extended her hand toward Simmad. "Bear up Falgar's flute, Simmad, and please give Khelya the poem so she may hold it in place for me."

Khelya took the scrap of paper with scribblings all over it and held in front of Shora. Simmad put on his gloves and took the silver flute from where he was keeping the velanachs in his bag.

Shora gazed over the poem, the crossed-out words, and Dask's random doodles. "May we meet again soon, alva," she said with a slight smile. "You have done very well." She laid a wispy finger on the page and began to read.

"Salty, boiling, strong-flavored soup;
the hands that stirred it,
that chopped the seasons—

"Freshly-baked bread tied in a loop;
the heart that made it,
with love the one reason."

As Shora spoke the words, they filled Falgar's cloth scroll. The sturdy boat remained still, but a ripple spread from its hull out through the water. Colors descended from the gems and luminescent moss to dance around the cavern. They formed flying alva, leaping animals, and winding plants, flowing into shape after shape. A gruff, unfamiliar voice joined Shora's clear tone.

"Welcome, taste the story I tell,
of fragrant forests
and the gifts they give."

"Take it, eat it, and use it well.
A meal is cooked
so that alva will live."

Matil could feel the warmth of food in her belly and spices lingering on her tongue. She relaxed as if someone had draped a blanket over her. Dask looked down into the dark water and then closed his eyes. The others, too, seemed comforted and wistful at the same time.

The moving images ran one by one toward the boat, and each crashed into it with a silent explosion of light. The light revealed a new figure sitting on the boat's prow, indistinct as fog. More light bursts gave definition until Matil could tell that it was Falgar, horned animal's head and all.

Shora respectfully bent at her waist. She was disappearing.

Falgar's face resolved out of the mist, purple eyes sparking and pulsing to life. He smiled. "Shora…"

The last creature galloped down, greater and more colorful than the ones before. It burst, and Matil had to close her eyes at its brightness. When she opened them again, Shora was gone.

"Ahhh…" A hazy Falgar stepped from his perch to the dock, leaving his physical body lying in the boat. The alva stepped back. "Dreams may show you all the possibilities in the world," he said in his nimble voice, "but they cannot make a single one true. They are not *life*."

19

Warrior Poet

"Real dramatic, isn't he?" Dask said under his breath.

"Yes, young one," Falgar said. "Dramatic I am. And why not? Being dramatic works miracles on a gloomy day. You should try it."

The phantasmal Elder stood a head taller than Khelya. His purple and red clothes were well-tailored to his muscular body. Thick horns spiraled around pointed ears filled with fur. His entire head and neck were covered in fur; he had the head of some creature Matil had never seen. His glowing purple eyes were set far apart on either side of his long snout, and his mouth smiled below a V-shaped black nose.

He held out his dark-skinned hands in a welcoming gesture. "And what are the names of my new friends?" he said.

Khelya sobbed and covered her face.

Falgar lowered his head in concern. "Am I frightening you?"

"She's excited to meet you," Matil said. "My name is Matil."

Khelya wiped her eyes. "I-I-I'm Khelya, Lord Falgar, sir."

"Please, dear child…I am Falgar, nothing more."

"Simmad," piped Simmad. He blew out through his mouth, trying to control his breathing.

"I'm Dask." He stood at the front of their group. "We're probably about to get jumped by a Saikyr featherhead, so let's get right into it, Falgar. It's been a long time since you fell asleep. There's all this trouble going on with the Book of Myrkhar and Matil doesn't have wings because of it. And Shora said you're planning to take us to Calo."

"Correct," Falgar said. "The Eldercount is many days' journey from here, so I shall transport us. Our travel will take but a moment." He began to lead them off the dock.

"'A moment'? Hang on, are you saying you can fly us across the forest with magic?" Dask's ears twitched in irritation. "Why didn't Dyndal and Shora poof us right to the velana stones? We had to walk the whole way."

Falgar chuckled. "Even at our greatest, we could not move physical bodies vast distances using only our own power. What I am about to do is call upon a bond that each of the Heilar have with our leader through the Eldercount."

"Then the Eldercount *does* exist?" Simmad said. "Lord Calo's record of the living Elders? The artifact that began the Hibernation?"

"The same," Falgar said. "We bound ourselves to Calo through it, as the Saikyr then bound themselves to Myrkhar through his accursed Book. Now—"

The cavern darkened. Pressure built in the air along with heavy warmth. Matil looked around uneasily, drew her knife, and saw Dask do the same. Her vision didn't extend as far, because fog now fenced them in. Dewdrop and Olnar huddled together. A broadsword appeared in Falgar's translucent hands.

A muffled scrape came from somewhere behind Matil. She whirled to face the noise and angled her ears back, shivers running across her skin despite the heat. More scrapes, shuffles, and clacks pushed through the fog. It sounded like something very large was pacing around them. The sounds got louder and quieter at random, garbled by the fog. It went silent before ringing out behind her again. She turned to face it and prepared to fade if need be. Simmad moved closer to the others, skin almost as white as a cloud. Khelya hunched over him protectively, but her eyes were wide with fear, while Dask adjusted his grip on his knife and looked over at Matil.

"We know you are there," Falgar said. "Speak."

A voice rasped from the fog. "In the generations that I have rested, I dreamt…of wondrous things. Of your body… destroyed, Falgar. Dead beside your wife."

Falgar brandished his horns. "Show yourself!"

"You survived the others, but Thosten knows you did not deserve to. You, Calo, Dyndal, Shora…and my brother. Each of you should have died."

"*Stal!*" Falgar's shout echoed strangely in the fog. "How does a traitor presume to speak of what others do or do not deserve?"

"Because though your memory is short," Stal said, "I remember. Though you close your eyes so that hearts will not be troubled…I keep count. If it is any solace, no one truly deserves to live. Not even I deserve life."

"Faithless prattle—" Falgar began.

"We are all corrupted! By *choice!* The stars that ran in your veins turned to clay long before I was born. No, the question is not how does a traitor, but how do you, who lived through the fatal decision, forget your own crime? And you wonder…you dare to wonder…why I hate you?" His laughter was like shards of broken glass. Its sound spread as he plodded around them, until the enveloping fog itself seemed to jeer.

"I will never forget," Falgar said, subdued. "None of us have forgotten. Even Calo bears the guilt of that day. I give no excuse. But I say to you, Stal, hatred is a poisonous cup—"

A shrieking roar split through Matil's head. Her ears went back sharply.

Out of the fog leapt a specter – a thickset creature covered in mottled black-and-green fur, with long, powerful arms and clawed hands, hind legs like those of a tail-less fox, a broad bat-like snout, eyes blazing orange, and a toothy jaw opened far too wide. When it landed on Falgar's upraised arms and slashed at his face, Falgar reeled back. His stumbling feet knocked Matil and Dask to the ground.

Winded, Matil struggled to get on her knees and look up. The creature tore the broadsword out of Falgar's grip and threw it into the fog. Falgar's lean, misty form dodged around the creature's furious attacks, but no matter how expertly he moved, its claws still caught him. Rather than harm Falgar's clothes or skin, every blow weakened his substance.

Khelya stood over Matil and Dask with a limp Simmad in her arms. She looked down at Simmad. "He fainted! Think he'll be okay?"

"Absolutely." Dask grabbed the beetles' reins and pulled them towards an area where the fog was thinner.

"Where are you goin'?" Khelya said, following him. "We need to stay with Falgar!"

"What we really need is to stay away from the fighting," Dask said. "I was thinking we could run for it."

Falgar launched himself past the growling creature and into the fog. He emerged a moment later wielding his sword. The two phantoms circled each other just a few steps away from the alva.

Khelya watched them with fear in her eyes. "Let's- let's wait a little longer, okay?"

"Is that really Stal?" Matil said, standing close to Khelya's side. Stal was the great hunter in the story Dyndal had told, the twin brother of Olen. This hunched beast looked completely savage, nothing like what she pictured. She could hardly believe the bitter, weary voice in the fog belonged to it. Then she imagined the voice – younger, maybe – saying to Olen, "We are brothers."

The creature swiped low with one arm as a feint and then pushed off from the ground, springing into the air. He wrapped his arms around Falgar's neck.

Khelya whimpered at the sight of Falgar choking. "I didn't get around to givin' you the scary stories about Stal, did I? To tell the- the truth, I never liked hearing those ones. But, um…that's him. Oh, thiffen." A shudder ran through her. "That's the monster from the scary stories."

Stal shrieked. Falgar had broken his grip and slammed him into the ground. The spiral-horned Elder threw himself over Stal and pinned his long arms. Stal lunged against Falgar's hold. Many shining bands of white light reached up from the ground and wrapped themselves around Stal.

Falgar elbowed him in the jaw. "As I was saying, hatred is a poisonous cup. Perhaps your object of loathing drinks from it and dies. Perhaps not. But it is certain that *you*, in holding the cup for so long, will drink the greatest amount of poison." He bashed Stal's face one more time with the hilt of his sword before jumping up and sprinting to the four alva. "Let us not keep my old friend waiting any longer!" he said.

Stal burst from the bands of light and hurtled toward the group. Falgar moved quickly, shielding the alva and the beetles with his back. He grunted as Stal barreled into him. Stal's sharp claws struck past and slashed Matil's shoulder. Falgar spun to face Stal and, kicking him in the stomach, sent him flying across the cave. Before Stal could recover, Falgar gathered the group close. Soft light rose up around them, and Matil closed her eyes.

The last thing she heard was a tormented howl.

* * *

Matil drifted in and out of sleep as the light continued to wash over her. She knew she was asleep because there were dreams, like Bechel in her arms, Crell flying with her, and Etsel laughing at a joke. When she could no longer see light through her eyelids, she opened them. Falgar lowered his arms slowly and everyone looked around.

The weather felt cold compared to the hot cavern they had left. The burrs, croaks, and chirps of nocturnal animals were lush to Matil's ears, as lush as the dark forest in which they stood. Ferns and bushes closed over the group. Simmad stirred in Khelya's arms, so she let him down and made sure he could stand.

His wings increased in brightness, creating an island of light. "Where are we? Is Stal gone?" A moth fluttered toward him. He yelped and batted it away. "Why did that moth come so close?!"

Dask jumped to face Falgar, whose substance was thin with fatigue. "Did you take us to Deep Valdingfal? The Kyndelin don't deal with the animals around here. We could get eaten!"

"In my day," Falgar said, "alva fought, tamed, or avoided animals if they did not wish to be eaten. Do you mean to tell me that the Kyndelin have changed things? Well, well. Alva can be quite powerful in their own right."

"You didn't answer my question," he said.

"It depends on where the borders lie in this age," the Elder replied. "We may or may not be in Deep Valdingfal."

"Talrach." Dask gestured at the others. "Let's keep close. The bigger we look, the scarier we look."

Something tickled the back of Matil's right shoulder. She clapped her hand over it, only to feel wetness and a pain that made her draw in a sharp breath. Her shoulder was torn and bloody.

"What's wrong?" Dask said. "Matil!" He took hold of her left arm to keep her steady. "Sit down."

Simmad glanced at Matil and then looked away, paling visibly. "Oh, dear."

Khelya squinted down at the wound. "I think Stal got her! Don't pass out, it's not good if more'n one alva passes out in a day. And don't die!"

"Khelya," Dask said, "get some bandages out, quick."

"Hold." Falgar knelt. "I cannot effect a full healing right now," he said. "For that I beg your pardon. I can, however, stop the bleeding."

He laid his palm gently over her wound. Underneath the slight pressure of a ghostly hand, her skin itched and stopped hurting. The shock was wearing off. When Falgar pulled back his hand, she looked at her shoulder.

"That is the biggest scab I've ever seen," Dask said.

Khelya wrinkled her nose. "I've had bigger scabs."

Falgar sat against the base of a potato plant. "If only Stal had not kept us from going out of the cave. I would have liked to see Tyr Tamryn again. To see how it changed or stayed the same."

"Tyr Tamryn?" Khelya said.

"The land where my body rests," the Elder said.

"Oh, that land's called Obrigi. It's where I'm from."

"Ah," Falgar said. "It is descriptively named."

"Yeah," Khelya hung her head. "Ever since your blessing disappeared…"

"Disappeared?" Falgar thought for a moment. "The blessing was certainly wearing thin. A shame it did not last."

"But couldja do it again?" she said. "Bless the Obrigi like before?"

"I do not believe it to be possible now," Falgar said, sighing. "Eventyr was young and I at the peak of my power when I first bestowed the blessing."

Khelya drew inward, fiddling with her fingers. "I understand, sir."

"It may have been for the best, in the end of it. I always wondered if my blessing took more away from the Obrigi than it gave to them."

Now that Matil's wound wasn't bothering her, she felt ready to move. "Is there a velana stone nearby?" she asked. Dask helped her to her feet.

"Yes." Falgar stood. "I suppose it is time. Where is my velanach?"

"I have it," Simmad said, reaching into his bag. "Oh, I do feel a bit of a twinge coming from it!"

"Then show us where to go, if you will," Falgar said.

The group followed Simmad through the overhanging plants and uneven ground, lit by his wings. Soon he stopped at the edge of a tangle of thick roots between the trunks of two ancient, moss-covered trees. The roots intertwined, half-buried in decaying plant matter and dirt. The tip of a pale stone stuck out of the tangle near his boots.

Falgar stepped forward, beginning to hum a simple tune, and stretched his hand over the roots. Soft wind blew past the alva. The plants, leaves, and soil covering the roots moved just a little. Falgar's humming strengthened, and then dirt, rocks, and vegetation swirled up, carried by the whipping wind. Within the mass of roots at his feet, the elongated stone was now mostly revealed, wedged on the slope of a pit. The floating halo of earth danced away to Falgar's music, finally dropping itself somewhere in the forest beyond.

Simmad crouched and, looking at Falgar first to confirm, touched the stone. The letters spelling out *velana* appeared on its surface.

He scuttled backward as the roots began to move. Smells of soil and damp wood permeated the air. Like the rocks at Falgar's mountain, the roots twisted and opened into a tunnel going deep underground. Looking down the tunnel was like looking into a bird's nest that wound its way into the earth.

Everyone walked cautiously down the round, fragile-feeling tunnel. Roots creaked under the alva's and beetles' feet until the walls became smooth clay and rock. The tunnel spiraled and steepened.

The curving wall grew brighter with faint orange light touching the rock from somewhere up ahead. They made the last turn, and Matil recoiled. Ahead of them, flames filled the tunnel and licked the ceiling. The fire crackled and whooshed and filled the air with a faint smell of smoke. There was no way to pass.

"How's it burning?" Khelya said.

Dask grimaced. "How do we put it out?"

Simmad stepped closer to it than any of them, fascinated by the wall of flames.

"You cannot stop it," Falgar said.

"Oh," Dask said, "so we have to turn around and go home, huh?"

The Elder chuckled. "You are taking my advice about being dramatic."

Dask crossed his arms grumpily.

"In answer, no. We must go through the fire. Yes, it is strange." Falgar shook his horned head at the flames with a fond smile. "But I know what this fire is, and it will not harm you."

Simmad held his hand out to the fire and then jerked it away. "It's hot!"

"Lord—uh, Falgar," Khelya said timidly, "are you *sure* it won't harm us?"

"Olnar!" Dask tugged the beetle back from the flames.

Matil realized that Dewdrop, wandering from her side, was also moving her antennae around *in the fire*. She yanked Dewdrop's reins to get the beetle out of danger.

"I am extremely certain," Falgar said.

Simmad went over to Dewdrop and examined her antennae. "No burning, no injury. She should have caught on fire." He approached the crackling blaze again, screwed up his face, and plunged his hand into the golden flames.

Matil turned away.

"After the initial heat," Simmad said, "it feels as though nothing is there."

"Because nothing *is* there." Falgar motioned towards the fire. "Let us go through."

"Ca-can I stay here?" Matil said.

Dask raised his hand. "I wanna stay, too."

"My friends," Falgar said, "you have already overcome much fear and placed yourselves in peril to wake us. If we are returning to war between the Elders, in time we will all pass through greater fire than this apparition."

Simmad took his hand out of the flames, still staring at the fire in fascination. "How about I go first and come back through, to prove it's an illusion?"

"Are you sure?" Dask said.

"I…I could go first," said Khelya.

Simmad looked over his shoulder at the group, smiled reassuringly, and stepped right into the fire. There was a long moment of silence.

"It's- it's *him*," came Simmad's awestruck voice.

Khelya put her hand over her heart. Matil and Dask sighed in relief.

Simmad's gangly figure appeared out of the burning wall and landed in front of them. "It's all right, come through!" He bounced on the balls of his feet, grinning. "Quickly now!"

Matil glanced at Falgar. His dark purple eyes turned to her and crinkled at the corners in a kindly way. She thought about what might be on the other side. A way to destroy Nychta and the Book. A way to make things right.

"Let's do this together." Khelya put her arms around Matil's and Dask's shoulders. "Ready?

Dask took a deep breath. "Well, Simms didn't die."

Matil saw him clenching and unclenching his fists, the caring concern in Khelya's eyes, and Simmad's face lit up with excitement. She fixed those images in her head. Her heart hammered in her chest. "Ready."

Simmad dashed back through the fire while the three others walked forward, Falgar close behind them. The radiating heat and light grew more intense as they closed the gap. Matil's legs were heavy, as if they didn't want her to move. She kept going. Just when the fire closed around them, the heat dissipated. The three alva stepped past the flickering flames without feeling a thing.

Khelya gave a yelp. "*What's that?*"

Directly facing the group was a huge wooden chair, and, sleeping peacefully in it, was the ethereal presence of a bear-like being. Unlike Falgar, this one was covered entirely in thick brown fur instead of clothes, with larger arms and legs and a larger girth. His ears were small and rounded. His deep chest rose and fell, as heavy as if it bore the weight of the earth.

"Is- is it Calo?" Khelya said.

Falgar dipped his head in confirmation. "It is his spirit. If you look behind and around us, you can see how, as ever, he makes his dwelling place his home."

Matil turned reluctantly. There was the tunnel-blocking fire, but she thought it would look scarier than it did. On this side, the flames sat in a giant fireplace of natural stone carved with unfamiliar words. The effect of the illusory fire being contained was surprisingly comforting. She still backed away. As she moved, she bumped into Olnar's shell by accident. His antennae tickled her arm. The beetles handled the fire much better than she had.

The rest of the cave, like the fireplace, was cozy. It was furnished with mundane objects such as a honeycomb press and a cutting board in what looked to be the kitchen, as well as a round dining table surrounded by unlit floor-standing candlesticks. Natural pillars and protrusions of rock marked the spaces from one another.

On the far left side, Matil saw a bed. It was low to the ground, a stone platform piled with thickly-woven blankets of every color in the fullest, heartiest hues. The same creature whose image dozed in the chair lay atop the blankets, fully solid, his great clawed hands folded over a prodigious stomach.

Khelya took it all in solemnly. Dask seemed unnerved by Calo's spirit sitting in the chair while his body lay on the bed.

"Why do you and Calo look like animals?" Matil asked Falgar, hoping she wasn't being rude. "Shora and Dyndal were more like alva, and Kanay switched from alva to animal."

"We have lived so long that Eventyr left its mark on us," he said. "The younger ones such as Shora and Kanay have not changed as much, but they still may transform when…"

He tapped the end of one horn as he searched for words. "…When the roots clutch at the heart."

Matil looked at Falgar with curiosity, but he started walking past the chair and towards the bed.

He turned. "Come with me, young ones."

They stood with him at Calo's bedside. Calo's bulk was a bit frightening, like he could crush them all by rolling over. Around his neck was a silver chain holding a large metal pendant that glinted in the firelight. The shape was odd: Three overlapping circles, two on top and one on the bottom, enclosed by a bar extending along the top and down the right side. Matil realized that the shape spelled out a word. "'Eev'?" she read.

"Yes," Simmad said eagerly. "'Iv' is a word used only in the most ancient scrolls to refer to the Elders."

Falgar lowered his head. "It is the Eldercount. Each Elder's name is engraved in its surface. Once, it was full. Now there are only a few of us left."

"*That's* the Eldercount?" Simmad said, his eyes opening wide.

Falgar nodded. "If you say 'velana', it will wake him."

The alva were quiet a moment, and then Simmad said, "Matil, you're the one who started all this. Why don't you say it?"

She hesitated, looking at the others. Khelya's excitement showed in her grin, and Falgar lifted his hand for Matil to go ahead. Dask smiled and shrugged. She wasn't sure she should be the one – would it even work, considering what she was? But if they all agreed…

"Fear not," Falgar said.

Matil stepped closer to the bedside and looked up at the sleeping king of the Elders. "Velana."

Darkness dropped over them as the firelight went out. She twisted around to see what had happened, only to find that the spirits of Falgar and Calo had disappeared. Khelya stared in shock, Dask apprehensively flicked his wings open and shut, and Simmad increased the light of his wings, watching Calo's body closely. Matil stepped away. She remembered the spectacular and terrifying things that happened when the other Elders woke. This time there was nothing.

Matil looked at her friends in dismay, but Dask's eyes lit up. He pointed to the bed.

Calo's stomach and chest moved slowly, up and down, like the spirit in the chair. He breathed faster. Then he opened his eyes and lifted his head to look at the face of each alva. His eyes had no pupils and were a deep, warm gold, with amber shimmering in the depths.

"You have called me back," he rumbled. His voice held such affection that it seemed like he had known them all for a long time. "You have brought me home."

20

Koselig

With a loud groan, Calo sat up. He turned to put his feet on the ground and stretched – his arms, his back, his jaw. Sitting on the bed, he was as tall as Khelya and twice as wide as her. "My friends." He smiled. "Who are you?"

Matil looked at the others to see if she should answer for them. They had been very quiet, after all. But Khelya had calm strength, Simmad stood up straight at his full height, and there was both bravery and uncertainty in Dask. He met Matil's eyes.

"We're his friends, but he doesn't know who we are," Dask said. "I'm Dask."

"My name is Matil," she said.

"Khelya, sir."

"And I'm Simmad, Lord Calo."

"Greetings to you all," the Elder said.

"Lord Calo," Matil said. "Eventyr is in danger. There's a new bearer of the Book of Myrkhar, and Bahantros the Slayer is dead." She detailed the rest of their story with the others' help.

They explained all that they knew, from the Book to Nychta, from Hasyl the hermit's disappearance to the stirrings of war. In Calo's kind presence, Matil felt guilt and found it harder than usual for her to mention her connection with Nychta. Calo asked clarifying questions and listened with an expression of increasing grimness, the gold in his eyes glowing like a hearth burned low.

At the end, he leaned forward and put his fur-covered, clawed hands on his knees. "Thank you. It seems the time has come for me to end the Hibernation. You must know that when I speak velana, both Heilar and Saikyr will awaken. But what you have said shows that we truly require the strength of the Heilar, for it is with or without us that the Book-bearer will work to bring Myrkhar out of his prison and back into this world."

The alva shared a worried look.

Calo dangled the Eldercount close to his eyes, letting it spin slowly as he read the names engraved in its surface. "My battle-brother Falgar, yes, he would have been here moments ago. Igsun…may you desire not the thrones of alva in this new age. Kanay the Wild, so long-lost from the path. Pure-hearted Olen and faithful Shora, and that chief of high spirits Dyndal. It gladdens me to see their names. Ah, Stal of torment and hatred, whose very mercy is cruel.

Jalt, the Sleeping Mountain…I hold on to hope that we will meet again one day. Calo, as expected. And…Myrkhar. Not one name has disappeared during this Hibernation."

He grasped the edge of the pendant in a clawed hand and said, "Velana." Presently, his golden eyes began to glow brighter. The Eldercount shone brightly as well, in a silver that was almost blue. The light of his eyes and the metal pendant's gleam strengthened to the point that Matil looked away. And then they faded, again leaving Simmad's wings as the only light in the room. Calo slumped over the Eldercount.

"S-sir, are you okay?" Khelya said.

When he didn't respond, Simmad took a step forward. "Lord Calo!"

A sigh came from the Elder's throat like a soft wind. "I am alive." He straightened a little to look at them with eyes of brown and glowing amber. "Now that they are awake, several of my fellow Heilar will come here in the same way you did with Falgar. However, neither Jalt nor Olen will join us. Jalt remains atop the Broken Mountain, holding back the Brandur; Olen guards the Heart."

Calo continued to ask the group questions until they heard footsteps echoing down the tunnel. Falgar appeared, striding through the empty fireplace. He ducked for his horns and broke into a long-snouted grin when he stood on the other side. Calo strode toward him and the two met in an embrace, pounding each others' backs.

"My brother!" Calo roared. "Are you well?"

"Weary," said Falgar. "I thought I would enter the great sleep and reawaken in what seemed the blink of an eye. It was not so. Though my body lay as death, my mind and heart keenly felt the years pass. How do you fare?"

"The same. I—"

"Falgar, Calo!" Dyndal's gregarious voice bounded into the room along with him. He grabbed the two in a hug, his orange hair and green wings bright against their gray and brown fur. "Come in here, Shora. I shall not let go of them until you join."

Calo laughed. "Dyndal, you fool."

Falgar tried to look over Dyndal's shoulder. "Is she here?"

Shora stepped out from the shadow of the fireplace. Her every movement was graceful as before, but her face held a mixture of joy and awkwardness. "Halsedys," she said. "How were your respective—ah!"

Dyndal pulled her into his hug, too, holding her by the head while her moth wings fluttered and the rest of her tried halfheartedly to get away. When the four pulled apart, they greeted each other further and spoke about whatever came to mind. They spoke of alva, Elders, and events that Matil couldn't recognize.

Simmad craned his neck forward. Khelya clasped her hands together, watching the Elders with stars in her eyes. Seeing them in the flesh was at once more real and more unbelievable than when they were spirits. They were tall like Obrigi, with Calo and Falgar standing above everyone else. Calo's and Falgar's animal traits made them seem like creatures from a strange dream, and the eyes of the four Elders glowed softly – gold, purple, gray, and green.

"They don't look powerful to me," Dask muttered in Matil's ear. "Just weird."

She nudged him. "They'll hear you."

"No, they won't," he said.

"Yes, we will," Dyndal called, turning around.

Dask nudged Matil back. "Apparently they will."

Dyndal darted over to the alva, patted their heads, and checked them over. "Our wakers! You are unharmed?" He saw the huge scab on Matil's shoulder. "Yenhali!" he exclaimed. "Matil, when did you receive such a wound?"

"It was Stal," Falgar said.

An image of Stal's slavering jaw and furious eyes appeared in Matil's mind. She pressed her own eyes shut briefly to clear her thoughts. "Falgar healed me as soon as we were safe," she said.

"Ah…I am sorry you bore Stal's wrath." Dyndal folded his arms over his bare chest. "But I see you are all in fine fettle. Well done, well done. What little wonders you are!"

"Little?" Khelya said, mystified.

"It is a term of endearment!" he said.

Shora bowed to them. "Thank you all for your dedication." She shot a glance at Dyndal. "And since he finds 'little' so endearing, call him 'Little Dyndal'. It just may shrink his arrogance to match."

"An impossible task," he scoffed.

Calo also bowed to the alva. "You have given us another chance to live. Thank you."

"We will repay your resolve with our own," Falgar said, "and again become Eventyr's guardians. I beg one more favor now. Would you return our velanachs?"

Simmad hurried to open the bag at his side. He respectfully presented Shora with her tulip weight, Dyndal with his toad pendant, and Falgar with his flute.

"What do you need them for?" Matil asked.

"Velana is complete," Falgar said, "yet these objects still mean much to us." He held the flute to his mouth and played a few clear, ascending notes.

Dyndal placed the pendant around his neck.

Shora stared at the little tulip weight in her long, pale fingers. "And mine has more than meaning. It is a heart-link, almost as powerful a bond as the one we have with the Eldercount – but it binds myself and my husband, Olen. He possesses the connected heart-link which allows us to speak to each other, as he cannot be with us now."

"Why not?" Matil said.

"He was sealed alone within the Heart Sanctum," Shora said in a somber tone, "and his charge upon waking is to keep it sealed."

"Until Calo finds the Sanctum and knocks upon its door," Falgar added. "Their heart-links – the tulip figurines – will help us to seek Olen and the Sanctum when it is time."

"I wish the Heart had chosen me as its guardian." Pain entered Shora's expression. "For one like Olen to be jailed away from all others…"

Calo gazed at the other Elders, his golden eyes turning dark around the edges. He gave a little sigh. "The Heart chose well. Now let us plan our next move. Falgar?"

With a motion of his hand, Falgar materialized a roll of pale green cloth out of the air and opened it up. It was a complex map of Eventyr with unrecognizable borders.

Calo lifted a claw. "The wakers told me of Ranycht who refused to join the Book-bearer. Let us find them, for our strength will grow through alva who defy evil."

"I'd hoped we were done traveling," Dask said. "If we're really in Deep Valdingfal, then getting to them from here will take forever."

Falgar gave Dask a sardonic look. "A very healthy alva may live to see only two hundred years! Young man, what do you know of forever?"

Calo beckoned at the map. "If they yet hide in the south of Nychtfal, there is a Path nearby that we can quickly travel. Is Jensym Grove a good destination?"

"Too far west," Shora said. "The borders are much changed, and now there is a high wall. Let us go…" She pressed her lips together. "Let us make for Twist Tree."

"No." Dyndal turned his back on her. "Never."

"Then stay here while *we* go on," she said savagely.

"Stay calm, my yofdani," Falgar said.

Dyndal turned again to glare at Shora. "I always forget your cold heart. How can you think of going to that place?"

"How can *you* not see what must be done, brother?" Shora said.

"Enough," Calo said in a growl like faraway storm clouds. "Shora has the right of it. Twist Tree is near the southern boundary of Eventyr and west of the Asta River – a good place to begin our search. Though I understand what it means to you both."

The planning was over soon, with Calo declaring that there be a time of rest before the next journey. The alva ate dinner and then made camp in Calo's den while the Elders went to the surface to talk. Matil's head was almost too full of hopeful ideas for her to sleep. The others tossed and turned as much as she. Eventually, sleep rolled along to each of them.

* * *

Velana.

Olen heard it…Calo's warm voice ringing in his mind. And after the sound faded away, after his dreams turned to darkness, he could hear the very soft sighing of air as it passed through the Sanctum. He smelled damp wood and rock – not musty, as this place did not grow mold, but damp. These things came to him sharp and clear, almost as though he were awake.

His eyes flew open. He sat up in shock and shook his head. Everything around him was calm and bathed in dim blue light coming from the floor and walls. Awake. Awake. He knew the first thing he must do, should he wake.

Olen closed his eyes. His senses expanded outward, giving him vague impressions of the rooms beyond. It stretched his small reserve of energy, but he was able to reassure himself that in all of the Sanctum, he was the only living being. The only one…

It would still be wise to secure the Sanctum's halls. With that decided, he yawned and stretched his wings. They were long and translucent like dragonfly wings, and torn in a few places. His face was lined with scars as well, extremely pale under his mop of brown hair. He looked around with azure blue eyes rippling like water and marveled at the feeling of being awake.

His room was hewn out of rock. Thin, conjoining lines of luminescent teal blue etched the floor and walls. There was faint movement within each line as the blue substance flowed ever upward to disappear into a ceiling of tightly wound tree roots. He had seen this room in his dreams many times. Dreams had been his reality for so long that he almost could not tell the difference.

He felt the smooth black cloth of his trousers and then studied his scarred hands, his right hand missing its little finger. They did not change form or number of fingers as they did in his dreams. He pressed down on the thin cushion between him and his bed of intertwined tree roots. The cushion sprang back like it was new. The waist-height shelves along the walls…they were full of scrolls and books in perfect condition. His body, too, felt almost the same as when he had lain down. The magic of the Eldercount had preserved Olen and his surroundings, just as Calo had said before the long sleep began.

And there, on the shelf closest to his bed, sat a small silver figurine in the shape of a tulip, with a cloth pouch lying beside it. Olen touched its petals with his fingertip. She must be awake as well. He did not know the situation in the outside world, so he would wait for her to speak first when she was ready.

Olen put the tulip in the pouch and then tucked the pouch under a cord tied around his blue silken tunic. He pushed himself up from the bed, wobbling as he tried to avoid straining his crooked right leg. To steady himself, he grabbed a polished walking stick leaning on the wall.

Olen left his room and started off down the curving hallways. His cane tapped the floor as he hobbled. The floor and walls here were the same as in his room, the blue trickling light ever-present. The other rooms he entered were just as lonely. The weight of the emptiness grew heavier with each room.

He arrived at a black iron door decorated with knotted iron symbols and bronze studs. It arched several heads higher than Olen, but the bar and latch that kept it locked were low enough for him to lift. He had locked himself in and would unlock the door when his fellow Heilar found the Sanctum. If the Saikyr found it first…he would never allow them to enter.

Olen went deeper into the Sanctum. The walls here were made of tree roots, like the ceiling, while the floor was uneven bedrock. At the end of the hallway was a stout, unassuming wooden door with iron fittings. He took a key that hung from the cord around his waist, opened the door, and crossed the threshold.

Entering the Heart's chamber always made him pause. The tall, circular cave overwhelmed with its heavy atmosphere. He stood at the top of a sloping walkway that led down to the floor. At the center of the room was the deep and still Heart, a roughly triangular pool of glowing blue water that gave just enough light to see by. The luminescent tendrils began there, spreading from the edges of the Heart across the floor and wending in and out on the surface of the bark-covered root walls.

Olen stepped off of the walkway and floated to the ground, his torn wings fluttering behind him. As he went towards the Heart, he reached out with his senses. He could feel its energy burning like the sun had come to rest beside him, unthinkably vast and frighteningly close. Yet he knew it would not harm him so long as he did not touch it. He leaned forward at the edge and looked into the water. If there was anything shown, he would receive it.

In the bottomless depths of the Heart, images formed of a black book and a Ranycht woman whose purple eyes were losing their color. The images changed and became two very different beings. One was a slim man with brown hair, leaning on a wooden cane. It was Olen himself, the same way he had appeared in the Heart when the Heilar asked who should rest within the Sanctum. The other being was a long-armed beast with snarling jaws and burning eyes of orange. Olen's twin brother, Stal, in a form created by his own rage.

Now the images combined into a black-furred figure stretching the length of the pool. The figure had a long snout and orb-like white eyes. A wicked crown of antlers grew from its head. A chill ran down Olen's spine. Myrkhar had spoken to him but once, on the night that Stal mutilated Olen. The night their father and mother had died in battle. The leader of the Saikyr had made an offer that Olen nearly accepted. He had refused…at the cost of his brother.

The dark image of Myrkhar stared at him now with the same amused look from so long ago. Just then, the white eyes turned to gold, and the fur went from black to brown. A gold band circled the new figure's hornless brow, and a silver pendant hung around his neck. Olen's heart settled somewhat. He recognized the good king of the Elders – Calo.

And, suddenly, the image vanished, leaving Olen staring into the lambent water. He felt a twinge of disappointment. The vision seemed to be…things he already knew. The Book of Myrkhar had a new bearer? Bahantros would slay him. Olen and Stal were at odds as ever? Myrkhar and Calo as well? Such was life before the long sleep. He supposed such would be life afterward.

At the very least, he had sensed no damage or taint within the Heart. He drew back from the water's edge and walked around the wall of the chamber at a sedate pace.

After ascending the walkway, Olen secured the door to the Heart's chamber. His work was done for now.

He turned to face the barren hall. He realized that his head was low and brow furrowed. Lifting his chin, he began to hum a jaunty traveling song on the way back to his room. It felt good to make music. On reaching his room, he didn't give himself even a moment to ponder loneliness, but went straight to the shelves for something to read.

"*Mu ola…*" came a voice in his mind.

A smile broke out on Olen's face. He went over to his bed and, making heavy use of the cane, sat down. He took the silver tulip out of its pouch. The metal was warm under his fingers, and he felt a faint vibration in the steady pattern of a heartbeat. Her heartbeat.

"Mu ola," he responded in a low voice. "Mu oshgir, mu maket."

She laughed, the most beautiful music he had ever heard. "*Mu oshtu. Nym wol mu hjardan. Stay with me a while.*"

"Until the last sun sets." Only his wife would know the next words.

"*Until the dead day rises,*" she said.

It was a way for them to confirm they spoke to each other and not an interloper.

"So we have returned," Olen said. "Are you and the others safe, Shora?"

"*I am safe with our brethren in Calo's resting place. We move on the morrow.*"

"Thosten be praised. How long has it been? Who brought us back and why?"

"*The four alva who wakened us are here as well, and through traveling with them we have learned that it has been a thousand years.*"

That news struck him. A thousand years. He had spent a third of his life in the Hibernation.

"*Eventyr in certain ways is much as we left it,*" she continued, "*but there is change. The alva have sought us out. Bahantros is no more, and the Book has taken another bearer.*"

Images from the Heart came back to him. The Book and an alva. "Bahantros…" he said. "How?"

"*He died from his wounds after slaying a Book-bearer two hundred years ago.*"

"No…" Bahantros had been one of the few alva who knew what it was like to live much longer than others. And now he was gone. Olen closed his eyes. He would bear the grief later. "Our power is truly waning. And what of the sword?"

"*Of the sword I know not. Strangely, one of the alva who came looking for us is the current bearer's double, created in the binding ritual. The bearer failed to kill her.*"

He frowned. "I did not know the double could survive the ritual."

"*It is remarkable,*" Shora said. "*Even troubling. Yet cause for hope, if the sword is lost. I have observed her to be a dedicated, considerate soul. She reminds me a little of you.*"

He chuckled. "I am sure she is better company than I."

"Silence yourself, Olen. You know I yearn for the day we find the Heart, for it is then that I will find my own heart once again."

He pressed the tulip to his chest. "And I will find mine." With a sigh, he said, "I trust the Heart's judgment in choosing me, but I do not understand it. Calo is the first of us. The best of us. The one who held fast against temptation."

Shora was quiet for a moment. *"I have seen the state of the forest, my love. War is a thunderhead on the horizon. Calo's leadership and power will prove necessary in the days to come."*

"I understand. However—"

"And if any beside him can hold against temptation, it will be you."

"I pray it is so," he said.

"I know it is so."

Olen smiled. She was kind to have such faith. "Now… please, tell me everything you have seen and done since we parted."

"Of course." The smile was clear in her voice.

They spoke for a long time. Not long enough by his reckoning, but it would do. Until he was free, she would tell him of the world and its alva and their fellow Elders. Until he could see her again, he would hold her voice close.

Olen could only carry out his duty and pray that Thosten keep watch over them all.

21

Blades and Breakfast

When the senior Council members needed to talk amongst themselves, they gathered in one of the trees connected to the Ambermeet. There was a spacious room with an oval-shaped table and large paper windows that let in creamy light. One windowpane was covered in jagged veins, patched after someone had burst right through it by accident.

Councilman Lorbryn floated about the room in agitation. "The king has barely been held back by his advisors. You're lucky he chose to leave you be, Lord Owynth."

A gaunt-faced Owynth drooped at the head of the table. He hadn't spoken except to call the meeting to order.

"Do you think that dear girl truly left the Accord?" Countess Sorigan shook her head, her bejeweled gray hair threatening to topple. "By Wuren, that's bold."

Lyria sat in her usual chair, staring at the ruined window. How was Annest doing? Would she ever return? Had she gone to her doom at Lyria's behest?

"Old hat," said Lord Adoc. "Right now we need to worry about our peasants and their rowdy demonstrations."

Lyria worked up an empty smile. "You know well *my* thoughts on the matter."

About half of the table gave her snide looks. Her gaze flitted coolly from Council member to Council member.

"I concur with Lyria," Councilwoman Rianna said. Now everyone looked at her in surprise. She was close in age with Lyria, but their political clashes, as well as Lyria's distaste of her methods, kept them from being allies. And…Rianna's sharp, intimidating eyebrows may have factored in at one point. "Sangriga should not have to shoulder such a burden, no matter how low they were born. Reduce the taxes, I say."

"But *how* will we get our money?" Lord Adoc said.

"From the Obrigi, obviously," Rianna said.

Lyria closed her eyes briefly. "The taxes we exact from our 'protectorate' have already flown up Mount Liangra, Councilwoman. They can't go any higher."

"Lyria's right," came Branneth's measured voice from the other end of the table. "Increase the taxes and we might as well call the Obrigi slaves. We need money, yes…but so do other alva. I wish there were a simple solution."

There *were* some fairly simple, if extreme, solutions, which Lyria was about to explain for the fortieth time, but Nider cut in after Branneth.

"Let us think on it," he said, "and move to a far more pressing matter. We have eased our stance against Nychtfal. Yet the Obrigi are mithering at us to reconsider, all the while keeping their soldiers in aggressive positions by the border. We cannot allow them to risk our chance at peace."

"They live on the front line, Councilman," Lyria said. "It's only natural they defend themselves when provoked."

Lorbryn waved his hand as he descended into his chair. "Our representatives in Obrigi are doing their best to convince the brutes."

Though Nider's eyes pierced Lorbryn, his voice was serene. "Perhaps greater measures are necessary. After all, what purpose does the Obrigi governor serve? He may as well be a Sangriga."

"You mean we'd scrap the Accord and take over Obrigi?" Councilman Wyll laughed. "Sir, you go too far."

"Are the pursuits of unity and safety to be taken lightly?" Nider said. "In such cases, actions which some fainthearted alva consider 'going too far' often don't go far enough."

Lyria could hardly believe what she was hearing, but Owynth didn't seem to care one bit. The other Council members murmured to each other and mulled over Nider's words. By the adjournment of the meeting, no conclusions had been reached.

After everyone filed out of the room, Lyria found herself beside Branneth on the Ambermeet bridge, which was one of the quickest ways out of the building from the senior room. Servants swept and scrubbed at the bridge, cleaning up filthy rags, splattered pieces of berries, and, eurgh, dungbasks – rubbish thrown there by commoners protesting the excessive increase in their tax rate. A few

Council members, ignoring the cleanup, took off from the bridge. Branneth was about to follow.

"Branneth," said Lyria. "Er…thanks. For speaking up earlier."

She turned around. "It wasn't much. How…have you been lately? I know you were close to Dalen and Annest."

"Close?" Lyria chuckled. "Not quite." She started to wonder, though, if she *had* been close with one of them. A good friend, Annest called her. "It's too bad about them, regardless."

"Too bad and sad," Branneth said. "Makes one wonder about Eventyr."

"Wonder what?" Lyria said.

"If goodness really exists here." She regarded the Ambermeet. "In stories, good alva are rewarded. In reality, they're killed or exiled."

Strangely, Lyria found herself caught between agreeing and wanting to make her reply…upbeat. "There *were* alva in the past who survived long enough to do good things," she said. Oh, dear. Annest must have infected her with some sort of sunshine and daisies flu.

"But you've noticed it, haven't you?" Branneth said. "Those ones survived by grabbing on to the bad in the world. By the end, they'd lost much of their own goodness."

"I see your point." The corner of Lyria's mouth lifted in a half-smile. "Yet I don't believe it's the whole truth. Why do the stories talk about goodness? They must have got it from somewhere. Good exists, I'm convinced. It seems near-useless, but it's there."

* * *

"All right, kid," said that wonderful voice. "This'll be your first real fight."

From the moment he said 'real fight', Matil had been a bundle of nerves. Down below her in a tiny side street, Etsel stood between three men and an old worker. A crate lay beside the worker, its contents spilled across the planks.

"Fly away now," Etsel said, calmly twisting his knife back and forth. "Your precious rat-face is in jeopardy."

"*Rat-face?*" one of the men spluttered. "You're dead, you soggy-wing—"

"Oh, that was rude of me, wasn't it?" Etsel put a hand to his heart. "I'm sorry, I can't believe I said such a terrible thing. Where's my manners, huh?"

Matil's stomach did a scared and excited flip. She dove from her windowsill perch and landed in a crouch at Etsel's side, stiletto dagger out.

He grinned. "There she is."

"You've got a hatchling for backup?" a second man said.

"That assumption's very wrong," Etsel said. "Very wrong, my friend. See, I'm *her* backup. Miss Hatchling wanted to take on all you fellas alone. I talked her into bringin' me with."

"Shut it, worm!" The first man jumped at them. The world went crazy.

Etsel did most of the fighting. He was able to slip around and around the three men, confusing them badly. Their refusal to acknowledge Matil as part of the fight cost them, though, and she dealt some effective stabs. She cringed each time her stiletto tore up their sides and backs. Only Etsel's training kept her from dropping the dagger. The men realized where the extra pain was coming from, but by the time they turned, she was out of reach and Etsel was clocking another jaw. They couldn't go on like that. Soon, they spread their wings and flew off, spitting and shouting over their shoulders.

"Thanks," the worker said as he scooped things into the crate. "Talk to the foreman if you want protection money. I don't got nothing."

Etsel smirked. "Thanks is enough. C'mon, Manners."

The two of them strolled away, but the old man's words bothered Matil.

"He was in trouble," she said. "Of course we'd help him. Why did he think we wanted money for it?"

"'Cause that's what our world is like," Etsel said. "Terrible place! Most alva act like they're the only alva that matters, and they expect everyone else to act the same way."

Matil dropped her gaze to the scratched-up ground, bitterness filling her mouth. "Yeah."

"You and me, though," he gently poked her in the head and then poked himself in the chest, "we're gonna make it better. Just by doin' the opposite of alva's expectations."

She gave him a hopeful look.

"You and me." He poked her head again. That time, she laughed.

* * *

Matil woke with a smile. As she saw the stone ceiling and remembered where she was, she held on to the dream like it was a precious heirloom. In time, she became aware of soft bubbling sounds. The reality of consciousness established itself. She sat up and stared. Reality didn't seem to be the right word.

The Elders were working quietly in the den. Dyndal and Shora had started a real fire in the fireplace and set over it a great big pot of bubbling liquid. Calo and Falgar stood back-to-back in the kitchen, the former chopping some cabbage leaves and the latter dicing a carrot that took up the entire counter.

Dyndal tore up a fragrant leaf and threw the pieces in the pot. He leaned over to Shora. "It feels grand to cook again," he whispered. "Does it not, sister?"

Shora answered him with a flat look while she stirred the pot.

"Aha, one of our wakers is awake." He waved. "Good morning, Matil."

Matil waved back.

"Welcome to breakfast," Calo said cheerily.

"Are those sparkling eyes as refreshed by sleep as they look?" Falgar asked Matil.

"Yes, sir, thank you," she said.

Still waking up, Matil sat for a while and watched Dyndal and Shora cook. They were brother and sister, but so different, one with leaf wings rustling behind his back and one with soft moth wings folded on hers. He was untamed, she was one who tamed others. He talked eagerly, asking about her journey with the alva as a spirit and sharing ancient memories of laughter and adventure. She responded carefully, her calm voice giving weight to the smallest of matters.

"This child holds the power to destroy the Book-bearer." Dyndal gave Matil a small smile.

"So she does," Shora said. "It is a curious thing…how she came to be. To my knowledge, there has never been an alva split in two where both sides survived. One might think Myrkhar's Book somehow created a new being, yet that does not seem to be the case." She set a finger against her temple. "Matil has dreams of her past."

Matil shifted uncomfortably. "Nychta's past."

Dyndal sprinkled salt into the pot. "Still, you are the one having these dreams. I wonder just how much of Nychta you are. How much of herself would she have put to death?"

Matil frowned and felt out the scabbed, raised line on her shoulder from Stal's attack. Below it was the older mottled scar. Something else she inherited from Nychta. But now she knew without a doubt that she was *not* Nychta. The dreams gave her a peek into Nychta's mind and she could simply never be that alva. Never think like her…never do what she had done.

"Hm," Dask said. He was sitting up out of his blanket. He looked around at the Elders absorbed in their culinary occupations. "Maybe I should try waking up again. I don't think it worked the first time."

Matil smiled. "Tell me if it works the second time."

"Nah, I'll keep dreaming," he said. "Were Dyndal and Shora talking about your dreams? Did you have a bad one?"

"No, I had a…" Matil traced a sad line on the floor with her toe. "It was a nice dream."

"Good." Dask yawned. "One less thing I have to worry about."

"You worry about them?" Matil said.

"Well—yeah, I mean…they're worrying, aren't they? Wow, that food sure smells good. Is it almost done?"

By the time the Elders finished cooking, the four alva were up. Shora began to speak over the sounds of everyone slurping delicious soup.

"Calo chose this den as his resting place," she said, "because the entrance to a Path lies near."

Simmad swallowed quickly. "Is this 'Path' different from, for example, a mundane garden path?"

"It is. The Paths are ancient ways that allowed us to travel from one part of the forest to another within a day."

"I haven't heard that one!" Simmad began counting off on his fingers. "The legends tell of transportation spells, magic objects, riding on the backs of hawks, and, oh, there was that odd one about Icto walking through a scroll."

Falgar elbowed Calo with a chuckle. "Remember the scroll?"

"We used the Paths sparingly and spoke little of them," Shora said. "They were particularly powerful, but dangerous, methods of travel. The magic that flows through the Paths touches every being in Eventyr, and Elders can sense when they are used. Hence, walking the Paths led to several battles between Heilar and Saikyr."

Dask groaned into his soup. "So that's the kind of adventure we're in for next."

"It is a risk we should take," Calo said.

Falgar stood. "We are weak, but so are the Saikyr." His broadsword sprung into the air before him and he caught it by the hilt with both hands. "It is time to stretch these old limbs."

Dyndal pulled his sharp blade of grass into existence. "Quite right, Uncle!" He whipped it downward. "Let them sense us."

Matil and Simmad shared looks of unease, one anxious and one queasy. On the other hand, Khelya's grin could not be matched.

"Do we get magic swords, too?" Dask said.

Khelya nudged him, almost tipping his bowl. "You can't *ask* the Elders for magic swords," she said. "Those are spirit weapons. *Their* spirit weapons."

Dask grunted at Khelya and held his bowl carefully while the soup sloshed.

"He is allowed to ask questions," Calo said, eyes twinkling. "You all are."

"*Thank you.*" Dask gave Khelya a smug smile.

Falgar hefted his broadsword. The hilt and crossguard were white stone, and one flat of its blade shone warmly with marbled white and sky blue. The other side was a deep, dawning purple. Stars seemed to glimmer across the metal. "If Jalt were here, he may very well have made you spirit weapons of your own. He forged ours."

"No blacksmith could match the Mountain Lord's skill," Simmad intoned.

Calo nodded thoughtfully. "I am confident that the fabled arms and armor he created have survived the years."

Simmad gasped. "I wonder how many of those attributed to Jalt are actually his handiwork!"

"I recall one from the front of my memory," Shora said. "The Rootsword. Jalt crafted it to kill bearers of the Book. Bahantros was the last one to wield it, so far as I know."

"The Rootsword!" Dyndal said. "I had forgotten! Bahantros and the blade were one in my mind."

Matil's ears pricked up. "What if…we had the sword? Then instead of me, could one of you use it to stop Nychta?"

Dyndal looked warmly down at her. "If we find it before the time comes."

"Even should we recover the blade," Calo said, "I advise you to let the ritual be reversed. You said that you feel drawn towards Nychta when you are near her. It is trying to undo what was wrongfully done through sorcery."

That wasn't exactly what Matil had expected. "Will Nychta die if I reverse the ritual?"

Calo paused. "Given that you have been apart for so long, I am not certain what it will do. The likeliest outcome is that you and she become one alva again, free from the warping influence of the Book. Regardless, it is nature trying to repair the wound. You may be happiest letting healing occur, whatever form it takes." He shrugged his massive fur-covered shoulders. "Or we can search for the Rootsword. Consider well."

Matil lowered her eyes. So Nychta being separate from her was a wound, and he didn't know what 'healing' it would do to her. Maybe it was a good wound to have.

"For now," Falgar said, "we must all prepare to protect ourselves. You may not have spirit weapons, but you have weapons of your own, and we shall bolster them with magic to give them more bite."

Shora and Dyndal took Matil's and Dask's knives. They each formed a shimmery substance like sparkling dust in their cupped hands and poured it over the knives. Falgar and Calo did the same to Khelya's Eletsol hunting spear and, for Simmad, an ancient knife from Calo's kitchen. The knife was nearly sword-length to the Sangriga, who looked extremely uncomfortable with it hanging from his belt.

The group packed up and left the den, passing through the empty fireplace. Matil looked up as they did and saw that there was a chimney stretching up to the surface. Once outside in the coolness of Deep Valdingfal, Matil breathed in the bracing forest air. Calo led them through the forest a short way, to a rock overhanging with viny roots. There was something about this place that danced and sang at the edge of Matil's perception. It felt like when she had stood at the Wall, the border of Eventyr.

"Mik lioth atgan enesel ir vanath," Calo said. The roots trembled and seemed to reach toward him. "Do not be afraid," he told the alva. "It is safe to enter." And then he stepped forward, disappearing among the roots.

Shora and Dyndal followed. Matil coiled Dewdrop's reins around her hand. She, Dask, Khelya, and Simmad looked at each other with nervous smiles – or just plain nerves – and walked in, Falgar following behind them.

22

Deeper Routes

Matil found it difficult to breathe at first because the bristly roots that hung in the way were so dense. She looked up. Was there even a ceiling? The air was filled with a moist soil smell that gave rise to thoughts of creatures lurking in the strands. As she moved through, she clutched Dewdrop's reins tighter and reminded herself that she could see. Even if it was only a step or two around her, it was still sight. At first she shuddered as the roots brushed by, but she became used to the feeling.

There was a faint glow beginning just ahead, rising up from the ground. Dyndal said something that Matil couldn't hear. The ground grew spongier and then her feet splashed into water. She stopped. Her boots were now soaked. The water, clear enough to see through to the bottom, was the source of the pale, blue-green glow.

"Matil?" Khelya said, panicked. "Dask, help her! Quick!"

"I'm okay!" Matil examined the strange water. "There's water, but it's shallow."

"It will remain shallow, as long as we stay on a Path," Falgar said from behind her.

Khelya came and stood beside Matil with a worried look at the water. "H-how do we know we're on a Path?"

"You will see," Dyndal called.

Only a few steps more, and the alva with their beetles emerged from the roots into an immense space. The watchful Elders stood beside them.

As far as Matil could see, the ground was entirely submerged by the glowing water. In shallow places, the water looked lighter from the stones and pebbles close beneath the surface, while the deeps to either side were a darker blue. Matil could see why they were called the Paths – the shallows looked like pale roads twining across the dark water. Short roots dangled from high above, where the cavern ceiling appeared to be entirely made of plant matter. Scattered clumps of long roots reached down from the ceiling to rest in the deeper water beside the Paths. The cavern was edged all around by thick jungles of roots, like the one the group had just come through.

"Stay close to us," Calo said. "We are now in danger." Out of three Paths splitting off before them, he chose the middle one, a twisting trail between the vegetation.

Matil looked across the dark, swamp-like cavern. It was a silent and lonely place, but calm.

"This water comes from the Heart, you know," Falgar said to the alva as they walked.

Simmad lifted up his foot. "Shouldn't we be dead, if we've touched it?"

Falgar smiled with his long face and shook his head. "The Heart lives in its Sanctum, isolated from the rest of Eventyr, and yet it shares magic with the forest. Its forbidden water has a way to flow out and be refined into drinkable, life-giving water in the Paths. Here, all the trees in Eventyr connect to the Heart."

"*All* the trees?" Khelya said.

"All of them. Through the trees and the air they breathe, the Heart's magic comes to permeate the forest…and the alva." Falgar's eyes were light and soft, like the water. "I visited the Paths often, before the Saikyr became a constant threat. It was a place I could focus, to write and mull over inspiration. Sometimes it was only an excuse to wander idly. My wife Chalena loved it as well." Falgar looked up at the high ceiling. "Primarily for its acoustic resonance."

"Chalena of the Song," Simmad said quietly.

"Wait," Calo said. His ears twitched.

Matil seized up. The Saikyr? Nychta?

Everyone stopped, though Dewdrop and Olnar kept scuttling with little swishes of their thin legs in the water. Matil and Dask tugged on their reins.

"It was the beetles I heard." Calo looked back at the alva with comforting eyes. "I was overly cautious. With the Saikyr sleep-weakened as we are, we would all know as soon as they were nearby." He started walking again.

'We would all know.' Thinking back to their confrontations with the Saikyr, Matil guessed what Calo meant. Kanay, Stal, and Igsun had each brought with them overpowering sensations. Venom, rage, a feeling like the seams of reality were unthreading. She relaxed a little. The Paths had so far been quiet. But she saw tension in the Elders' faces.

Though the water soaked Matil's boots and skin, it was somehow more refreshing than bothersome. Her boots weren't any heavier as she pulled them up and set them down, and her feet didn't feel clammy. The beetles' antennae were strangely still as they followed the alva.

Khelya stayed in the very center of the path, far from the deeps to either side. "Can't believe this water comes from the Heart," she said. "I mean, I *can* believe it. But I can't believe I'm steppin' in it."

"It's like a dream," Matil said.

"A boring dream," Dask said. "I was hoping we'd get attacked."

Khelya turned pale. "Don't say that."

"*Dask*," Simmad said. "You are scaring the lady."

Khelya looked down at Simmad in surprise.

"Oh, no." Dask swept into a bow. "My lady, how dare I?" He snickered. "Sorry, Khel. I'm used to us getting into fights, so joking around takes the edge off."

"No, it's…fine," Khelya said. She was still staring at Simmad, who walked along obliviously.

There was another split in the Path. The Elders took the curving right turn. Dyndal lingered at the turn and curled his hand around the toad pendant. Shora looked over her shoulder at him. Her face softened.

The group approached the curtain of roots swallowing up the edge of the cavern. Calo stood to the side as everyone stepped through, and then he followed. The openness of the Paths vanished among the thick roots, and in that damp, stifling jungle, Matil tried to hold on to some of the peace she had felt surrounded by the water.

Solid ground rose out of the shallows. This time, going from the Paths to the outside, she sensed with a shiver that they were passing through a doorway of sorts, a doorway both beautiful and stern.

* * *

Matil and Dewdrop left the hanging roots and entered a world of sight, open air, and chattering birds. Light streaming through the tree canopy had the low, golden quality of late afternoon. The group had spilled from the Paths into a cavity between bark-covered tree roots arching over them. Matil lifted her foot and marveled that her boot was dry.

Shora strode forward to look out into the forest. "We must hurry on," she said.

"Yes, geviyof." Dyndal eyed their surroundings. "Away from this place."

They stood on a huge slope. Descending the slope would be a long trek through tree roots snaking in and out of the ground and dark grass bursting out from between. Pine trees, firs, and oaks lived atop the mossy maze of roots. Matil looked up. More roots curved above the alva's and Elders' heads. Farther up the slope, lording over the hill, was a ponderous, knobby mountain of bark – several trees wound tight together. Twist Tree.

The Elders led the alva on a westward march down the slope. While everyone walked and spoke to each other in low voices, Matil fell in beside Shora.

"What is it, Matil?" Shora said.

Matil thought about how to word a question. "Why… doesn't Dyndal like this place?"

"The Chivishi tells of it. You have not heard?"

"Oh, n-no," Matil said. "I'll ask Khelya instead. I'm sorry to bother you, Lady Shora."

Shora gave her an almost-smile. "Stay by my side." She slowed her steps so that she and Matil dropped behind the others. "Twist Tree was the site of one of the Heilar's last summits before our long sleep." Shora's gray eyes darkened. "Nine Heilar met that day, including me and…Hanem of Heights. The one who used to be my younger sister. She had joined the Saikyr in secret, and that day she wielded powerful sorcery. When we nine were gathered, Hanem cast a terrible spell. She and the other seven died. I had seen something strange in Hanem for a long time, which gave me enough warning to shield myself." Voice sinking into a murmur, she added, "Not enough to protect the others."

Matil's eyes welled up. "Do you know why she joined the Saikyr?"

Shora's tone was gentle. "I have many guesses, but I do not know. That was my greatest mistake. Should not the elder sibling look after the younger? It was my duty to guide her, to keep her from straying. *My* duty, and I failed. Sometimes I fear that neither Thosten nor Dyndal will ever forgive me for it, for how can one repay such a debt? I asked forgiveness a long time ago, and I know they must have wiped the debt clean…yet a part of me still perversely thinks their forgiveness is not enough to balance the scales of justice." She glanced down at Matil and chuckled, an unusual sound coming from Shora. "My apologies. Now you know too much of the story."

Matil's heart hurt for Shora and Dyndal. "It's all right. I want to know the past."

"A wise aim. What about your own past? Would you like to know it?"

Yes or no? Matil couldn't answer. "Is there…a way I can know it?"

"There may be," said Shora. "When our power is replenished, there may well be a way."

Matil let her gaze fall to the slope. Then, startled, she closed her eyes tight and reopened them. Her head was swimming and the ground felt like it was moving.

Shora looked up sharply. Her long, moonlit glaive appeared in her hands. "*Saikyr.*"

Matil unsheathed her knife. And there it was, all at once. Bitter anger rose up in Matil's heart as her stomach turned with the forest's unsteadiness. She glanced at Shora and the Elders, and then at Dask, Khelya, and Simmad, struck with sudden fear that any one of them might turn on her. She shook herself. Her eyes flicked over the roots surrounding them. None of what she felt was real – or at least, it wasn't her.

Dewdrop and Olnar tugged frantically on their reins.

Calo waved toward the beetles. "Let them go."

Matil and Dask reluctantly dropped the reins, letting them scuttle down the slope into the roots and hanging moss. Matil felt something else suddenly, past the Saikyr's mental oppression. Twitching in the back of her mind, pulling her somewhere. She knew that feeling. Dread pooled in her gut.

A distant voice came from behind the group. "*Mu thruvai velana!*"

The sound of buzzing began to spread through the dark meadow.

They all whipped around, looking back towards the hidden entrance to the Paths. Matil could almost feel the thrumming under her skin. Flying down the slope was a swarm of Skorgon armed with sabers. Their wings and carapaces glistened in the low light.

Shora pushed Matil backward, where Dask, Khelya, and Simmad stood. The other Elders moved in front of the alva to head off the oncoming wave of Skorgon. Falgar and Dyndal brandished their swords as they ran, Falgar to the left and Dyndal to the right. Calo followed Dyndal. He also drew his weapon into his hands; it was a massive war hammer of knotty wood and shining bronze. Seeing them ready their weapons, Matil winced at how tiny and unthreatening her own knife looked. Should she fade or fight?

Calo swept one of his clawed hands toward the four alva. A shining golden sheet rose up from the ground in a circle around them and formed a transparent dome over their heads as Skorgon descended to attack. Some of them made it past the Elders, but none touched the alva; they skidded across the golden shield and landed in the dirt with hisses.

Matil saw Falgar sweep his broadsword through the attacking Skorgon. Those that he hit spewed green blood from their gaping wounds. In front of the shield, Shora spun and slashed with her glaive, her movements flowing and precise. Dyndal fought in a flurry to her right. He jumped and kicked and jabbed with his grass blade. Hollers and whoops flew out of his mouth when Skorgon fell from his skewering blade to the ground. Calo stayed closer to the shield he had made, letting Dyndal defend their section while he quickly surveyed the ambush. A Skorgon landed on Calo's arm, raising its sword, but the Elder swept it off easily and crushed it with his hammer.

Simmad's chest heaved, but this time he was still conscious. He fumbled for the knife in his belt. Dask pivoted, watching the Skorgon that surrounded the shield. Khelya's knuckles were white around the shaft of her spear. Matil turned from the Skorgon and looked up the slope to their source.

A heavy cloud of gray dust billowed up and sank to roll along the ground. Skorgon emerged one at a time from the cloud, and the longer Matil looked, the more she could see that the dust was swirling together, forming shapes, growing thicker, until each four-armed, glowering Skorgon was summoned.

The cloud faltered, perhaps blown aside by a breeze. Matil stared. There she was. A small shadow amidst the dust, standing with both hands raised and wings halfway out. Gray dust poured from her palms.

Matil stood transfixed as though in a nightmare. The twitch in her mind, the pull toward that shadow, nagged at her. She wanted Nychta to stay where she was, far away. She didn't want to see those cold lavender eyes.

A woman's sharp laugh broke in on Matil's panicking thoughts.

"Well, *hello again*," the woman said, much too near.

Matil jolted and Simmad yelled.

Behind them, the Elder Kanay's wide smile and blurring yellow and red eyes pressed close to the golden shield. Her vulture wings folded up as she curled her snake-like body around the dome. She was in her reptilian form, with scaly green skin and a long tail full of crushing muscle. She traced the shield with her talons.

"Oh, how I wish you would come out of that bubble and let us carry you away," Kanay crooned.

"You, Kanay, are the one getting carried away," Falgar said. He swung his broadsword at her midsection.

She squawked in surprise. The sword went straight through her. She giggled. "Kanay is not here at the moment, but I will inform her that you wish to speak with her." Her body dispersed into air.

Falgar snorted angrily and snapped his head around. Out of the storm of Skorgon shot the brown and green serpent, Kanay. She whipped Falgar's legs with her tail, toppling him. He rolled to the side and sprang back up to strike her, but she was gone.

"They are upon us," Falgar shouted to the other Heilar.

There was a shrieking roar from a tree trunk to the right. A huge, dark green form threw itself from the trunk onto Calo's back. Calo stumbled.

It was the wild-eyed beast, Stal. He sank his fangs deep into Calo's shoulder.

Calo grunted in pain and then reached around to jam his claws into Stal. He flipped the Saikyr to the ground and hefted his hammer.

"It is useless," Stal said.

Calo glared at Stal and rested the hammer on his good shoulder. The fur on his other shoulder was smeared with blood. "Speaking in the midst of battle, Stal? How unlike you."

To the left, Dyndal joined Falgar in the fight against Kanay. Shora meanwhile opened her moth wings, pushed off from the ground, and flew up toward the gray cloud of dust and Nychta. She fought her way through the Skorgon as she flew. Green blood splashed onto her gray robe with every stroke of her glaive.

A man in black clothes appeared from her left, gliding over the roots with white feathered wings outspread. That was Igsun, the Saikyr who had appeared in Shora's resting place. He swiftly reached Shora and lunged at her with a gleaming red rapier. She spun to avoid it but grunted when it cut her leg. They spiraled off, locked in a grapple.

Stal's eyes flared orange like flames. "You know it is useless," he said to Calo. "Give to us the wingless Ranycht and we will save this fight for later. You do not need her. You need your strength."

Matil felt cold hearing his words. Stal was right. They didn't need her to stop Nychta if they could find the Rootsword.

Calo swung his hammer and a flying Skorgon *crunched* into the other end. He chuckled down at Stal. "You are not confident that you can win."

"Win?" Stal said. "I am confident that we can snatch the prize and send you running like frightened rabbits. You are weak. *We* have received strength from the Book. But…I despise…wasted time. I despise it on behalf of all involved. Be kind to everyone, then, and give us the girl."

"Stal, do you understand what she and the other alva have done for us?" Calo glanced at Matil through the golden shield. "They have returned us to Eventyr. You should desire to protect them. Indeed, *we* will protect them. We will protect her, for we are hers, and she is ours."

Stal growled, curling his lip back over his jagged teeth. In the blink of an eye, he was back on his hands and feet and Calo was swinging his hammer. A group of Skorgon swarmed around Calo, hiding the fight from Matil.

…We are hers, and she is ours.

Her heart grew full. So these were the Heilar.

But even as that thought gave her hope, she realized that none of the Heilar were within view, and the cloud of dust had descended toward the magical golden shield. The dust flurried closer and closer until it touched the shield and pressed up against it but did not enter. The twitching in Matil's mind grew almost unbearable. *No.*

The gray cloud encroached over the shield's surface, and the small figure that Matil knew was Nychta stepped through the dust with arms raised. A larger Ranycht walked beside.

Nychta's arms lowered halfway, and then her shadowy form fell to her knees. The dust began to lessen and clear away.

"Matil," Khelya said, stunned. "It's you."

23

Wings

The dust fell enough that the two Ranycht were fully revealed. Second-in-command Crell was tall and strong, wearing a chain mail hauberk. His heavy-lidded orange eyes squinted at the group through Calo's transparent shield before he bent down to help Nychta to her feet.

Nychta was breathing heavily and her head barely came to Crell's shoulder, but she was the one who made Matil want to run and hide. She looked identical to Matil, from dark hair to pointed nose – except for her brown wings, deep red doublet over black hose and boots, a leather satchel strapped across her torso, and a pale stare that promised torment. She straightened up, seeming to regain her strength unnaturally fast.

"That…that's what you meant, then," Simmad said as he looked from Nychta to Matil.

With Skorgon hovering all around, Nychta put her left hand on the satchel. "*Hurach Calomyr,*" she said.

"*Hurach!*" She lifted her right hand and lowered her palm toward the ground.

A small circle opened in the top of the golden dome and continued to grow. Skorgon began to crowd the opening.

Khelya thrust her spear at the first Skorgon crawling inside, hitting his armor plating hard enough that he shot up and out of the receding dome. Matil, Dask, and Simmad stood around their giant friend, blades drawn. The shield continued to wane. As more Skorgon climbed over, Khelya's spear whirled around and kept most of them away from the smaller alva. Simmad protected her legs and torso with unexpectedly savage slashes of his long knife. Dask stayed close to Matil, who had frozen up.

The pull to Nychta was like a drumbeat in Matil's mind, steadily urging her to run forward and make contact. To heal the wound that created her.

"Look at you," Nychta said. Her cold, lavender-white eyes bored into Matil's. "Pretending you're someone else."

"I *am* someone else," Matil said in a low voice. The last of the shield dissipated.

Nychta smiled. "Sliva." She lunged at Matil with her dagger.

Matil sidestepped the lunge. She heard grunts to her right – Crell attacking Dask. She hooked her foot around Nychta's ankle to unbalance her, but Nychta hopped lightly out, wings catching the air, and landed farther away.

The pull seemed to speak to Matil with its insistence, and she knew that if she could grab on to Nychta and give in to the pull, they would merge. Calo had suggested she let it happen.

"Name one thing I've done that you wouldn't have," Nychta said.

Matil thought of Amacht looking at her as he died. "Everything."

Nychta laughed. "Really? Think about it. Go back. I know you remember." The smile fell from her face. "In my place, would you really have done anything differently?"

As much as Matil didn't want to remember, the memory dreams flooded her mind. The things that happened in them, the thoughts and feelings she had, the choices she made…the more she dreamed, the more she understood.

And the less she wanted to be Nychta. She would find the Rootsword herself if she had to. She just couldn't go back. She couldn't let this wound heal.

Behind her, Khelya jabbed her spear from Skorgon to Skorgon, the blade ringing out against their shell plates. Simmad hacked ceaselessly with his long knife, keeping them away from Khelya. The fear had left his face, replaced with narrowed eyes and clenched teeth. Dask and Crell grappled on the right in a flurry of feathers, Dask's quickness pitted against Crell's strength.

"I'm glad you got rid of me," Matil said to Nychta. "I can do things right. I can fix your mistakes."

"You're the only mistake I ever made," Nychta snarled. She leaped into the air and flapped her wings once to hurl herself at Matil.

A green-winged blur hit Nychta in mid-air. Dyndal. He threw her to the ground and then landed standing over her. He slashed down with his blade of grass.

"*Aharjen!*" Nychta shouted. A ball of flame formed in her hand and shot into the Elder's face.

Dyndal recoiled.

Nychta slipped out from under him. "Rakath," she said, and she faded instantly. Not a trace of her was visible.

Matil's blood ran cold. Nychta could use the Book to make her fading stronger.

"Craven," Dyndal spat.

"Crell, Skorgon!" came Nychta's voice from above. "Hold her for me!"

Crell wrestled Dask's knife out of his hand and elbowed him in the side of the head. Dask fell.

"Dask!" Matil said. Skorgon descended on her and she spun into motion. Green blood covered her arm as she plunged her knife between the carapace of an attacker.

Someone yanked her wrists behind her and forced the knife out of her hand. She kicked and strained against her captor's huge arms. He pushed her to the ground. She breathed hard from the impact, getting a face full of dirt. She turned her head to see.

Crell was kneeling on her back, still gripping her wrists with his callused hands. He looked down at Matil and met her eyes. Crell…her best friend. As they stared at each other, the deep furrow in his brow lessened slightly. His expression became a questioning one, and he looked just like the boy in her dreams.

Dask tackled him from the right, rolling the larger man off of Matil. He stabbed his retrieved knife into the base of Crell's wings. Crell howled in pain.

"Cover your eyes!" Dyndal yelled, very close by.

Matil looked back down at the dirt and squeezed her eyes shut. Light burst at the corners of the darkness. As soon as the light disappeared, she opened her eyes and pushed herself to her feet. Nychta, fully revealed, was gliding toward Matil.

Dyndal passed over Matil's head and again hit Nychta with all of his weight, slamming her into a tree root. She hit the root with a cry.

Light-dazed Skorgon stumbled around Matil. The best thing to do was get to the others. She ducked and dodged and backed up until she reached Khelya's side. Simmad stood, panting.

"What happened?" Matil said. "Did you use your light?" She flinched as Khelya bashed one Skorgon into another.

Simmad nodded. "With Lord Dyndal sharing his magic, I created enough light to banish Nychta's fading."

From beyond the surrounding Skorgon, Dask barreled through to Simmad and Matil. They helped steady him.

"You're all right," he said hoarsely.

Matil surveyed his wounds. "So are you. And…Crell?"

"Collapsed. If he's not dead, he's close to it."

Matil's heart sank, but she showed Dask a hopeful face. "Thank you for saving me."

"It's nothin'," he said, slightly smiling. "I always come back, remember?" He looked up at Khelya mechanically swinging and stabbing her spear into the Skorgon. "Great job, Khel!" he shouted.

"Mm-hm," she managed, her lips pressed shut in concentration.

Something heavy landed behind the group. Matil turned. The long-armed, beastly Stal towered over them. His upturned nostrils flared and hot breath poured between grimace-locked teeth.

"Move, little specks," he rasped. "Give to me the one you call Matil."

Matil looked around the dusky slope filled with Skorgon soldiers and clouds of dust. Here and there she could see flashes of the Heilar and Saikyr locked in fierce battle. Kanay twined her snake-like tail around Falgar. Calo defended a wounded Shora against Igsun. Explosions lit Dyndal's form as he twisted to dodge the fire Nychta threw at him. The alva were truly alone this time. Just them and their puny weapons, alone with Stal.

"*Move*," the Elder said again.

"Sure," Dask replied. He stepped between Stal and Matil.

Simmad was trembling, but he stood beside Dask and lifted his green-spattered blade.

"We won't leave her!" Khelya shouted, still holding the line at their backs.

Matil shook her head. They couldn't do this for her. They should get out of Stal's way. She looked down at her empty sheath and a thought came to her. Hadn't Dyndal just shared magic with Simmad? And hadn't the Elders enchanted their weapons?

"Simmad, your knife," Matil said.

He looked at her in confusion, but quickly passed her his long blade.

"What are you—" Dask began.

"Everyone, hold on to me," she said. "Share your magic." She felt her three friends grip her shoulders. A new reserve of energy flooded her tired body. Matil reached for her magic, not to fade, but to strengthen Simmad's Elder-enchanted knife. Light and shadow rippled into being along the blade. The back of her neck tingled.

"You are as foolish as the old ones," Stal said. His eyes turned from orange to yellow, burning with greater intensity. He lifted his fur-covered arm and swung down at the alva. His claws cut toward Dask like five black scythes.

Matil jumped in front of Dask and thrust the knife into Stal's descending forearm.

The rippling elements exploded. Nearby Skorgon cringed away. Glimmering radiance and swirling shadows fell like rain between Stal and the alva. As energy rushed through Matil into the blade, the tingling spread down her spine. Her heart swelled because she knew the energy meant her friends still stood at her back. She drove the knife in all the way to its handle, thinking of them so ready to protect her. Stal's jaws opened in a thunderous roar of agony.

He lifted his arm, ripping the knife from Matil's hands. The chain broke, the energy left her body, and she fell backwards into her friends. Dask, Khelya, and Simmad helped lower her to the ground, where she knelt to catch her breath.

Stal's yellow-orange eyes shone in the growing darkness. He looked from the alva to his right forearm. Blood soaked the fur around the knife. Tearing out the knife, he backed away with a feral growl. "The alva have injured me!" he shouted. He leaped into the swarm of Skorgon.

After a moment, Nychta's voice pierced the air in a scream of frustration. "Fall back to the Paths!" she yelled.

"What?" came Igsun's voice.

"The creature is mad!" Kanay said.

"The Book *demands* that we fall back to the Paths!" Nychta replied.

Kanay hissed. "In *that* case…fare thee well, my sweetlings!"

"Crell! Crell, where—" Nychta paused. "Skorgon, cover our retreat and then fly to the fortress!"

The Skorgon drew closer together, obscuring vision of the slope. One slashed a saber at Khelya's head, but she whipped her spear up to block it. Another went for her back with a dagger. Dask dragged it to the ground and stabbed it, its transparent wings buzzing and mandibles chomping. Simmad dashed out to grab his knife where Stal had dropped it.

Matil struggled to her feet and saw her own knife in the dirt not too far away. She ran and, retrieving it, took a feeble swipe at a Skorgon. Her target bolted to join the remaining swarm rising out of range. All of the Skorgon began to fly north through the trees. The buzzing grew fainter and fainter until deafening quiet filled Matil's ears. Her mind, too, went quiet. The pull to Nychta was gone.

With the slope exposed, the four Heilar were visible, scattered around the group of alva. Dyndal flew to Calo's side where he tended Shora. Falgar followed on foot. Gray dust rose slowly with the breeze as dead Skorgon dissolved away.

Khelya's arms dropped to her sides and she let her spear fall.

Simmad's voice shook. "Let's sit for a moment, shall we?"

The four alva sat in the dirt. Matil found that the other three were looking at her.

She looked back at each of them. "What's wrong?"

"Nothing," Dask said. "Just…what *was* that? How'd you get wings?"

Matil's breath caught in her throat. "Wings?"

"Yes," Simmad said. "In addition to the explosion, it- it rather seemed as though you had wings, with feathers of white light and black smoke."

"You looked like an Elder," Khelya said slowly.

Matil remembered the tingling down her spine. Could it have been…real wings? Her heart beat faster. *Her* wings? No, they weren't only hers. She wouldn't have been able to hurt Stal on her own, and she couldn't have formed wings on her own.

"It wasn't just me," Matil said, beginning to smile. "We shared magic. I felt your strength, and all I did was use it."

Khelya blinked at her hands. "So…when we share magic, we can do *that?*"

"Incredible," Simmad murmured.

Dask rubbed his blood-smeared face. "I need a nap, this is too crazy for me." Then he winked at Matil. "Looks like we're even on saving each other. Thanks."

Sitting with her friends on a dark slope in the middle of nowhere, Matil was so happy to be alive that it she felt like she had wings again. If only the wings had stayed, at least a little longer. Long enough to see if she could fly.

Footsteps crunched in the dirt as the Elders trudged towards the alva. Brown-red cuts patterned their bodies. The green bloodstains on Shora's robe turned to dust as she walked.

Calo limped over to the alva. "My deepest apologies for leaving you undefended. I had thought that my shield would hold, but the Book of Myrkhar's power is great. And now each of you has suffered injury."

"You're worse off than any of us, sir," Khelya said.

"It is only exhaustion. Wounds such as these will heal soon. Alva are more delicate."

Dyndal slammed his blade into a nonexistent sheath at his side, causing it to vanish. "My only regret is that we failed to end a single one of them rightly."

"Indeed," Falgar said. "Our foes will someday return in force." He walked to Dask. "May I heal you?"

Dask eyed him cautiously, but offered the Elder his scratched-up arm. "Thanks."

Falgar passed his hands over Dask, closing many of the cuts he'd sustained. The other Elders did the same for Matil, Khelya, and Simmad.

"Myrkhar's ilk retreated after Stal cried out," Calo said, sitting down beside Khelya. "Dyndal reports that powerful light and shadow magic originated from the four of you just before their retreat."

"Stal was about to attack us," Matil said. She explained how Dyndal sharing magic with Simmad had given her the idea to use her friends' magic. Dask, Khelya, and Simmad described what had happened next.

On hearing their story, Calo sat back. "Magic shared between alva is indeed powerful, and I have seen it accomplish wonders. But I have never seen it used to gravely wound an Elder, except through sorcery."

"Wounding to the point of fear, too!" Falgar said. "Stal, despite his talk of death, does not wish to speed the process for himself. This night, he feared the possibility of a mortal blow."

Simmad and Khelya looked at each other, mouths open in shock.

"I feel no pity for him." Shora put her hand over the pouch on her belt where she kept the tulip weight. "He gave his own brother a taste of death. It is time he savored it for himself."

"Spirit weapons, sorcery, and heartsickness have brought Elders low in the past," Calo said. "Is it possible that there is another way? That the power of alva combined with Elder magic – such as your enchanted knife – could kill an Elder?"

Simmad's eyebrows drew together and he looked down. "Is this how the prophecies will be fulfilled?"

Dask interjected. "I was wondering something. You all made a big deal about how dangerous the Paths are, but we were only attacked once we got out. Why?"

"I am certain it was due to the Skorgon," Falgar said. "Nychta and the Saikyr used distraction, low visibility, isolation, and overwhelming numbers to their advantage. The Skorgon were integral to their plan, and they cannot be used within the Paths."

"They would be destroyed the moment they entered that sacred place," Calo said. "The Book's Skorgon are dead things, creatures animated by sorcery that cannot withstand the Heart's power."

"They're *dead?*" said Khelya.

He nodded heavily. "Long ago, Myrkhar attempted to create his own alva using an army of Skorgon who had pledged their souls to him. They sacrificed their lives for his promises of power and immortality. His experiment failed, but he discovered that the Book-bound Skorgon could always be summoned to serve him."

Dask shuddered. "We've been fighting dead guys. That explains some things."

Calo and the alva got to their feet, groaning with exhaustion. The Elder put his heavy, clawed hand on Matil's good shoulder and bent down.

"You faced her this day," he said quietly.

Matil hesitated.

He gave a low chuckle. "Your decision is already made, then. You and Nychta will remain separate. And once we have found allies, we will seek the Rootsword."

She met his pupil-less eyes. "Would that be…okay?"

"Yes, Matil," Calo said. He patted her shoulder.

They were rejoining the group when Shora cried out.

"*No!*" she said. "He stole it!"

Shora held a small weight in her palm, but instead of the tulip it was a goblet. The same goblet Igsun had picked up in Shora's resting place.

Calo closed his eyes and Falgar's nostrils flared.

"Igsun," Dyndal muttered. "Lowly fiend. Disgusting thokiri."

Shora's fingers closed around the goblet and she hurled it at the ground. She stared at it, her gray eyes darkening like gathering storm clouds. "I could overtake them. Keep hidden and secretly retrieve—"

"We cannot afford to take that risk," Falgar said. "After the battle today, you know we cannot. Olen would agree."

Dyndal stepped forward. "Shora and I can pursue them together."

"Once you have found them, how do you expect to take the heart-link from them? Would you attempt it through trickery? Force?" Falgar shook his head. "We are all that is left to stand between the Saikyr and the alva, yofdani. If any one of us falls, it will be an immense blow."

"I am loathe to let them have the link," Calo said, "yet Falgar speaks truth. We can make better plans to retrieve it once our power has returned to us. What say you, Shora? Is there any chance they may convince Olen that you are speaking to him through the link?"

Shora sighed. "No. I…hear what you are saying. It is fair."

"When it is time, we will find Olen," Falgar said gently. "Or die in the trying."

She gave him a firm nod.

"Then let us away," Calo said. He cupped a hand to his large mouth. "Beetles! Kind beetles, return!"

"Ha-ha," Dask said. "Seriously, though, how are we supposed to find…"

Dewdrop and Olnar appeared in the distance, scuttling over tree roots and boulders.

"We have our ways," Dyndal said with a grin.

Dask rolled his eyes. "I'm starting to get that."

And after the alva reunited with their beetles, the ragged group left Twist Tree behind.

* * *

It was a rare day for Lyria. No Council business, no personal business. A free schedule meant a brisk flight-and-walk was in order. Many things had come and gone throughout her life, but her firm belief in exercise stayed put. She flew down the grand, stone streets of the city, directing her course on whims, when a wish surfaced in her mind. At first she resisted; to act upon it would be humiliating. But it was the right thing to do, wasn't it? Father would have said so.

She took the turning into Councilwoman Branneth's neighborhood and thought about what she needed to say. Not far down a quiet street, Lyria saw Branneth shuffling onward with two heavy-looking ceramic containers in her arms.

"Branneth," Lyria called as she approached. "What in the leafy heavens are you doing? Don't you have alva to help?"

Branneth shrugged, nearly upsetting the ceramics in her attempt to appear casual. "I'm on my way home. I sent the servants out on holiday and went shopping for antiques. Lovely haul, isn't it?"

"You haven't changed. Here, give that blue one over." Lyria reached for a vase perched in the crook of Branneth's arm. When both of them held the antiques comfortably, she looked down at the vase. "There's a chip in the rim. I hope you didn't pay full price."

Branneth leaned closer to see. "Oh, *blast* it. I thought the store owner was such a nice man, too. At least it's a good piece. Age of Goec, by my reckoning."

Lyria couldn't look at her. She swallowed. "I'm sorry."

"It wasn't your fault," Branneth said.

"No, I mean, I'm sorry for…for acting like…a badger. All these years."

Realisation dawned in Branneth's eyes. She smiled. "Long past time you admitted it."

"You must want to know why," Lyria said. "Why I stopped talking to you."

"Actually, I think I know."

Lyria gave her an edgy glance. "Do you, then?"

Branneth turned the urn she carried. "You've been afraid."

They began to walk, each in her own bubble of silence while birds sang in the trees and a mouse-drawn carriage rattled by. Hope and distrust tore Lyria in two. She looked up, seeking the sun's rays past the pillars, domes, and trembling tree branches of Corwyna. This weather was the kind Annest would enjoy.

"I've been terrified," Lyria said. "After the Riot, I was always in danger. So I reduced that danger by any means."

"Those means…they did hurt." Branneth also looked at the sky. "Lyria, you were my only true friend."

"And- and you were mine. I apologise."

"I suppose I'll accept. Not much we can do about those years now." She looked at Lyria. "Almost there. Did you have anything else to say?"

"Well, perhaps…" Lyria began. "Can we…"

"Be friends again?"

She froze. "I wouldn't presume—I'm aware that the distance between us—"

"I see you still have got mud in that head of yours." Branneth pointed her nose at the blue vase in Lyria's hands. "Did you think I'd let anyone but a friend touch that vase?"

Suddenly, scarily, happily, Lyria could remember how optimism felt.

"Ah, home," Branneth said. "You'll be staying for tea, of course."

Lyria hesitated, starting to calculate how safe it would be. She stopped her mind in its tracks and dipped her head to Branneth. "Of course."

She'd done a lot on her own. Maybe it was time for another ally.

24

Sun Up

After their battle against Myrkhar's forces, the group continued their course westward in search of the rogue townships. Dask offered his services to help find the rogues as soon as possible. That same night, he visited a few rural tree-villages that they passed. His mustache disguise kept him from being recognized, and he had past experience looking for those who didn't want to be found by the wrong alva. He went to the markets and taverns and listened. He asked innocent questions until someone seemed like they knew something. He pried, and eventually one alva suggested he talk with another alva in the next village to the west.

Dask located that alva as morning broke. This one said that if Dask really was a friend of the wingless Ranycht, he should bring her to a farmer even farther west. He was given something to say as well, a pass phrase that the farmer would respond to. Dask returned to the group to tell what he'd heard, and then they rested for a couple of hours before continuing the search. The Elders and alva combed the forest together, Dask flying through the trees while the others stayed near the ground. A few times they hid quickly from Kyndelin – a squirrel man scurrying down a tree, a robin landing and changing into a girl. They saw a few Ranycht from far off, but none fit the description of the farmer.

In the afternoon, Shora gave the alert. The others gathered around her, concealed beneath an ivy bunch. She pointed out a very dark-skinned Ranycht some lengths away, leaning against the stalk of a tall mushroom and fanning himself with his dark brown wings. He wore a wide-brimmed grass hat and held a shovel. Though they watched him for a while, he didn't move from his spot. They didn't see any buildings in the tree above him. Behind him was a large thicket of bushes.

It wasn't quite the farmer's homestead they were expecting. Dask quietly took to the air. He came back after a short time.

"I flew down the thicket that way and saw two more guys hanging around," Dask said. "Can't see inside, though. Leaves are too thick."

Shora narrowed her eyes at the man holding the shovel. "It could be a trap set for us."

"Hmm." Dask looked at her. "Can you disguise me? Please? I'll give the pass phrase. Watch my back." He slipped out of the ivy. Disguise rippling into place, he approached the man and spoke with him. A few moments later, Dask waved for the group to come forward.

"Think it prudent, all of you, for us to show ourselves?" Calo said.

The Elders and alva agreed to leave the ivy and brush, ready to fight if need be. They ducked under the leaves and began walking. The man caught sight of them. His light green eyes popped open.

"Nack!" he called behind him into the bushes. "Nack! I need backup!" He held his shovel with a tighter grip. "Stop there," he ordered the group. "Who are all of you?"

"It's hard to explain," Dask said, "but, basically, these are your new overlords."

"And that is the last time we let Dask speak for us," Shora said.

"The small one jests, good sir." Falgar put his hand on his heart and bowed gracefully at the waist, his curling horns on full display. "We are Valdri – what you may know as Elders. We have of late returned from our long sleep. I am Falgar."

The watchman brought his shovel closer to himself.

Calo lowered his head in a bow. "I am Calo."

Shora gave the man a curtsy. "Shora."

Dyndal smiled and bowed at the waist. "Dyndal!"

After a pause, the watchman said, "Oh, you betcha. Lemme just bow on down to the ground. Might take a while, is that okey-dokey with you? My knees aren't what they used to be." He guffawed. "Like bald rabbits you're Elders."

A much younger Ranycht burst from the bush behind the watchman. He had brown-and-gray wings, big hazel eyes under a flop of brown hair, and he held a sharpened stick taller than him. Three men followed, one with a pitchfork and two holding bows.

"Private Nack," the watchman said, acknowledging the young Ranycht with the stick.

Nack stopped beside him and stared at the Elders. "What's going on, Pop?"

The watchman shrugged. "They don't seem hostile, but I think it's a bunch of Kyndelin and Obrigi getting smart with us." He turned to the other men. "Rimmer, check around the line in case this is a distraction for something else."

One of the bowmen promptly stepped into the bush.

The watchman looked at the group. "This isn't your land, folks. You should just go home before anyone else sees you and starts a hunt."

"But they really are the Elders!" Khelya said.

Nack gasped. "The Elders?"

"And I guess you're an ancient Obrigi princess come back to life," the watchman said.

Her face started turning red. "No!"

Dask sighed. "Un-disguise me."

Dyndal cleared his throat.

"*Please*," Dask added.

After he spoke, his mustache vanished and the hair on his head returned. His face changed back to its true shape.

"You might've heard that the Dominion's after four travelers," Dask said. "An Obrigi, a Sangriga, and two Ranycht, one of them without wings." He gestured to Khelya, Simmad, and Matil. "That's us."

"That's *them?*" Nack asked the watchman.

The watchman studied the alva carefully. "Thiffen. It could be."

"Now why would the Dominion go looking for us?" Dask said. "Because we were gonna wake up the only things that could stop Nychta Olsta." He pointed over his shoulder at the Elders. "And we did."

The watchman lifted his gaze to the giant, alva-like beings whose strange eyes glowed in the forest shade.

"Pop," Nack whispered. "I think they *are* the Elders."

"Private Nack," the watchman said calmly. "Go ask the general to come meet these nice folks."

"Yes, sir." The young man turned around in a daze and tripped over a branch on his way into the bush.

When his son had gone, the watchman swung his arm stiffly. "So…how was the Hibernation?"

* * *

They spoke with the watchman while they waited, until they heard a woman's perky voice through the bushes.

"How many are there?" the woman said.

Matil cocked her ears. She'd never heard a Ranycht talk that way. The woman's accent sounded like Simmad's. Did that mean…?

"Umm, seven or eight," came the voice of Nack. "I think."

"Yes, you think," the woman said lightly, "but we do need to know these things before we go into a potentially dangerous situation. I mean, really, Private."

Nack whimpered a little. "Sorry, ma'am. I'm not used to the daylight shift yet."

"I suppose none of us are used to any of this yet," she said. "But we must get used to it soon."

"Yes, ma'am," he said.

The leaves rustled, soft light emerged, and three alva extricated themselves from the bush's leafy branches. One was the slim Nack, the second was a brawny man with white-edged black wings, and the other, as Matil had guessed, did not have bird wings at all. Instead, the woman had the oscillating light rays of a Sangriga, along with pinkish skin and honey-colored hair in a braid. Interestingly, she wore a short, Ranycht-style blue dress and coarse pants.

The watchman saluted. "General."

"Corporal, I've told you, I'm not a genera—*oh-good-Calo*." The woman stepped back, narrowing her blue eyes at the travelers.

"Oh, good alva," Calo said. He gave her a stately bow. "How did you know I was Calo?"

Dask, Simmad, Dyndal, and Falgar exploded into laughter. Khelya looked mortified, but it was Shora's unmoved expression that sent Matil into fits of giggles. They were all very tired.

The woman goggled at them. "I'm dreaming," she said. "I must be, because there's no way this is…real…"

Everyone made brief introductions. The Sangriga woman was called Annest. She was a former Corwyna Council member who remembered Matil, Khelya, and Dask from when they had been to the Ambermeet. The black-winged Ranycht was her bodyguard Doss, and the watchman, Nack's father, was Corporal Lorick. Lorick stayed at the entrance while Annest, Doss, and Nack led the rest of the group through the dense bush for some time. They arrived at a huge place where the undergrowth had been cleared between the trunks of three large trees. It was the rogue settlement.

The settlement consisted of a large number of temporary shacks leaning this way and that in the clearing and among the tree branches above. In the center of the clearing, the rogues had driven thick stakes into the ground, to which they tied work insects and animals alongside plump mice and shrews kept for food. Makeshift stables partially encircled the creatures, and five Ranycht stood watch atop the stable roofs. The watchmen gawked.

"If this is the army fighting Nychta, we're in trouble," Dask muttered.

Most of the settlement would be asleep during the day, but Matil also had expected something…more.

Annest turned and faced them with Doss ever-watchful behind her. "Private Nack," she said, "Wake the mayors, please, and tell them…" She took a deep breath. "I'm not sure anything you say could prepare them. Tell them to attend the meeting hall as soon as possible. I will be there soon, along with some *very* important guests."

"Yes, ma'am," said Nack. He saluted and flew up toward the shacks in the trees.

Annest's wings brightened when she looked at the Elders. "Er…receiving you is a great honor, my lords and lady." She curtseyed deeply. "Our humble encampment cannot compare to the marvelous estates and palaces you have graced in times past, but I will provide you with the best of our hospitality."

Calo inclined his head. "Our thanks, my lady."

Annest smiled, and she continued with more confidence, "I don't yet understand what all this means – your return, and your coming to *us* instead of an established and well-armed nation – so it would be a great kindness if you would explain the circumstances. I do recall some things from religious studies in my youth. Old, dusty writings warning of fabled evils which now seem…frighteningly real. Prophecies of battles, night and day, fire and water, the end of the world…"

"Oh!" Simmad said. "I don't know whether to worry about that last bit, not currently anyway. I had calculated my own estimations based on the prophecies you mention, and due to recent revelations, I believe I may be mistaken about the imminent destruction of Eventyr. Thus, battles? Most likely. World ending soon? Perhaps, perhaps not."

Annest nodded slowly. "Good- good to hear such reassuring…uncertainty, Scholar Simmad. Erm…and so, great Elders, I ask if I may know more of your tidings, as my own tidings are rather dire."

"You may know all that we know," Calo said. "Myrkhar's goals are the same as in the past: to break free of the bonds that stop him from joining the Saikyr and to enslave the forest. We come because he is rising in power. The brief tale is that these four alva journeyed bravely to end the Hibernation, hoping for our help in opposing the Book of Myrkhar and its bearer. We have awakened due to their efforts, and now we seek worthy allies. And if allies we find, we will 'pitch in', as the young ones say."

"Young ones my right horn." Falgar laughed. "You are the only one who says it, Calo."

"Faugh!" Calo waved a clawed hand at him and turned back to Annest. "General Annest, are you?"

"Just Annest," she said, cheeks reddening.

"Very well, Annest the Just," Calo said.

"N-no, Annest...*only*."

Calo opened his mouth again and Shora nudged him. He snorted through his snout. "I was simply going to ask, given the state of Eventyr at present, how a Sangriga found herself in this gathering of Ranycht."

Annest dipped her head. "I'm...a bit of a runaway, but the Ranycht mayors took me in and gave me the task of keeping track of business here. If you would, I'd like to bring you to them and further discuss what must be done. Your companions are welcome to join us."

Khelya yawned.

"If you would like to come," Calo said to Matil and the others, "you may. But it seems as though you four need rest."

"Yeah, I've been 'velana' for way too long," Dask said.

Simmad looked torn. "I *am* right knackered. I beg of you, my lords and lady, please excuse me for not attending. I would be grateful to learn later what transpires."

"Of course, sir scholar," Falgar said.

Annest lifted her eyes. "Good, Private Nack is here."

A moment later, the scrawny Ranycht landed. "Ma'am, the mayors are going to the meeting hall."

"Our meeting hall is over there, in the far tree," Annest said to the Elders. "We have loading platforms, unless… you all can fly?"

"Yes, we can," Calo said, "though I know it does not appear that a brute such as I should be capable of flight."

"I hope you were all listening," Falgar said. "He did it. He called himself a brute. I did not need to say a word."

Calo clapped the horned Elder on the shoulder. "And you still do not."

"Private Nack, "Annest said, "please show these alva where to sleep."

"Yes, ma'am."

The Elders bade Matil, Dask, Khelya, and Simmad a restful slumber, and Annest smiled at them.

"I look forward to speaking with you all soon," she said.

Matil felt a weight start to lift from her shoulders as she realized that she could go to sleep…and someone else would take care of things. "Thank you."

Khelya wanted to go with the Elders, but now, standing in a safe place, the journey's toll was crashing down on her. It made her limbs heavy and her eyes itch.

Nack looked around the settlement and then at Khelya and the others. "Wait here, okay? I'll check the ground shelters for you."

Khelya watched him jog into the ramshackle shelters. The buildings were so small and flimsy. She couldn't believe whole villages were crammed together in them.

She looked above at the trees. "The shelters up there aren't sturdy enough."

"Ranycht aren't like Obrigi," Dask said. "We don't weigh nearly as much, so places like those are just fine."

"I know, but they're still too rickety. Next storm that comes along'll blow them clean outta the trees. I'm not used to Ranycht construction, but I bet I could…" Khelya trailed off, the beams in her head lifting into place as she applied some formulas. She stepped backward to get a better view of the tree-shelters and bumped into a large someone. "Oof, sorry!" She whipped around. "I'm sorry, sir, are you—"

The man's height was surprising; he was taller than Khelya. Another Obrigi in Nychtfal? No, he had ears like an animal's. A Kyndelin, then, and she recognized his face. But from where? Rusty red hair and copper eyes…

"It's you!" she said. It was the raggedy Kyndelin she had seen at the tater patch in Fainfal. He'd groomed his pointed beard much better since then. His clothes – mostly leather and dark cloth wrapped around him – were travel-worn, but no longer grungy.

The man turned away slightly. "I don't believe we are acquainted," he said. There was a burr to his cool voice.

"You don't remember?" Khelya squinted at him, making double sure that she wasn't mistaken. Yep. Definitely him. "In Fainfal, not too long ago. I saw you, an' you ran off." Her friends stared at her. "How, uh, how are you, sir? I'm sorry for hollerin' at you when we met the first time. I didn't realize you were—"

"Ah, han. I recall." He wasn't looking at her. "Don't be worried. I take no offense when an Obrigi shouts at a stranger. It is only in their nature."

Khelya frowned. "No, I don't usually—see, I thought you were a wild—"

"But I'm not," he snapped, his sharp ears going back. Then he relaxed. "I still take no offense. I don't expect other alva to know the difference between wild and reasoning Kyndelin. Particularly not Obrigi, whose observational skills are far from celebrated."

Heat rose in the back of her neck. How could he say that? In front of everyone else, too. "Seems to me like you don't think very well of us Obrigi."

"Why should I?" the Kyndelin said. "You are foreigners."

"Well, I never had an opinion on Kyndelin till now," she said, "but I guess you're all either rude or bandits, huh?"

He looked at her straight on for the first time. "And I guess Obrigi are all lunks and boors, just like I had heard."

Tears sprang up in Khelya's eyes, so she blinked fast to get rid of them. Lots of alva didn't like Obrigi. The Obrigi didn't like them back. And she didn't even know this man. Then…why did his words feel like a betrayal?

Matil put a hand on Khelya's clenched fist and looked up at the man. "We don't want to fight, sir. Are you waiting for something?"

"Yes." He glowered at each of them. "But I'd rather not be."

The Kyndelin who'd smiled at Khelya in the forest wouldn't have spoken with so much poison. But apparently she was wrong. Maybe all the time she spent with other kinds of alva was spoiling her. The rest of Eventyr was practically at war, after all.

"Now, look here," Simmad said shakily.

The Kyndelin looked down at him. "What is it?"

He cleared his throat. "You're…you're not…being very… polite."

"Your sort has never been *polite* to mine, even after all we've done for the forest. Why should I be polite to you? And why must I listen to a dullard Obrigi ramble on about Fainfal and wild Kyndelin?" He rolled his eyes. "Braksaheh lani feh…"

Khelya was sorely tempted to let her fist fly.

"Hey," Dask said, "life's not fair, is it, Whiskers? And if it so happened we lost our tempers, that *fight* wouldn't be fair, either. Four to one, got it? So leave off my friend. She's a better alva than you, and whatever she says is worth saying. All I hear comin' outta your mouth is a pile of worm guts."

Khelya smiled, surprised.

The man stayed silent and unreadable.

Sudden wind stirred Khelya's hair. Nack was back. He landed and stared at the Kyndelin.

"Is he an Elder, too?" Nack whispered to Dask.

The Kyndelin glanced sharply at him.

Dask shook his head. "He *thinks* he's an Elder."

"I am a magician from the Kyndala nation," the Kyndelin said. "I've come to speak with those in command, on behalf of Torak Sa."

"That sounds important," Nack said, furrowing his brow.

"It's very important." The Kyndelin leaned down. "Did you understand a word I spoke?"

Nack thought for a moment. "Your accent's kind of funny, but I got that you're a Kyndelin magician and you want to see the General and the mayors. What's a 'torocksa'?"

"I'll tell you if you bring me to this 'General' in all quickness."

"Okay, okay," Nack said. "Hang on."

The Kyndelin seemed impatient, but at least he didn't start calling Nack names.

The young Ranycht gave the others an apologetic look. "I'm really sorry. We don't have room in the shelters for you right now. Alva keep showing up, so it's hard to keep track of how many we have. We're planning more shelters anyway, but they take a while to build."

More shelters? It wouldn't take a while if Khelya helped.

"It's all right," Matil said. "We can make camp with the supplies on our beetles."

"That works! Sleep over there." Nack pointed. "That's where we're going to build the new shelters." He turned to the Kyndelin. "Sir, the General is in the meeting hall right now. If you'll get on a loading platform, I can bring you up to see her." He indicated a few square wooden platforms below a tree on the other side of the settlement. They were attached to the branches with ropes and pulleys.

The Kyndelin's fox ears twitched. "I will be…going up? Into that tree?"

Nack shrugged. "That's the fastest you'll get to see the General, sir."

"Pretend you're floating on a cloud," Dask said.

"A really big one," added Simmad.

They both snickered.

The Kyndelin once again glared at the other alva. His gaze came to rest on Khelya. Then he turned away and followed Nack.

"Good riddance," Dask said. "Let's go find a place to collapse."

While they walked toward a clearing by the shelters, Khelya reached up to adjust her headband and then remembered it wasn't there. Her heart sank. Funny that the Kyndelin would make an issue out of her being an Obrigi when she wasn't hardly a proper one to begin with.

"Why would he try to pick a fight with us?" Matil said.

"I bet he's one of those grumpy loner types," Dask said. "Khelya bugged him just by talking."

"Whiskers." Simmad laughed. "That one makes more sense than Sparkles. I don't sparkle, by the way. I really don't."

Dask gave him a side-eyed glance. "How long's it been since I called you Sparkles, huh?"

"I heard you say it last nigh—"

"Hey, hey, no, you know what? I was saying it in a friendly way. Jokingly."

"Nicknames are fine," Matil said in the *please-don't* voice she put on sometimes. "But please don't insult alva, Dask. Even if they deserve it."

Dask grinned. "I'll keep that helpful advice in mind."

Khelya looked at Matil, Dask, and Simmad before smiling at the ground. "Thanks, y'all." She should forget about what Pa and the Kyndelin said. Her friends were here, and she couldn't ask for anything better.

25

Guardians of Eventyr

Matil and her friends found a spacious area beside a shelter and put down their bedding. She wondered what the Elders and the mayors were talking about, but trying to imagine it just lulled her further into sleep.

* * *

"Say my name."

"Nipba."

Matil leveled a suspicious look at Bechel. "You're saying it wrong on purpose."

"Nipba." He grinned. By now he was a scrawny child, just out of toddling. He could pronounce all kinds of words and he *should* be able to say her name.

They played catch together, and then they helped Mother bake bread to sell. They learned all the herbs in Father's garden, and then the whole family sat in the little rosebush house for tea.

Matil remembered hearing Bechel say her name right only once.

"Help! Nychta! *Nychta, hurry! There's fire!*"

* * *

Dyndal woke the travelers at midnight.

"Oh, Matil," he sang. "I recall you promised me a feast!"

Matil rubbed her eyes. "What?" She looked around in surprise, remembering where they were; Ranycht men, women, and children were starting to fill the clearing. They were getting ready for something. What had Dyndal said?

The Elder floated above their camp with leaf wings riffling. It was a familiar sight from when they first traveled together, but he was solid and vibrant – no longer a ghostly form. "We will have a feast tonight, little one. A one-day feast! I tried yet again to bargain for more," he added.

"Hey, a feast is a feast," Dask said, sitting up and stretching. "Sounds great to me."

"Indeed!" Dyndal crowed. "Praise Thosten. And thank you. Now clean yourselves so you may join us! It will begin soon." He spun away into the night.

Some Ranycht women came and took Matil and Khelya to a shelter with water for washing and offered them clothes to change into. Soon Matil was happily dressed in a long, blue-and-green skirt like she'd seen on the dancers at that festival up north in Locka. The women cut the torso off of a large red dress, turning the rest of it into a knee-length skirt that Khelya fastened around her waist with her belt.

They left the shelter and found the open area filled with long tables and illuminated silhouette art. The sounds of musicians playing cheerful tunes drifted through the settlement. Big pots of food sat in lines by the cookfires. A swarm of fireflies danced overhead, where Dyndal played chase with some children.

Matil and Khelya looked for Dask and Simmad while they soaked in the anticipatory buzz of the place. On the fringe of camp, Matil saw two bright copper eyes in a red-bearded face watching the festivities and she realized that it was the Kyndelin they'd talked to. Their eyes met; Matil resisted the urge to make a face at him. He turned and disappeared into the nighttime forest.

"I found our fancy ladies," Dask called from up in the air. He flew to the ground, folded his wings, and gestured for Simmad to hurry over.

The two of them wore vests and colorful tassels like the Ranycht men, and they, too, were noticeably cleaner. Simmad's goatee was trimmed. Dask's hair was shorter and more neatly cut. Matil knew she was smiling too much, but she couldn't help it.

Dask held up his hands in exasperation. "Why do you always laugh when I change my hair?"

"I'm not laughing," she said.

"You're laughing on the inside. I can tell, ya know."

She crossed her arms and turned away dismissively. "You look nice."

"I...you look nice, too," he said.

"Can we eat?" Khelya said, staring at the food. "I'm gettin' one of everything."

"Even the mushrooms?" Dask elbowed her in the hip. "Eh? *Ehh?*"

"Not the mushrooms." She shook her head firmly. "Never the mushrooms."

"There are mushrooms?" Simmad asked, delighted. "Is it soup? I love mushroom soup."

Khelya sighed. "Maybe...I'll...try some."

The group flocked to the food like so many others were doing, though Khelya and Simmad's presence startled a few alva out of the way. Khelya had to bend down for the cooks to spoon food onto her plate.

With plates full, the four made their way through the maze of tables and ducked under flying dancers. Matil swayed to the music as they went. They sat in an empty spot and began to dine on foods like savory mouse and bird meat, fresh dense breads, and fried potato cakes.

Dask glanced at the tables filled with Ranycht, their feathered wings hanging off the benches. "I don't wanna be a rain cloud," he said quietly, "but I can't see this lasting very long. This, uh, rebellion. We're facing an army here, and this...it's barely a gang. It's not an army. Not enough fighters. It's a handful of families who should be kept safe behind city walls somewhere."

The thought brought Matil down from her height of joy. She stared at the delicious food on her plate. "Well…I thought *we* were too weak, and then we learned how to share magic. I thought we were alone, but we found this place. So maybe there are more alva out there who want to do the right thing. Who can join us."

Khelya shrugged. "Maybe. But even my kin didn't believe me."

"What about the Eletsol prince, Ansi?" Simmad said. "You spoke of him uniting his clan. And…ah! The Councilwoman who helped you in Corwyna. There *are* others, and with evil growing bolder and the Elders here now, standing as a beacon in the dark, I believe alva will gather to fight."

"Like the bedtales, huh?" Dask said.

"What else?" Simmad gave a small smile. "I hope so, anyway. With all my heart."

Dask picked up a hunk of dark bread. "For the sake of everyone here, I hope so, too." He bit into it with gusto. "Mm."

Simmad sat up, wings brightening. "Right, yes," he said. "I've got something to, er, express." He alternated between staring down at the table and looking up at the others. "To be perfectly honest…I think that if you hadn't kidnapped me back in Tyrlis – if instead you'd left me tied up – I'd have been stuck in my flat for days. Before…before anyone noticed me. And I'm not saying you should go about kidnapping alva on the chance they might prefer it to what they have, because asking how my day went and sitting down for a cuppa would've done it. But thank you for allowing me to join you. For taking me in. For making me…one of your own."

The three of them looked at him, speechless, while he turned redder and redder. Khelya beamed first, followed by Matil.

Matil realized that these alva were her family and the fight against Nychta and the Book was her life. It was everything she needed to know. Learning about her past only brought pain.

"You're all right, for a Sangriga," Dask said.

Matil poked Dask in the arm.

"Okay! He's all right! Simms, for an alva…you're all right."

Simmad smiled bashfully. "Does that mean you'll stop playing tricks on me?"

"Nope," Dask said. "Gotta get used to—"

"Halsedys, alva of Eventyr," Calo boomed from his place standing on a fallen log. The festive sounds hushed and the crowd turned to see him.

The other Elders stood on the ground to his side. Falgar smiled, Shora was solemn, and Dyndal had a hard time keeping still. Annest and three older Ranycht stood on his other side, puffed up with pride.

"We give thanks to Thosten for this food, this companionship, and this cause." Calo's eyes were reddish-brown and gold, shimmering like leaves on a tree. "Those gathered here have become warriors against an evil force. And we must now prepare ourselves for the worst, as evil is not afraid to make war." He looked out over the now very quiet gathering. "Beware the Saikyr, for they are working with Myrkhar to wreak havoc on all of Eventyr. My fellows and I have been called to stand with you against their power. Called from our millennia of slumber. Yes, friends, what you have heard is the truth. We are the Heilar, and the Great Hibernation has ended!"

The entire camp of alva burst with jubilation. As bellows and expressions of hope buried Matil's ears in an avalanche of sound, she and her friends looked at each other with the same, almost disbelieving look that said, *'We did it.'*

Calo held up a clawed hand. "This camp is now home to Ranycht, Sangriga, an Obrigi, Elders…and perhaps others soon to come. Together with your mayors and Judge Annest Ren, we Heilar discussed the adoption of a name. Rather than name our alliance after a king or queen or a type of alva, we remembered our own name of old – Valdri. Protectors…guardians of Eventyr. Is that not what each of you are, whether you wake with the sun or the moon? This name may encompass us all, if you will it. The Valdri. What say you?"

"Valdri!" someone yelled. "Valdri!" A few others did the same, and then many more, until everyone in the crowd was caught up. "Valdri! Valdri!"

The chant turned into triumphant cheers. Matil listened with a big smile on her face, looking around at all the alva from whom she no longer needed to hide. Dask shouted and Khelya cheered her throat hoarse. Simmad shook his fist approvingly, but at Dask's urging he threw both hands in the air and waved them around. The musicians started playing again, alva got up to dance and fly, and the celebration went on through the sunrise.

The story will continue in

Flames of Eventyr

About the Author

Ellias Quinn is a Christian and a storyteller. In her childhood amidst the rain and the woods, she stumbled into Eventyr's border – bruising her head in the process – and through the years has had the great fortune to learn from the bantam residents about its history and cultures. Now, she is humbled by the privilege of relating certain great events from Eventyr's past for the benefit of humankind.

Ellias's favorite time of year are the days just out of Vana, when the sun shines warmly through the cold air, as Thrual creeps in and paints the leaves. On those days she enjoys sitting down with her family to a meal of thick squirrel steaks broiled in the Obrigi tradition.